Stunned by Light

Richard Napam

Papua New Guinea

Paperback ISBN: 978-0-6459322-6-3

First Published in 2024 by

**First Nations Writers Festival International Limited
T/as First Nations Publishers**

A Registered Charity (ABN 79 655 932 979)

2/53 Junction St, Nowra NSW 2540, Australia
Phone: +61 491 851 353
Email: firstnationswritersfestival@gmail.com
Web: www.firstnationswritersfestival.org

FB: www.facebook.com/firstnationswritersfestival.com

Cover Design: Busybird Publishing
Typeset: Busybird Publishing
Line Edited: Anna Borzi AM 2024

Printed and bound in Australia by IngramSpark

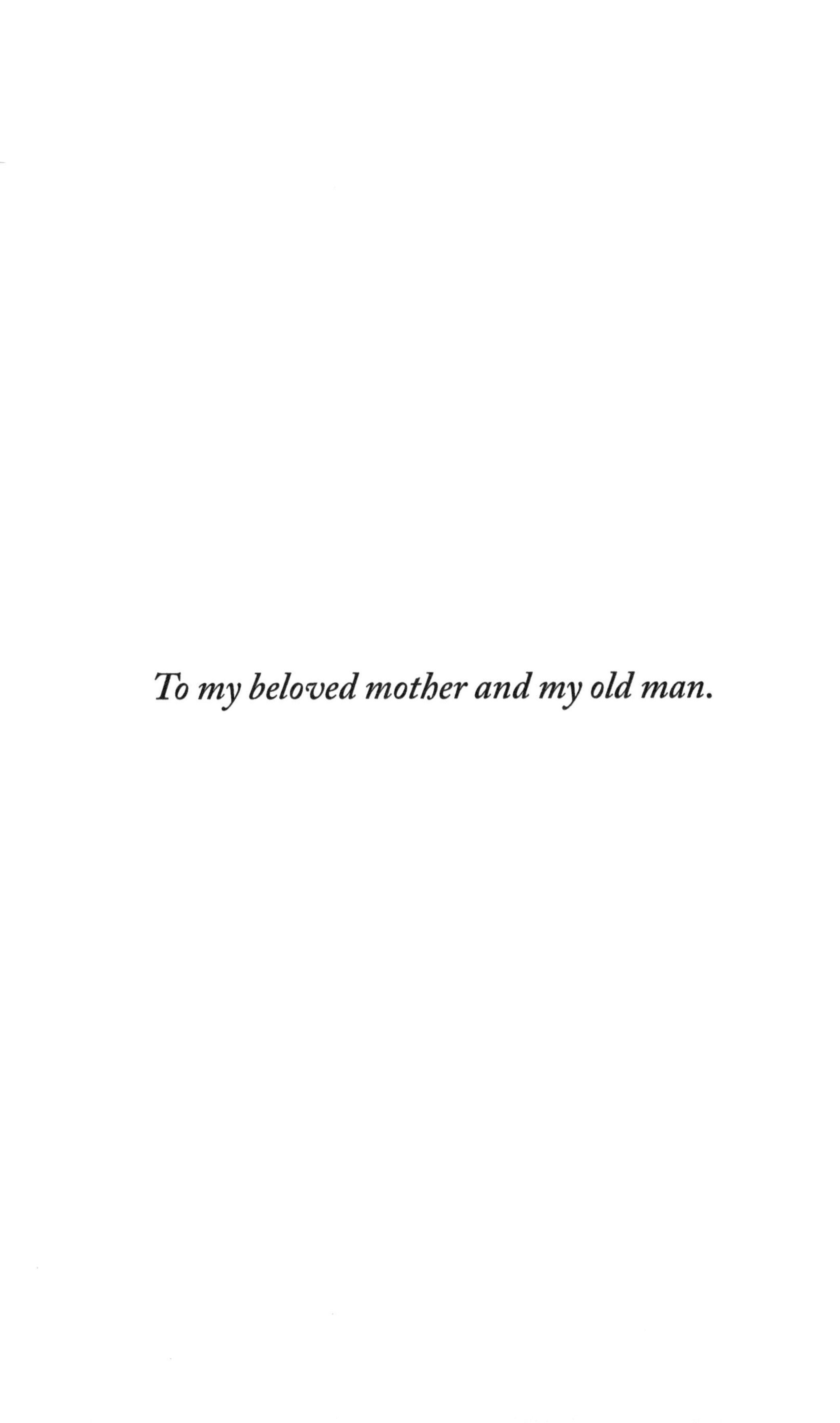

To my beloved mother and my old man.

Chapter 1

My stepmothers' anger exploded two days later. They found my mother alone in her garden and emptied all the anger that had been keeping them sleepless for the last two nights. They even threatened to murder my mother whenever my father went away on a long journey.

Two days earlier when my father brought home a pig from Kandep, my stepmothers cast envious eyes and spoke between themselves in low voices as my mother led the pig away to our pigpen. They each had eight or nine pigs but that didn't matter much to them. They were only interested in whatever was passing through my father's hands. They had every reason to attack my mother that afternoon because they knew my mother's pigs had gone up to seven.

Besides the pig, my stepmothers probably had other reasons to attack my mother. One time the second wife said my mother had stolen her husband from her and was keeping him for herself. That was probably not true because my father spent most of his time with the men in the men's house or elsewhere attending to important tribal issues.

My stepmothers couldn't interrupt us because my father lived with us. They were however in a constant search for reasons to argue and call names to my mother when my father was not at home. That afternoon, my stepmothers didn't know my father would return home. It was too late for them to escape my father's rage.

"This is not about the pig. They are talking about something else," said my mother when my father came home that afternoon. "My husband gave it to me. He gave the pig to me with his own hands. I didn't pull it out from their houses. What wrong have I done against them? I have given them a row of sweet potatoes each from my new garden. I also allowed them both to select a piglet of their liking when my sow gave birth to seven piglets last moon. Just imagine, do they receive such favours from their fathers and brothers? Ungrateful, selfish women! If they are complaining about the pig, wait…" She stopped midway and searched with her eyes.

"Where is Maip?" she called for me. When she spotted me beside my father, she said, "Go and pull that pig out. Cut it in two. Let them have half each."

My father ignored her and continued to file his axe but when her voice changed to an outburst of tears, he lost his patience in ignorance. It was as if he had been waiting for my mother's words to bring the anger out in him.

"Tell the women to come here," he shouted.

My elder brother Katopa sprinted off to fetch my stepmothers. Their houses stood on the other side of the ceremonial ground. We would live under the same roof as some families did but my father built separate houses for my two stepmothers. He probably didn't want to be the centre of women's pointless arguments. He however visited my stepmothers whenever it was convenient for him. I wasn't sure whether his visits were convenient for my stepmothers too, but my stepmothers didn't chase him away. He preferred to pay them quick and separate visits either on his way to the men's house or in the evenings when the children were out playing.

My father's first wife Poikaamb was said to have approved of my father's marriage to my mother. She was barren herself. But because women's hearts are as unstable as waves, she wasn't a different breed of a woman. The second wife influenced her so much that they both hated my mother.

The second wife, Engaamb, was said to have fought hard to keep her place in my father's house when he married my mother. My mother said that was a normal thing women did. My mother said the first wife would fight to keep her man but if her husband succeeded in taking home the new wife, the first wife would reserve her vengeance until when her husband married another woman. The first wife would then take sides with the latest wife just to see the other woman experience what she had suffered.

While Katopa was still away, my mother removed some sweet potatoes from the ashes and scraped off the blackened skins with a bamboo knife. She slapped the dust away and handed the largest to my father. He broke it into two halves and placed them on a flat piece of firewood near him to cool off for a while. My little sister Konopu grabbed my father's bamboo container and ran off to the creek to collect water.

My father had nearly finished the sweet potato when Konopu returned from the creek and handed him his drink. He drank the contents in one gulp and leaned the empty container near the house post. Konopu laid her head on his thigh while he plaited her hair. My father said how pleased he was to have a lovely little girl.

"Papa I have helped Mother in the garden. We pulled the weeds out of our sweet potato garden," said Konopu. She said more of such things children say when they are happy.

"You are a good girl. Always listen to your mother. Never disobey her," said my father.

Katopa arrived before dark and my father enquired why it had taken that long.

"I had to check Poikaamb in the garden," said Katopa.

"And Engaamb?" asked my father, referring to the second wife.

"Both are leaving their houses."

When Poikaamb and Engaamb appeared on the tracks a few moments later, my father asked Konopu to go out and play with the children at the ceremonial ground.

My stepmothers came in and sat quietly at the doorway with their heads bowed. My father rolled a tobacco and ignored them. He grabbed a glowing firestick. I thought he was going to throw it to my stepmothers but he brought it to his mouth and set his tobacco alight. He blew a cloud of smoke towards the rafters. This was his habit. When he was angry, he would take his time to speak. And when he spoke, his words were clear and deliberate so that none of his message was lost. He, however, had a limit to which his anger stayed inside his crazy mind. Whenever his temper overran his patience, especially in the house, he would release anything his hands came into contact with.

He never talked hard about my mother. It was probably because he did not want to break my mother's heart, a heart everyone said was as soft as her voice.

"Come inside or else you'll catch the axe," said my father and turned to the wall where he kept his stone axe. The women came in and sat near the door.

"So you have attacked her again?" said my father. His eyes floated to Poikaamb and then to Engaamb. Poikaamb lowered her head but Engaamb was the sort of woman who wouldn't allow their husband to go unchallenged. She mumbled something to herself but my father silenced her.

"Each one of you has a house of your own," said my father. "You also have enough gardens to grow your food. How is it that you are…?"

"But Amboama got the pig again," cut in Engaamb. "She got two in a moon now. What special woman is she? What has she done to merit such favour? She must have done something you can't forget, eh? That's why you are allowing her to have the best of you. She is…"

"Shut up your mouth woman," shouted my father, fixing his eyes on her. She avoided his eyes. They both avoided his eyes. They probably didn't want to hear him also, but they couldn't avoid his message. His words were direct and to the point, to them.

Engaamb put her hands on her cheeks and looked as if my father was speaking to someone else.

"I own this household," continued my father. "No woman here should dictate how things should be used in this house. I have married all three of you to support me. You will not make decisions for me."

This contest for wealth ended a few days later when my father died during one of his trips out of the village. His death plunged us into a world of turmoil and confusion.

My mother was the most devastated of the three. Life threw its toughest challenges her so early. I wasn't sure how she would take us through the uncertain times ahead of us. It took every bit of my mother's life, ingenuity and wisdom to raise me, my baby brother Yando and my little sister Konopu.

Chapter 2

One night as I was lying awake in bed, my father came home late in the night and was speaking to my mother. He said he was going to Kandep the next morning and asked my mother to cook some sweet potatoes over the fire for him.

"I'm making a moka. I am going to see if Wane could help me with a pig or a kina shell," said my father. Wane was the elder brother of Engaamb.

"Another moka, eh?" said my mother. "You have given seven kina shells to that Sipaka man, just eight moons ago."

"Oh, that was my sixth moka. I have repaid twice Napulge Olko's kina shells and pigs. Is there anything wrong with that?" My father's voice rose a little.

"There's nothing wrong with it, but I thought our small pigs would need some time before you pull them out to the ceremonial ground."

"I'm ok with pigs," said my father. "Pepena's father has made two mokas in the last ten moons. I think I'll be able to make three in just eleven moons. Poikaamb and Engaamb have some pigs too so that should help. If Wane gives me something, I'll be thinking of my seventh moka. And that seventh one will be to repay Wane. He owes me four pigs and three kina shells. He'll be happy if I repay him more than twice."

My mother said nothing more of my father's obsessions on giving away pigs. It was she and my stepmothers who raised the pigs but none of them resisted whenever my father demanded the pigs.

My father returned to the men's house. My mother divided the hot ashes with a wooden thong and buried the sweet potatoes (which she had been roasting over the flames) inside the ashes.

Next morning when my father, Yare and Katopa got their axes and bilums ready for the trip, I ran down the creek and hid in the tall grasses near the track. My mother had stopped me earlier when I wanted to accompany my father to Gia for a pig killing. This time I didn't want to miss the trip. Katopa who had been to Kandep twice said Kandep had many shallow pools with a lot of fish.

My father and the men arrived at the creek. My father said nothing when I followed them. We crossed the creek and when we climbed the hill, my mother called for me to come back to her. She warned me that the tree roots along the tracks would break my legs and the creeks would float me downstream like a feather. My father looked at me for a while but said nothing. "Katopa take care of Maip," said my mother and returned to the house.

Kandep was a day's walk from our village Malke in Tambul. If one left home at dawn, he would arrive at dusk. Many young men had speedy legs which helped them to see some sunlight in Kandep. If one carried some load, he would use a light to reach Kandep.

By the time we left the grassland and reached the forest, the sun emerged on the horizon. Mt Giluwe rose above our village and the sun's golden rays began to splash on the mountainsides. My father gave me his two burning pieces of bark to keep my hands warm.

When we reached the top of the mountain overlooking the Kaugel River, the sun was spreading throughout the valley. The river cut through the mountains and thick jungles before it meandered through the Kaugel Valley. It divided the valley into two unequal sides which were inhabited by powerful tribes. Our village was the first the river touched on its way down to Piambil.

A long vine bridge had been floated above the river. Two thick bundles of ropes ran parallel across on either side of the bridge with their ends fastened against huge branches at either side of the banks. Small saplings were fastened at the base of the bridge and countless ropes ran from the ropes down to the saplings. The bridge would sway from side to side, forcing one to hold the two ropes to maintain balance. It was a mammoth task to cross the bridge when one had to bring live pigs across.

We crossed several fast-flowing creeks and climbed some steep hills before we travelled through a thick flatland of forests. After we climbed a mountain, we reached a plateau which was covered with short grasses. The top was all swamp. We continued to walk across the swamp until we reached the top of a mountain overlooking Kandep.

Kandep sat still in a valley. A large river ran along the mountainsides without disturbing the village. A large area of forest near the river had either been slashed or burned to make way for new gardens. Several clouds of smoke were rising on the mountainsides beyond the river. Just on the other side of the river a thick forest raced up to the mountain. Tall casuarina trees blackened one-third of the village while grassland covered a huge portion of the land. Two huge lakes sat still at the edges of the village. My father said they were male and female lakes.

"I think that place used to be a forest of casuarina trees," said Yare, pointing to a clear area at the end of the village.

"Yes, that was the home of a large village until a few moons ago when a tribal fight displaced the villagers," said my father. "The tribe that lived there fought with another tribe beyond the river. The river tribe flattened the trees and burnt that village to ashes. The pig that I brought home last moon, which the women were arguing over, was one of the four that were given to us for negotiating peace talks for the two tribes."

"I don't think all the displaced villagers have returned. Their place still appears empty," said Yare.

"They are rebuilding their lives slowly," said my father. "Battles are exciting but recovering from a battle is like starting life all over again."

We descended the mountain and after crossing a creek, we reached the village ceremonial ground. The houses stood on all corners of the ceremonial ground with their doors opening towards the ceremonial ground. The men's house stood several spaces away from the ceremonial ground behind some fencing. It was bigger than the rest of the houses. It was where men discussed important tribal matters like pig killings, battles and bride prices. Women were not allowed into the men's house. Whenever women brought food for their sons and husbands, they would leave it outside for the men to pick up.

When we exited the ceremonial ground, we met three young men who were returning from the forest. They said Wane was still in his garden. The eldest of the three dispatched the youngest to fetch Wane while the other young man disappeared behind a sugarcane garden near the track.

"We are coming back from the mountains," said the eldest to my father.

"Have you been out hunting all night?" asked my father.

"No, we've been cutting posts for my new house in the forest."

"Taking home a young woman soon?" said my father, laughing.

"Oh no," said the young man quickly as if he was covering up something. "We are replacing my old house which is rotting away."

The young man said after his father died from a battle wound, he had been caring for his mother and two young sisters. My father said the young man was the son of one of his former trading mates.

They were still talking when the young man who went to the garden returned with a heavy bundle of sugarcane. The sugarcane swayed from side to side and the young man tried his best to maintain the balance. He dropped the sugarcane in front of us and removed the tubers.

"Help yourselves," said the young man," leaving the entire sugarcane bundle to us.

He collected the shoots and went to the creek to leave them there for some time before he planted them.

"You can finish the sugarcane and come later," said the eldest young man and left.

The sound of our teeth tearing away and smashing the sugarcanes replaced our words.

My father quickly peeled away the skins for me to help my young teeth.

By the time we had only one piece of sugarcane each, the sun sank behind the mountains and the place became colder. We walked towards Wane's home.

As we passed through the different houses, mothers returned home with their small children bouncing on top of the bilums. One childless mother rested her bilum on raised ground at the wayside to call for her pig that had gone off track. As more people returned, the village came alive with children playing and chasing each other and men splitting firewood for the afternoon fires. Smoke from the afternoon fires leaked out from the blackened roofs and swam above the houses.

When we were some spaces away from Wane's house, Wane arrived from his garden. He was a tall middle-aged man with broad shoulders and muscular arms. His sharp nose had been pierced in the nose thrills. His bearded face was strikingly handsome.

A large piece of firewood rested on his right shoulder. And on top of it laid a brown spear which may have scared away enemies and nocturnal spirits. Behind him walked a middle-aged woman. She carried a heavy sweet potato bilum on her back. She held the rope of a pig in one hand and the bilum's handle in the other. Two kids, a boy and a small girl, were chasing the pig that was trying to go off the track in search of worms. Whenever the pig ventured off-track, the woman pulled the rope, which was tied to one of its forelegs, and the children chased it with two broken branches. Their mother was young but appeared much older.

Wane leaned his firewood against a tree and apologized for coming late.

"Karimbi, I'm sorry. I've been clearing a new garden for my latest wife," said Wane.

"You added another one?" asked my father.

"Yes, she is the fourth. I acquired her five moons ago," said Wane.

"With new women comes new responsibility," said my father.

"That's it, my man. A double responsibility," laughed Wane.

Katopa carried Wane's firewood while Wane and my father talked as we walked over to Wane's house. His wife shook hands with us and hurried away ahead of us with the two kids and the pig.

Wane, Engaamb's elder brother was advanced in age but his appetite for young women was blind to ageing. His latest inclusion in his line of wives reflected his ability to acquire wives. His latest wife, I found out the next day, was half his age, but what was age when a man had the bride price to acquire wives? So long as a man had a bride price, age couldn't stand in the way of a man whose heart ran after younger women.

Wane lived in his own house but his four wives lived in their own homes with their kids. Their houses were close to Wane's but not too close to each other. A clearing was in the middle for feasts and gatherings.

Katopa and Yare quickly broke the firewood outside Wane's house while I went in with my father and Wane. My father leaned his stone axe near the wall and rested his back against the walls. Wane opened the hot ashes with a thong and built the fire. His little girl came back and sat beside him; casting curious looks on us from time to time. Wane sent her away to check with her third mother if she had prepared something for dinner. The little girl slipped out of the door like a wind and disappeared in the darkness. Moments later, a woman appeared at the door with some cooked sweet potatoes and sugar cane. She placed the food before Wane, shook hands with us and left.

My father and Wane spoke in both the Kandep language and ours. I understood their language but couldn't reply because my mouth was too heavy to utter a word.

It was through my stepmother Engaamb that we came to understand the Kandep language. She spoke the Kandep language at home with her children. Many of our mothers also spoke the language as they also came from Kandep.

Wane's accent in our language was like that of a child. He couldn't pronounce the words well and would often switch to his native language whenever words failed to come out quickly. My father must also have appeared like a fool to Wane when he spoke in their language.

The men talked on other topics until well into the night when my father informed Wane we had come to seek help from him for a moka in the coming moon.

"You have come to the right place and to the right man," said Wane after my father had spoken. "I am not saying I have all the pigs and kina shells to give you. I have a problem and the problem is, you have come to me when the whole world has been turning mad against me lately. I am not going to lie to you. I did have some pigs and kina shells but I used them all in some recent marriages and pig killing occasions. I have exhausted the remaining pigs in marrying that woman, the woman I told you earlier. I don't know whether she will give me a son."

"You will see all the empty spaces in the pigpen tomorrow," continued Wane. "My people here see me as the source of pigs and kina shells to solve their problems. They see me as part of their problems."

"I know what it's like to be a chief," commented my father. "As a chief, your tribe's problems are yours. Back at home, a pig in my house belongs to the tribe."

"That is very true," agreed Wane. "Your people's problems won't exclude you. And you can't even escape their problems too."

Both men talked for some time about the similar challenges they were facing in leading their people. Well into their talks, he called for his little girl.

"Where is the little girl? Mono?" called Wane.

"I'm here Father," said Mono who was sitting quietly beside her father, struggling to chew a piece of sugarcane.

"Oh, you are here," said Wane. He was so carried away by the conversation that he forgot his little girl.

"Go tell your mother to come here quickly. Say Papa wants to see you. Be quick little girl."

Mono threw the sugarcane away and disappeared into the thick darkness. She wasn't afraid of the darkness or spirits.

Now the wood had burnt out and cold had crept in. Wane reached for the door and returned with a load of firewood. He rested the firewood on his side and placed them onto the fire one by one as he spoke with my father. The fire bellowed some smoke and soon rose up and the house was warm and light again.

Mono arrived with her mother moments later, holding her mother's grass skirt in one hand and a small glowing ember in the other. She waved the ember from left to right to shed enough light on the path. The mother and the child talked to each other, with the child's voice rising above its mother's.

"Is the river carrying you downstream?" said her mother. "Don't pull my grass skirt like that. It will break loose."

"Mama I'm afraid of the spirits," replied Mono.

"Ah don't be a silly little girl. There's no spirit here to grab you."

"But there is one holding a light and coming up the creek." There was a short silence.

"Your little mind is tricking you," said Mono's mother. "There is no light at the creek."

When they entered the house, Mono threw the ember into the fire and went straight to the corner where she had left her sugarcane. She searched for it in the dark and found it. She brought it back to her mother and cleaned the dirt away by rubbing it against the back of her hands and chewed it. A little while later, Mono left the sugarcane aside and rested her little head on her mother's lap. Her mother played with Mono's hair until she dossed off to sleep.

Wane explained to his wife that we had come to seek help. His wife eyed us for a while and said nothing.

"This great Kaugel Chief has come a long way with his little boy and his sons. It's not good if we send them back the way they had come."

"I only have the red pig," said his wife.

"Shall we give that away?" asked Wane.

"Will they go back with the red pig alone?" said Mono's mother.

"That's what I'm also thinking," said Wane.

"The other two pigs are for Tambanda's bride price. We have talked to the girl's father saying we'd show the bride price in six moons' time."

"We'll kill them both. We'll take care of the bride price when its time is due. Let's not bring future concerns to the present."

Wane said no more. He picked up a small firestick and set his tobacco pipe on fire and inhaled several puffs before releasing a cloud of smoke simultaneously though his nose and mouth. He inhaled three or four more puffs and killed the fire with spit when the fire reached the tobacco pipe.

Mono's mother stared at the fire as if she was collecting words to say something but not a word came out of her mouth. Wane turned to Mono and asked for his water but seeing that Mono was asleep, her mother gently set the sleeping child aside and slipped out of the house and returned with a bamboo full of water and handed it to her husband.

Mono's mother must have been upset with Wane's decision to give both pigs away. She waited for a while but when Wane resumed his conversation with the men, she scooped up the sleeping child into her arms.

Wealth was measured by pigs and pigs were mostly reared by women. It took many, many and many more moons to raise pigs. Pigs were second babies to women. Mono's mother would have protested but perhaps it wasn't proper for her to argue in front of visitors.

"You are an insane man," said Mono's mother when she was well away from the house. "You have already promised to the girl's father. Now you are giving away my pigs. We'll see how you will marry your son's wife. You are the chief so your people will buy your son's wife for you. My man is a wealthy man."

Mothers opposing their husbands' decisions wasn't something unique in Kandep. My mother would sometimes disagree with some of my father's decisions. She, however, gave in when her words failed to change my father's mind.

"Women are here to support us," said Wane after Mono's mother had left. My father concurred with him that women were subjects under men's control.

"She is the second wife," said Wane after Mono and her mother left. "She wins my heart because she supports me. I get my strength from her and talk in public."

Chapter 3

Next day, we followed a stream until we arrived at the pigpen hidden under some tall casuarina trees on a hillside. There were five pigs snoring in their small enclosures. The two smaller pigs woke up and grunted when we neared their home. Mono plucked some sweet potato leaves and threw some to the pigs. The smallest of the pigs jumped up and snatched the leaves from Mono's hand and missed her little fingers narrowly. She screamed and ran to

her mother who picked her up from the ground and comforted her.

One of the pigs was so huge that it rested on its belly to feed. The pig's two front teeth pushed their way out above the mouth. Mono's mother tied a rope on its arms and slowly

edged the pig out of the pen. She also led out another pig and tied it under the casuarina trees.

"You can kill that one," said Wane, pointing to the biggest of the two. "I don't think it will walk to Tambul."

"I didn't expect this much from you," said my father.

"Never mind," said Wane. "Pigs and kina shells are nothing if they can't meet man's needs."

My father thanked Wane and Mono's mother. He promised to repay them twice in a moka later.

The sun was already up when we arrived at Wane's home. His children returned from the bush with leaves and ferns for the mumu. His four wives and the three elder daughters peeled sweet potatoes and dried in the sun. Wane's two boys and Katopa split the wood while my father and Wane dug a rectangular cooking pit for the mumu. After the cooking pit was completed, the men built a small fire in the pit. We were killing two pigs, one for Wane's family and one for us.

Yare sharpened a huge stick, about the size of a man's hand and dried the moisture over the fire.

"Bring the pig near the fire," said Yare.

Katopa pulled the pig near the cooking pit and tied it to a short stick. Yare raised the stick and when he was about to smash its head, the pig turned its head away, forcing Yare to swear and rest the stick aside.

Katopa threw a small sweet potato to the pig and while the pig was munching it, Yare swung the stick and smashed the pig's forehead. A stream of blood seeped out from the fractured nose and mouth.

After hitting the pig's head several times, Yare set the stick aside and felt with his fingers whether the bones in the head were broken.

"Ready to go," said Yare.

He and Katopa washed the blood off and lifted the pig onto the burning fire. As the flames licked the pig's hair, the men rubbed two split woods hard against the burning hair. When all the hair came off, the men brought the pig over to my father. My father placed the pig on its back on some banana leaves and ran the sharp edge of a bamboo knife around the neck and along the chest down to the tail. He ripped open the pig's thick skin and white flesh, and removed the intestines, and the heart, and chopped off the ribs and the head.

We placed round stones at the base of the cooking pit and crisscrossed the firewood over the cooking pit. We heaped the remaining stones on top of the firewood. As the flames licked the wood, some of the stones, which could no longer withstand the intense heat, exploded, sending sharp pieces of stone flying everywhere. My father cautioned me to take cover behind the house while he cut some small branches and placed them over the stones.

My father ripped out the ribs on both sides of the pig and roasted it over the fire on two long sticks. Me and my father ate one while Yare and Katopa had the other. My father also chopped some meat into smaller pieces and packed them inside two bamboo containers with some soft greens. He said the greasy parts were the best, so he placed a little extra fat on the top. He secured the lids tight with some leaves and heated the bamboos on the stones.

Moments later the woods collapsed with the stones and settled at the base of the cooking pit. Sharp purple flames like the tongues of many snakes flickered among the gaps in the stones. As the woods disappeared, smoke began to diminish and whitish ashes settled on top of the hot stones.

"The rains won't wait for us," said my father. "We need to be quick."

When the sun passed above our heads, we removed the hot stones with long tongs and heaped them near the cooking pit. We left a third of the stones inside the pit and later covered them with large leaves. The stones were so hot that they burnt the fresh leaves when we placed them inside. We threw the ferns and cabbages on top of the meat. Katopa and Yare brought the two halves of the pig and laid them flat on the ferns. My father opened the pig's mouth and placed a red-hot stone in it and another underneath the pig's head.

Mono's mother and her elder sister brought two bilums of peeled sweet potato and emptied them into the cooking pit. When all the sweet potato, ferns, pork and cabbages entered the cooking pit, we covered the top with soil, letting no steam escape. Thus, we buried everything for the hot stones to do the cooking for us.

My father wiped the sweat away on his forehead and retired under a casuarina. He drank some water and rested for a while before he asked me to bring the bamboo over.

Placing some leaves on the grass, my father gently tapped the bamboo's mouth against a wood. A mixture of delicious pork and steaming vegetables spilt onto the leaves. The smell of cooked meat floated in the air. Katopa and Yare joined us for the meal.

As soon as we completed our meal from the bamboo, it started to rain. We retired at Wane's house while his wives and children returned to their homes to cook the intestines and some of the leftover meat.

Talk becomes food when men meet. We talked about many things that afternoon. My father said the increased intermarriages between our tribe and Kandep had strengthened the bond between our tribes. He said he was coming back to Kandep to look for a wife for Katopa in a few moons' time. Wane joked that he wouldn't give away any more girls in his land unless he received some in replacements.

"There should be some fairness," said Wane. "It's unfair if you take away all our girls without us marrying your girls in exchange. There should be some replacements. I'll come to

Tambul when I have enough wealth to buy a girl."

I was unsure whether Wane meant to buy a wife for himself or for one of his sons. Wane was determined for replacements so long as affordability concerns were taken care of. My father said he was pleased to receive Wane and accord him the same hospitality if he came to Tambul.

Now the rains subsided and the weather cleared a little. Light clouds floated downstream above the river. A cool breeze splashed off the raindrops on the leaves. The men sent us boys out to remove the food while they continued their talks.

When all the soil and leaf coverings came off the cooking pit, the food was exposed. A delicious smell brought everyone to the cooking pit. Two of the smallest kids sat closest to the pork as if they were taking ownership of the pork. The hot stones had cooked everything, pork, cabbages, sweet potatoes and even leaves.

Wane cut half of their pig and shared it with his four wives and children and reserved the other half for their neighbours. While the children sat with their mothers and ate, Wane cut his neighbours' meat according to the number of houses. When he completed the cutting, his wives wrapped the meat with ferns in the cooked leaves. Wane's two daughters and one of his young boys hurried away and distributed the meat to their neighbours' homes.

"Papa we have forgotten the Papes," said Mono after their neighbour's meat was taken away.

"Ok we'll give them our share, the backbone," said Wane.

Yare and Katopa split our pork into two halves and packed it inside two big bilums. My father placed the head and spine in another bilum.

It was before dawn when we left Kandep the next day. Katopa and Yare carried the meat while my father held the rope of the live pig and the small bag which had the spine and a shiny kina shell Wane had given to him in the night.

We were nearly out of the village when my father rested on a hill and beckoned

Katopa to rest his bilum near him.

"Can you see that house on the hill," said my father, pointing to a house on the other side of the creek. Smoke was rising early in the morning.

"That house belongs to my father's last sister. The lady is a very old woman. You will see her awake and making bilum. Take your bilum plus this spine for her. Tell her I will visit her sometime."

When Katopa ran back, the old woman came out of her house and waved at us.

"She didn't recognize me," said Katopa. "After I had explained who I was, she sobbed and hugged me on my feet. She was not happy because she didn't see you. She wanted you to come to her home first before going to other's houses."

"Oh, sorry for my old aunty," said my father. "I will visit her sometime. Now we have a long way to go. We have to be quick."

Katopa and Yare split Yare's pork into two and carried a quarter each.

When we reached the forest floor, the track was still wet from the downpour of the previous day. Beautiful sunshine poured above the treetops after midmorning but was short-lived as storm clouds scooped up the sunshine and darkened the skyline. My father said we had to get out of the Kandep side of the jungle quickly as heavy rains were imminent.

The pig stopped here and there to search for warms. I hit it with a stick.

"Don't hit the pig," said my father. "It will make the pig too lazy to travel."

Judging from the way the pig travelled, my father said we would reach home at nightfall.

By the time we reached the plateau and the swamp, the clouds got heavier and darker. Then raindrops began to hit the leaves and ferns. The rain became heavier and heavier when we reached our side of the forest and headed towards the Kaugel River.

Once we crossed a flatland and arrived at a creek, there was a dry shade under a huge tree. I suggested we could rest for a while but my father said we had to continue because we had the two mountains to climb before we reached Kaugel River.

The rain showed no signs of abating. We slashed off huge leaves and covered our heads as we travelled through the rain. My father would scoop me up and carry me on his back whenever we came to a flooded creek or a steep slope.

By the time we reached the Kaugel River, the clouds cleared and the rains stopped. A gentle wind whispered through the leaves and splashed off the raindrops. In the valley below, the great river bounced from rock to rock, shooting and splashing its currents everywhere.

Yare and Katopa arrived at the banks ahead of us. Katopa was fastening his bilum on a bending branch at the bank while Yare had gone upriver to check the bridge.

"I have never seen the floods this high" said my father, resting his bilum against a tree.

There was excessive rain in the mountains where the river began its journey. All the creeks collected all the rainwater and emptied into the river, so that the river swelled and swelled to its brim and swept away anything that interfered with its flow. No bending branch or a giant tree could withstand the sweeping might of the great river as it rushed its way towards the valleys.

Yare returned only to inform us that he couldn't locate the bridge.

"What do you mean? It should be there" said my father.

We all rushed upriver and found the banks empty. The floods had uprooted and washed away the huge trees on either side of the river where the vines had been fastened.

"This is the second time the river has taken the bridge," said my father. "We have been concerned about the bridge lately, when the rainfalls were heavy. Now we need to find a way home. Check if you can locate a spot where we can cross."

Yare and Katopa went downriver where the river widened but they returned a while later and said there wasn't a place shallow enough for us to cross.

"See if you can find a tree then," said my father.

Katopa and Yare identified a huge tree further up the river and immediately began to cut it. My father and I went to where we had left our things. He removed his kina shell from his bilum and held it up with his left hand.

"This is of the purest and the highest quality," he said. "This must have been taken out from a great lake where all the rivers meet."

After wiping the shiny treasure with a soft leaf, he wrapped it inside some ferns and gently placed it back inside the bilum again.

"Father, how many will you have now?" I asked.

"Oh, I should own seven but I have used four in a moka and threw one away to buy that stupid third wife of Yopai. I have wasted that kina shell. I should have kept it for other purposes rather than casting it off to a woman who wouldn't give us a son."

"But Tarapi has three beautiful girls. You should be happy, Father."

"Ah what are girls going to do?" said my father. "Will they defend your land in battle? Will they inherit the land? I would love to have many boys to fill the edges of this land. Our tribe must be huge and fearful."

"Then you don't love my little sister Konopu?"

My father thought for a while and said, "Son that is not what I am saying. How could one forget the child of his bone and blood? He who forgets his daughters is a fool.

"I have all those huge land and trees I've shown you last time. I need more sons to dominate the land. Our tribe needs sons who will defend our land. When Konopu grows up, she like every other girl, will marry away to another tribe. Girls have a home elsewhere but you boys will inherit the land when I am gone."

"Father you should be happy because you have Katopa, Koukera, and me."

"I am a proud father of you boys but our tribe must have more men."

I asked my father how the bridge was built. He followed the currents with his eyes, inhaled a deep breath and looked away to the heavy waters as if he hadn't heard me. I guessed he was consulting his memory to recall how many vines were employed to construct the bridge.

"Katopa was a baby when we built the bridge," said my father.

"Your mother and the women brought food here every two days for the men."

"How many days did you take to complete the bridge?"

"Oh, how many days? Son, it isn't that easy to pull the ropes over the river. We were lucky because other tribes helped us to fasten the vines on the trees and get the bridge suspended over the river. When we completed the bridge after a moon, we slaughtered seven pigs to celebrate its completion. We invited all those who helped us to the feast."

I couldn't believe how they managed to collect the loose vines together and pull them across the great river.

Now Yare and Katopa were halfway into felling the tree. But every sound of the axe made me more desperate to see my mother. I had never left my home before. Those three days were like moons to me. I was missing my playmate and little sister Konopu so much that I persuaded my father to take me home after the first day in Kandep. The longer it took to cut the tree, the more desperate I became to go home.

At length, Katopa shouted that the tree was falling.

My father and I were watching from a hill when the giant tree flattened everything to the ground on its way across the river. Some branches broke off immediately and floated downriver as the tree landed across the river with a massive fall. The one-log bridge was narrow for two people to pass each other but was wide enough for one to cross safely to the other side.

Now the sun sank behind the trees and the place got dark. We had flatland of thick forest to cross before we reached home. My father said we would leave the pig behind for some boys to pick up the next day.

After Yare and Katopa brought their pork bilums to the other side, Yare returned and crouched down with his hands behind him. I climbed on his back and wrapped my hands around his neck. I clung to his back as we slowly crossed the river.

I hid my face against his back for I didn't want to see the huge body of water which was rushing downstream, bouncing and breaking on the boulders.

My father brought his bilum handles to his chest and stepped onto the bridge. I thought I would ask him to give me the kina shell and the head of the pig when we arrived home so I could proudly carry them to my mother and my sister. My mother would hug me and Konopu would insist on hiding the kina shell in my mother's room.

The long journey had drained my strength. I pulled out a sweet potato from my small bag and as I got the second bite, my father cried out for help.

His bilum was falling ahead of him. He slipped off the bridge and headed into the angry currents. His hands scrambled to get hold of something but he was too late. He landed in the flood with a heavy splash.

I sprinted to the spot where he fell but the currents rushed him away like a light log.

Parts of his body appeared and disappeared as the heavy floods carried him away.

Yare and Katopa jumped towards him but the closer they went, the further the floods took him away. They came out of the river again and sprinted ahead on land and waited for my father where he would appear. When my father arrived, the men jumped in but the great river tackled Katopa's legs and flattened him into the currents. Katopa disappeared for a while and when he re-emerged downriver, blood was all over his forehead. He raised his head above the waters just in time when he neared a protruding rock. The currents slapped him hard against the sharp rock and floated him downstream. His hands rested on the waters without any movement.

Now the currents tossed both Katopa and my father here and there against the rocks until I lost sight of them both at the section where the river turned a corner. Yare wrestled with the angry currents to rescue them, but when he realised his own life was in danger, he made his way out of the river. However, the currents slackened his muscles and floated him down until he reached a bending vine at the riverbank. He grabbed the vine and pulled himself out of the river.

I knew I had lost them both because the great river was known for squashing the life out of those who interfered with its flow. It was famous for vomiting disfigured and lifeless bodies. I was lost and hopeless. I was like a bird with broken wings.

A heavy silence permeated the land. Echoes of death and hopelessness resounded in the forest. Darkness, which had fully settled, completed the river's work and ended any possibility of searches or rescues.

Yare vomited out some water and after he recovered his breath, he picked me up and carried me on his back as we journeyed home.

Chapter 4

Aweak moonlight spilt thinly through the canopies and shed a little light over the track as we felt our way through the swollen streams and slippery tracks.

By the time we reached home, it was midnight. The whole village was dead quiet. Yare said it was good to announce bad news from a distance because revealing such news at a close range would shock some recipients to death. He yodeled and announced the deaths while we were at the creek.

My mother must have been awake all night. As soon as we delivered the message, a little light moved from her side of the fireplace to the door.

"Amboama," Yare called again, "Katopa and Karimbi have drowned in the river."

My mother held two glowing embers in her hands and watched the tracks when we arrived. She could confirm the deaths because my father's voice was missing. Whenever he returned from a long hunting trip or a faraway land, my father would indicate his arrival with a unique whistle from across the creek. We children would rush to meet him at the creek.

That whistle which preceded his arrival was missing that night.

My mother left the door and walked out slowly to the field to meet us but she stopped and stood motionless near the door. She opened her mouth but words died on her lips. Then the ember in her left hand dropped and then the one in her right. She stood motionless for a while and then slumped backwards to the ground. She was rushed to the creek and was submerged underwater for a long time before she regained consciousness.

Shouts echoed from one end of the village to another and brought the entire village to our home.

My mother wept and applied dirt and mud all over her body. She crawled in the mud and pulled out the hair in her head but that couldn't take her grief away. She then rushed into the house and brought out my father's axe. Before anyone could snatch the axe out, my mother placed her fingers on a log and sliced off the last two fingers on her left hand. The detached fingers crawled on the ground, spraying blood everywhere.

Pepena's mother quickly came in and tied my mother's damaged arm at the wrist with a rope to stop further blood loss.

"Oh, my sister it's very, very bad for you to lose both son and husband. But please don't do this again to the rest of the fingers," said Pepena's mother. "Your fingers are your strength. They are innocent. They'll look after you in the future."

Pepena's mother washed my mother's wound with warm water and applied pig fat before she covered the wound with some soft leaves. She then wrapped the wound with a rope.

Pepena's mother and two young girls were instructed to watch over my mother in case she ended her life.

Next morning a search team was dispatched to retrieve the bodies. They searched all morning and found the bodies at noon.

My father's corpse was washed out at a corner where the river vomited logs and sediments. His skull was fractured with a sharp wound across his forehead and his right eye was knocked out of its place. My brother's bruised body was found inside a cave where the river hit the rocks and bounced back. Both corpses were severely disfigured with various injury marks.

The retrievers wrapped the bodies inside tree bark and brought them into the ceremonial ground and were suspended on two long poles at the ceremonial ground. When the bodies were rested on the poles, the mourners raised their voices and wailed. The voices blended and shook the foundation of the village. It was the beginning of a sad day. It was the day of mourning. It was the day of sorrow.

My mother, my stepmothers and the village women wore black mourning clothes for the occasion.

For the next two days, mourners from distant villages poured in for the funeral service. Some painted their faces with charcoal and others smeared their bodies with clay.

As the mourners entered the ceremonial ground, our people welcomed them with wailings and embraces. After the cries subsided, the visitors were given time to share their condolences.

Famous chiefs from the visiting tribes consoled our tribe for the loss. They said they were equally as devasted and shocked as us. They would stop for a while for our people to welcome new visitors when they entered the ceremonial ground.

Some described my father as the string that held the tribes together. Others said my father had nurtured and raised many young men to become great leaders. Anzue, the Tendepo chief and my father's cousin said my father was a big tree.

"Many birds come to the tree for its fruits and some build their nests in its branches," said Anzue. "Now the tree has fallen. Its fall is shaking the entire land. It has gone with all it provides."

"I am shocked by this news. I couldn't believe Karimbi has died," continued Anzue.

"Karimbi was the strength of the Yanos. I'm sorry your strength is gone. Your wings are broken. I thought I would enjoy many great days with my cousin but death has its own way of ending things."

While Anzue was still speaking, his tribesmen pushed two huge pigs into the ceremonial ground and tied them in two short sticks. Anzue and his men added three kina shells. Other tribes also comforted our tribe and contributed valuables. My father's trading mate and his cousin from the Sipaka tribe, Napulge Olgo delivered a moving tribute. He said my father was the wings under which the Yanos took refuge in times of chaos.

"The whole Kaugel valley will miss this great chief," said Napulge Olgo. "Karimbi has left behind a huge space. If he was part of a fence, I would replace it tonight. But it takes ages to raise a man. It takes a tribe to raise a man.

"However, I want to assure you that when a tree dies, a young one grows in its place.

In your chief's death, many great leaders will be born. The sun has set for Karimbi but will rise with his sons. The darkness of death has fallen on Karimbi but the light of hope will glow with his sons.

"If it was possible to get my cousin's life back, I would be the first one to pull in the pigs and kina shells," concluded Napulge Olgo.

The crowd applauded Napugle Olgo. His speech assured us that my father had not taken everything to the grave with him. Napulge Olgo and his Sipaka tribesmen presented two pigs and three kina shells.

Now, Yopai, one of our young chiefs thanked everyone for comforting our broken hearts with their words and contributions.

"I am pleading with you all," said Yopai. "Please do not expect similar treatment when you have a death in your tribe. We might not come to you in the same way you've come today. Problems don't remind people before they come.

"We also extend our gratitude to everyone here who has come to shed your tears with us. You know adults wouldn't cry for nothing. Your tears are coming out from within the depth of your hearts. There is no lake in your eyes but tears have been put in your eyes for a purpose. Tears are precious gifts that are used to express sorrow and heartbreak. You are doing just that today and we are grateful."

While he was yet speaking, war cries emanated at the end of the ceremonial ground where the track came into the village. Yopai stopped for a while. The voices grew louder and louder until men and women with painted faces came running into the ceremonial ground. They were mad. They grabbed sticks and stones and even spears (which they had brought with them) and aimed at us. Some of the young men kicked the dust and shouted at us.

"Just observe," said Yopai to the panicking crowd.

"They are expressing their anger."

"Why two? Why too early?" they demanded.

"Who are they?" I asked Pepena's father.

"Oh, they are your grandmother's people," he said. "Why are they angry with us? They should be crying."

"They are expressing their pain for losing your father."

The youngest brother of my father's mother was also among the crowd. He was a grey-haired man with a long beard. When the noise died down, he stepped into the middle of the ceremonial ground with clenched fists and aimed his spear at us. Then he brought the spear to his right knee, and holding the spear at its ends, broke it in the middle with a bang.

This signified a fight. Whenever an elderly man broke his spears, young men would take to the battlefield. They wouldn't care who married their wives or took their land when they were killed. But his men watched on.

"Me and my men would die with the two if they had died in someone's hands," said the grey-haired man. His tribesmen brandished their weapons in agreement. When my father's uncle completed his speech, another man spoke, then another. After the fourth man, Yopai comforted them all.

"We are sharing with you the same pain of loss and heartbreaks," said Yopai. "The same knife that cut us has cut you. Death did not say, "I have taken the father. Let the son live for I will come back for him when he is old." Death's appetite is not quenchable. It has no limits for how many it can take. Death can take a loved one today, and another tomorrow. Whoever death puts its hands on, it claims for itself."

Now it was getting late. Those who had come from distant villages began to leave. The corpses were lowered from the poles and were taken away to a secluded house to be overnighted. Some of the distant relatives spent the night in the village.

Next morning, the bodies were brought out again and suspended onto the same poles.

Those mourners who hadn't turned up the previous day arrived. Some of our distant relatives couldn't make it on time because they were still unaware of the deaths. Some even came after the burials while others apologised to us moons later that they hadn't heard of the deaths.

It was at the end of the third day when we buried my father and brother in the village cemetery.

After the burials, the neighbouring tribes brought firewood sweet potatoes and vegetables for us to use during the entire mourning period. Four days after the burial, the funeral was dismissed and we returned to the house to continue the mourning. Most of the distant people left but our close relatives remained with us.

We threw a great funeral feast to end the mourning. Every family killed a pig or more depending on how many they could afford. A bachelor killed five pigs. Some of our people sought help from their distant relatives to increase the numbers. Only two men couldn't afford any pigs to kill. They helped the bachelor and others prepare the feast.

On the day of the feast, everyone pulled their pigs into the village ceremonial ground before daybreak and slaughtered them. By midmorning, all the pigs were slaughtered, cleaned and dried in the sun. Soon the stones were spread on top of the wood in the cooking pits and the wood went up in flames. After midmorning, the thick smoke from the many cooking pits blocked the sun and caused shadows.

While the stones were heating, the men cut out the ribs plus some meat and distributed them among the people. Some old women cooked their meat inside bamboo containers with tender greens. They said their teeth were not good enough. Young children roasted their meat over the open fire.

By midday, we buried all the meat and hot stones inside the cooking pits and covered them with soil. We removed the meat at sunset and piled it alongside the long ceremonial ground. Others who had cooked in their homes brought their meat to the ceremonial ground.

The line of pork stretched from one end of the ceremonial ground to the other. Each of our men stood beside his pork and began cutting the pork into smaller portions.

A crowd of guests had gathered at the ceremonial ground, some by invitation and others by will, to witness the pig killing.

Now as each clan's name was called, a representative received the meat on his people's behalf and brought it back to his people. Then their leaders cut the pork into smaller pieces and distributed it to their people. We gave special pork like the backbones or a quarter or half a pig to eminent persons of high standing in the society like chiefs and orators

We also gave some pork to my father's maternal people and my mother's family.

Giving to one's mother's side of the family following a death was said to strengthen family ties and avoid curses.

A brief speech preceded when handing out the pork to my mother's people. Our chief

Kipingi said to my mother's people, "My Yana brothers, I am sorry that we've lost our son Katopa too early. His death has broken all our hearts. You've been with us during the entire mourning period. Now this feast is marking the end of our mourning.

"Your expectations are high because a chief's son has died.

"If his father was alive, he would acknowledge you better. We are, however, not using Karimbi's death as an excuse. How could one forget his origin? We have put together these few things for you. Pigs and kina shells will not take Katopa's life back nor will they heal our broken hearts. Please accept the little we have here."

We gave my mother's people some pork, two live pigs and three kina shells.

"We are not chasing you away with the things," said Yopai. "Please you can visit your sister and the children anytime. The children and their mother will need your support as well as ours."

The Yanas thanked Kipingi and echoed similar concerns about keeping our relationships with them intact.

"The deaths have not broken the link our sister's marriage has forged with your tribe," they said. "We will maintain our relationship."

After the feast, everyone left for their homes. Our home became lifeless and gloomy. My mother covered her face with her hands and wailed for the deaths had thrown a mist of uncertainty and doubts over our future. From that moment on, she became our mother and father. I was unsure how she would take us through the unknown days ahead of us.

Chapter 5

A few moons after the deaths, we received two visitors one morning, an old man and a little girl. The little girl walked beside the old man with her right hand locked in the old man's hand. When they neared the house, the little girl refused to walk. The old man picked her up and carried her for a little while before he lowered her to the ground. He knelt before the girl and after speaking into her ears, he straightened her hair which was like that of a corn.

Moments later, he pulled her close to his heart and embraced her. They both appeared to be crying but I couldn't tell because they were some spaces away.

My mother raised her eyes to the track and cried out.

"Oh, that's my old man," said my mother and ran to meet them. She threw herself into the old man's arms and sobbed.

"Oh Papa, oh my dearest Kepambo. How could you come like this?" cried my mother.

The old man hugged my mother and cried. He was coughing badly. The little girl had signs of tears in her cheeks and eyes. They both were a pack of bones.

Kepambo was my mother's youngest sister. She was left motherless when her mother (my mother's mother) died. My grandmother did not have any children after Kepambo. Her health deteriorated rapidly until she passed away a few moons before my father and my brother died. I could remember Kepambo clinging onto her mother's lifeless body and called for her mother to come back. Kepambo couldn't let go of her mother's corpse when it was taken away to be buried. Every morning and afternoon, she would sit at the graveside and weep saying, "Mama come back to me. The house has grown cold without you."

Kepambo's cries and pleadings must have been too much for my grandfather to bear so he brought her to my mother.

"Daughter," said my grandfather to my mother, "I've come to leave her with you. She had been deepening my grief lately. She is yours now."

My grandfather returned to his village alone that afternoon. My mother sobbed seeing his back. Kepambo cried a lot that afternoon too and over the next few days. Sadly, her father's visit was the last one. He passed away a moon later.

Since Kepambo came to the house, my mother treated her as her firstborn daughter and she was part of our small family.

As one is not immune to challenges, we had ours as well. Several moons after the deaths, Yopai's wife accused my mother of courting her husband. He was my father's closest friend and was a father figure to us after the deaths. Yopai and his youngest son helped us with firewood and other work in the house after the deaths but when his wife became suspicious of his visits, he avoided coming to us.

My mother had disputes with my two stepmothers, especially with the second wife. Engaamb would spill her anger whenever she felt like it because my father was no longer there to quell tensions or restore order in the family.

One-time Engaamb exchanged words with my mother over a piece of land. She alleged that my mother had used a portion of her land to make our sweet potato mounds. My mother denied the accusations. She maintained that she had never touched Engaamb's soil. This tension quickly developed into an altercation before the village elders intervened and settled the issue two days later.

"You both must respect each other," they advised my mothers. "Don't take what is not yours."

Another incident happened one day when my stepbrother Koukera broke Konopu's nose while my mother was away in the gardens.

Koukera asked for a piece of sweet potato from Konopu and when she refused, he punched her across the face and broke her little nose. Konopu covered her nose with both hands but blood leaked out from her fingers and wet the earth. Koukera's little sister Pindaka, who was of Konopu's age and her best friend, cried with her.

Everyone fled into the bushes when they heard Pepena's mother shouting. She was in her garden nearby when she heard Konopu crying in pain. She ran after the children with a stick but when she couldn't catch any of them, she came back with heavy breaths.

"Oh, Mama why has he done this to you?" said Pepena's mother, examining Konopu's wounds. "Will I ever see that boy again? I'll teach him a lesson he will never forget."

After wiping the blood away with some soft leaves, she squashed some leaves in her fingers and allowed the greenish liquid to dip into the wound.

"Is it hurting you?" she asked Konopu.

"Oh Mama it's hurting me more now," cried Konopu.

"That is good. It will dry the wound quickly. Now go home and don't play anymore."

Our mother and Kepambo were still in the garden when Konopu and I returned home. The sun set and rain began to fall. We were so hungry that we searched for sweet potato remains that escaped the pigs' jaws in the pigpen. We found a few dried pieces and chewed them raw until we dozed off to sleep.

My mother and Kepambo arrived at sunset. She learnt of the incident and was very cross with Koukera.

"Why would he do this to you? Is she not his sister? Are you not his sister?" cried my mother.

"I'll talk to Engaamb about this," said my mother.

After dinner, my mother demanded an explanation from Koukera. Koukera came to the door and returned quickly to the house again. His mother came to the door with her hands crossed behind her and threw a quick look at my mother and laughed.

"I didn't hear you. Did you say a broken nose or a broken eye?" said Engaamb.

"Why would Koukera do this to my little girl? Is he not supposed to take care of her?"

"You stole my husband," said Engaamb. "And you had him for yourself all those times."

"I'm not talking about our husband. It's your son's behaviour."

"Ah," said Engaamb giving a fake smile. "I am sorry for you my sister. No one will defend you now."

"So you are encouraging evil, right?"

"Listen now," cut in Engaamb. "When Karimbi was alive, you were invincible. Nothing could harm you because he was always there for you, you owned him. Now you are nobody. We will survive according to our individual strengths."

The words hurt my mother so much that she cried on our way back. Kepambo and Konopu cried along with my mother. Koukera's little sister Pindaka also cried with the girls and cursed her mother for making my mother and the girls cry. My mother warned us to avoid Engaamb's children.

"Don't go any closer to her children," she said. "Her children's bad blood will come to you."

Without my father, life became tougher and tougher every day. One day we didn't have enough firewood and another day we were short of hands to cultivate the land. Work was easy when my father was alive. Men did most of the hunting and mended our fence. His death took all those helping hands away with it. No one was there for us. Even my mother's people who had offered to care for us during the funeral, weren't there for us when we needed help the most. We had to cut down the forest ourselves, we had to clear the land ourselves, we had to dig the ditches ourselves. My mother worked twice as hard to raise us.

Despite those setbacks, we persevered to survive until we came to a time when a great famine swept through the land and smashed all our food crops and killed our pigs. It scattered our people to distant villages in search of food. Many died along the tracks, including one of our own.

This sudden turn of events unfolded one morning that no one, even the oldest man in the village, expected.

Chapter 6

Several moons before the frost fell, the skies were torn open and the land was flooded for three full days. Every ditch and creek swelled until they could no longer take in the excess water. The surging creeks and drains vomited out the excess water onto the land. The runaway waters ran aground and devoured the crops, leaving only the leaves floating in the middle of the pools.

When the rains subsided, the water level shrunk back into the waterways. The weather cleared over the next few days as the clouds became lighter and thinner. A light wind rose from the east and gradually dried the land.

Now the sun, whose strength had been washed out by the rains, splashed its rays happily onto land again. The crops spread their leaves open and feasted on the sunlight from morning to sunset.

Day after day, the sun poured its rays over the rivers, crops, mountains and swamps. It rose very early in the morning and set very late in the afternoons. The sky withheld its showers and the rains, which were supposed to arrive on the third moon, were held back in the clouds by some invisible hand. Some children said the rains were afraid of the scorching sun and had retreated behind the mountains to take shade in our ancestors' land.

The temperature dropped so low that it froze out the night fires. We would leave our beds at night and would crouch over the fireplace at midnight to warm our hands.

The prolonged dry weather culminated in a frost fall one night. An old man who lived at the ceremonial ground noticed this and alerted everyone.

As old as Mt Giluwe, the old man knew all the seasons of the moons. His ageless eyes could predict seasons by the look of the clouds and the turn of the winds, but that morning, his warlike cry shocked the whole village. It was as if his ability to foresee things had abandoned him six moons ago.

"The enemy has struck again," cried the old man. The strange tone in his voice brought everyone to their doors and straight to their gardens.

I rushed to the door where we piled flat slabs of wood one on top of another horizontally. I removed the wood piece by piece and piled it near the door. When the last one came off, I sprinted to the old man's house and found him in a very sorry state. He had smeared clay and ash all over his face and beard.

"Oh, why have you waited until this day to take away the fruit of my labour?" he cried. The old man had spent over two moons to cultivate a small piece of land near his house. His sweet potatoes were only maturing when the frost arrived. He mourned for his sweet potatoes for the next few days as the frost continued to wreak havoc on the land. Sadly, he did not live to enjoy the great harvest after the frost. He was one of the seven people who perished in the great famine.

Now as the daylight grew lighter, the frost became clearer. The thin ash-like substance obscured the sweet potato leaves and the bare earth. It appeared as if someone had sprinkled white ash thinly on every surface. Frost covered every leaf, every grass and even the bare earth.

Mothers with their little crying babies came out of their homes one by one, trembling and shaking with cold in the freezing morning. They all knew one thing. Their lives would be cut short now. However, the children seemed not to understand the situation. They did not know that a thief had intruded the village in the night to steal, kill and destroy our produce.

Soon all the food crops would be gone after the frost had visited the land.

The sun crawled out of the horizon, much quicker than it used to do since the dawn of time. It was as if it had lost something in the previous evening, and had been awake all night this last night. The unhindered sun quickly scooped up the congealed frost on the leaves and on every surface. In no time the sun melted away the frost.

By the time the sun was above the head, the leaves turned light green to dark green as if they had been thrown into a steaming pot. The leaves withered in the next few days and fell off their branches. Massive piles of dead brown leaves accumulated under the trees, and gathered around rocks and piled up in the grasses.

The beans cooked on the vines, corn mushed inside their combs, and sweet potatoes melted underneath the soil. My mother's expert knowledge of matters regarding harvesting and planting became obsolete. We plucked out the beans and corn before they fell off the stems. We also dug out the young sweet potato tubers before they became watery and unsuitable for eating.

We fed on the frost-stricken food but when that was depleting, fears of starvation haunted us. Konopu grew thinner and thinner every day. My mother lost half of her weight as the famine gradually squashed the health of our people. It forced all social activities like pig killing and bride price ceremonies to an indefinite suspension. Many of our people abandoned their homes and sought refuge elsewhere where the famine was said to have been less severe.

Koukera and his family fled to Kandep in his mother's village of birth to avoid starvation while others migrated to Mt Hagen.

We also fed our pigs with the spoiled sweet potatoes but when the supply petered out, the pigs gave out desperate cries in the nights and passed out. Konopu would cry when she heard the pigs cry in the night because she knew one of her favourite pigs would be gone in the morning. One of the pigs that died one morning was Konopu's favourite. It was a piglet that used to live with us in the house before. The pig grew so big that we took it to the pig pen and left it with the big pigs. Konopu embraced the dead pig and sobbed for a very long time.

All our five pigs died when our sweet potato supply petered out. At first, we lived on meat but soon we ran out of meat as well.

We laid down in the nights with memories of times when food was bountiful, those good times when food decayed in the gardens, flooded our minds. Nights were empty and dark as a moonless night at midnight.

When empty nights faded into daybreak, daybreak brought no hope, but fear of tomorrow, where there was no tomorrow for us. There was no reason to live for tomorrow because tomorrow was the same as today, and today was the same as tomorrow. We wished for a better tomorrow but feared that a better tomorrow might not be for us, as we feared we might not see tomorrow at all.

One morning my mother gathered us all together and said, "It's hard for us to survive here. We must move into the forest. Maybe we may find hope there."

So we left for the forest in search of food that morning. Our neighbours, Pepena, his mother, his younger brother Laipe and their elder brother Lip joined us in the forest later in the day. Pepena's father preferred to stay in the village with a few other old men. We never knew the forest would be our second home for a very long time.

Chapter 7

It was midmorning when we reached the mountain above our village. The entire Tambul Valley was below us and smoke fires were rising in several villages. Further towards the mountainsides, untamed fires had pushed the tree lines further away from the villages.

Black spots were visible in the areas where vast areas of grasslands had been burnt out.

"This is terrible," said my mother. "We never burned down our land like this. Why would you burn your land which supports you? The land is our mother and our strength. We only slash and burn only a small portion of the land when we need a new garden. When you look after the land well, it will sustain your life.

The sun was above our heads when we arrived in the forest. We searched around and found a shady spot under a huge tree where we would build our shelter. It was near the Awilimalke Creek.

While the girls, my mother and Pepena's mother went away searching for mushrooms and edible roots, we boys pulled in saplings and erected a small shelter next to the huge tree. The tree's huge trunk served as a wall on one side. We fenced the other two sides with leaves and ferns, leaving the front open towards a small clearing. The leaves above and around the sides blocked off the winds perfectly. We made a fire inside and it was warm.

Konopu, Kepambo and our mothers moved into the shelter while we boys played a cat and dog race under the moonlight, chasing each other in the trees until nearly midnight. We didn't realise it was already daybreak when we woke up the next morning.

The day burst open with beautiful sunshine. It was a perfect day for hunting. Lip said we were hunting at the top of Mt Giluwe. We were excited to try out our hunting skills.

"Today is my happiest day," said Laipe, Pepena's small brother. That was his first hunting trip and he was so happy. He ran ahead with our two dogs while we were still fixing our bows and arrows.

The sun had risen moments ago but the trees were still blocking off the sunlight from reaching the forest floor when we left for Mt Giluwe. We followed the Awilimalke River to the top. The higher we climbed, the smaller and thinner the trees became. At length, the sky became clearer and the trees gave way to fine grassland. We reached the top of Mt Giluwe!

The top of Mt Giluwe was breathtaking. One could see all the villages in the entire Tambul Valley and beyond. It wasn't as steep and narrow as I had imagined. Huge areas of grass-covered flatlands ran from one hill to another. Among the grasslands sat pools of forests made up of short trees and shrubs. Wallabies, possums and large flightless birds lived in the forests. The ice on the grasses and inside the creeks remained solid although the sun had hit us on the face.

Straight ahead of us stood a lofty rock. It cast its huge shadow on the valley below when the sun splashed its yellow rays onto one side of it. Its base was wide but narrowed as it rose to the skies. A small house would sit comfortably on its top. Two creeks issued forth out of the rock and flowed together for a short distance before they fell off a cliff to form the head of the Awilimalke River.

"The rock's name is Owapelg Koou," said Lip. "It is where wild dogs live." "You mean that's their home?" asked Laipe, pointing to the huge rock.

"Yes, there are caves underneath the rock. The dogs live there with their puppies and their chiefs."

"What do they eat?" asked a curious Laipe.

"They feed on possums and wallabies. Their home is full of the bones of the animals they hunt," said Lip. "If you stay here in the night, you would hear them barking.

"Please let us go to the caves. I want a puppy," said Laipe.

"Man, you are saying take me to the death lands," said Lip laughing. "I'm afraid. No one has ever lived after seeing the dogs.

"Their leader is Kiluwe Peandi. Legends say Kiluwe Peandi is a giant of a dog. If you see him, you will die."

"How big is Kiluwe Peandi?" asked Laipe.

"Oh too many questions," said Lip. "This is one of the reasons why I don't like taking young boys around with me."

No one said anything for a while. We stared at the rock. Then as if he didn't want to ignore Laipe's question, Lip gave us a picture of what Kiluwe Peandi looked like.

"Kiluwe Peandi is like our biggest pig that died in the famine," he said. "But it is longer than the pig and has very tall legs. It can reach my waist."

Now it was midmorning. Lip said we would hunt in the grasslands.

"Are we going to hunt with fire?" asked Pepena.

We would hunt with the aid of fires but Lip said our fathers would reprimand us. Hunting with fire was the easiest and most effective. When the grasses went up in flames, the wallabies, flightless birds and possums would collect themselves inside the unburnt portions of the grasslands, surrounded by fires at all sides. The hunters would close in upon the frightened animals and hunt them down with their spears and hunting dogs. Lip said this hunting method was greatly condemned because it angered the gods of the mountains. Whenever the smoke ascended to the skies, angry storm clouds would gather over the mountaintops. Then the winds would gather up speed and hailstorms and floods would destroy food gardens. Our fathers reprimanded those boys who hunted with fires. So many preferred bows and arrows and dogs instead of fires.

While we were listening to Lip, one of our dogs barked in the valley. Then both dogs barked incessantly and ran over the grasses, jumping here and landing there. We sprinted towards the dogs, but before we reached the valley, a huge brown bird flew out of the grasses and floated across the grasses for a little while before it descended again.

We quickly broke off strong branches and ran after the bird. The dogs pursued it until they forced the bird out of the grass again.

As soon as the bird took to the skies, Pepena swung one of his sticks and knocked down the bird. It was when we were running towards the bird that the dogs sent feathers flying into space. Lip quickly ran in and pulled the bird out of the dog's teeth before the dogs tore it into pieces. Laipe played with the dead bird for a while and placed it inside his bilum.

We left the valley and went over to the other side of the hill where we continued to hunt for birds and possums. It was at sunset when we wrapped up our hunting. We killed four more birds, all huge brown birds with massive wings, and four wallabies.

Now the sun was standing over a mountain ready to sink. We followed home a small track that ran along the head of the Awilimalke Creek.

As we descended further down the mountain, the dogs ran off into the woods, sniffing here and there. By the time we arrived at a huge leafy tree, the dogs sniffed around its base as if they were curious to investigate and question the tree of any wrongdoing. Then they barked towards the branches with their eyes fixed on the top.

"Oh, look at this," said Lip raising something with his fingers. It was a cuscus dropping. There was a heap of dropping nearby, some appeared recent and fresh. The ones underneath were dry and black. It appeared that the last time the cuscus had dropped its waste was earlier that morning.

Lip sniffed the waste for a moment and then raised his eyes towards the branches.

There was a small hole like a man's fist on the trunk below where the tree split into two huge branches. The moss around the fist-sized hole was gone, apparently due to frequent stepping by cuscuses.

Lip quickly made a loop out of a strong vine by running the rope in and out of the loop until the loop was firm and strong. Then he placed his feet inside it and embraced the tree. However, he couldn't get his arms around the tree because it was too large for him to climb.

Fortunately, there was a smaller tree nearby where he could climb with ease.

"If the cuscus escapes, shoot it down," said Lip before leaving the base of the small tree.

The loop kept him intact with the tree as he hopped up the tree like a wallaby. Within a moment Lip was right opposite the hole. The hole was now slightly above his head. He was right at the entrance but was still on the branch of the small tree.

Breaking off a strong branch and stripping its leaves off, Lip plunged the stick into the hole. He removed the stick and thrusted it deep inside the hole violently again and again but there was no sign of life inside the hole. He rested for a while and said,

"Boys, we have wasted our time. I am coming down again."

"No. Please, please please please don't throw the stick away," cried Pepena "Just try one more time, just one more time. You are too close to the cuscus. Please try again one more time."

Lip didn't say anything. He stayed there for a while. He seemed to forget about the hole and the cuscus and instead commented on what he was seeing on the other side of Mt Giluwe. He said smoke was rising everywhere on the mountain on the other side.

"Is that Mt Hagen," asked Pepena.

"I think it is because Mother says the opposite of Mt Giluwe is Mt Hagen. They are sisters," said Laipe. He sounded happy.

Lip plunged the stick into the hole again. This time he pushed the stick right up into the tree until half of his hand was buried inside the trunk. He assaulted the cuscus' home for some time and removed the stick. As soon as the tip of the stick left the hole, a fatty cuscus ran out and made its way to the top. But before it escaped any further, Lip was more alert than before. He threw the stick away and grabbed the cuscus by its tail. The cuscus used all its four limbs to edge away but how could it escape the strong hands of an alerted young man? Lip dragged the cuscus toward him from the tail and grabbed its legs. The cuscus snapped its sharp teeth at Lip's fingers twice but missed them narrowly. Lip broke the cuscus's limbs against the trunk.

"Escape down there," said Lip and plunged the cuscus to us. It landed with a heavy fall near Laipe and stretched its injured limbs to get away. In its escape attempts, the cuscus collected some leaves on the ground.

Out of pure excitement, Laipe grabbed the cuscus by the tail and before he caressed its furs, he screamed in pain and threw the cuscus away.

I did not know whether Laipe had realized the cuscus was still alive. The joy of holding the cuscus blinded him that he failed to notice the living cuscus. Laipe's innocence provided a perfect opportunity for the injured cuscus to take revenge for its broken limbs. As soon as Laipe had his hands on the cuscus's furs, the angry cuscus sent its two sharp teeth deep into Laipe's finger and drew a pool of blood.

Pepena was fitting his string onto his bow on the other side of the tree when his little brother cried out in pain. He left everything behind, rushed to Laipe, picked up the cuscus in one hand and smashed its head against the huge tree. He then picked up his axe and smashed the cuscus's head on a giant root before he plunged the half-dead cuscus away to the dogs to finish it off. Pepena took Laipe's torn finger into his hands and kissed it. They both cried.

When we returned to our forest home that afternoon, Laipe went straight to his mother. She nursed his wound at the fireside while the meal was prepared.

My uncle Ponenge, Pepena's father, had arrived from the village and was at our forest home making a fire when we arrived. He commended us for a successful hunting trip but wasn't pleased when he noticed we had killed both the mother and child wallabies. He said even if the forest supplied unlimited meat, we should be mindful of how much we took.

"If you hunt all the wallabies today, where will you get your meat tomorrow?" said Ponenge. "You should have let the child go. You boys think only of today. Will you marry elsewhere like your sisters? You should be ashamed of yourselves for overhunting.

Remember, if you don't die today, there is always tomorrow."

Ponenge and our mothers cooked the cuscus and some ferns inside a cooking pit. We had our meal at midnight.

Two days later when we asked Laipe if he was accompanying us for another hunting trip, he said he was no longer interested in hunting because the cuscus would bite him again.

He went back to the village with his father.

We spent our days in the village and the forest. One night when we returned from the forest, my baby brother Yando cried and cried. My mother breastfed him but the child refused the breastmilk and continued to cry. We gave him water but he spilled it. His skin was very hot as if he had been taken out from the fire. We poured one container of water after another on his little hot skin until all our water was gone.

My mother sent us away to the creek to fetch water in the night. Kepambo and I carried a pumpkin container each. We asked Konopu to stay back but she cried and came after us. We had to go further up near the forest where there was a little pool between two boulders where we drew water.

It took us a long time to return to the house after our light went out midway through our way back.

My brother's cry was gone when we neared the house. There was a sobbing, and it was our mother's voice. We stopped at the wayside and listened. There were several voices, clearly of mothers crying inside the house.

"I'm afraid," said Kepambo. "This time it must not be our little brother." "No. Not my baby brother," cried Konopu.

"There must be something wrong with little Yando," said Kepambo.

Pepena's mother came out of the house with a light and took Konopu into her arms. "Daughter it's another bad story again," she said softly. "This time our little one has left us."

Yando's little lifeless body was placed on a pandanus mat near the fireplace. Two traces of tears ran back from his eyes.

"The famine has taken my boy away," said my mother taking Yando's warm body into her arms.

Yando was born a few moons after my father and brother drowned. We called him Yando as he replaced the deaths. He was a happy little boy who became our favourite. The child was my mother's treasure. She did not allow Konopu or any other children to hold the child, fearing they would drop him. She only allowed Konopu to carry the child in the bilum when Yando crawled. Whenever the child cried when we were returning from the gardens, we would stop by the wayside and mother fed him quickly. Sometimes when darkness caught up with us or when it was raining, my mother would hold the child in her arms and breastfeed him while walking.

Konopu went straight to the lifeless child and whispered into its ears.

"Wake up baby brother. Wake up," she cried.

Yando's death tore our hearts into pieces. We mourned our little brother for the whole night and buried him at sunset the next day near the ceremonial ground.

Konopu would visit the graveyard every morning, hoping Yando would come back to her. Her visits moved my mother to tears. It was hard for us to convince her that Yando wouldn't come back again.

One day when we came home from the gardens, Konopu told me and Kepambo that she had talked with Yando.

"I was alone playing around the house when he came," she said.

"We played all day until at sunset when he said he had to leave. I was sad to see him go but he said he had to leave. He was not the baby I knew. He was like Maip."

"Did he say anything to you?" asked Kepambo.

"He said he was sorry because I was playing alone. He said he would come back to me tomorrow. But he told me not to tell anyone."

"We won't tell Mama then," I said.

This news excited us so much that we avoided going to the garden with my mother and stayed around the house the next day. But when Yando didn't turn up, we went home crying.

My mother found this out days later and said we would never see him again.

"Mama why has my little brother died too early?" cried Konopu.

"Baba, that's the thing I don't understand," said my mother. "I don't know why death is taking away my loved ones too early."

"Death is only interested in this family and not others," added Kepambo. "I don't know whether we will have a good time to enjoy as a family someday."

"Life is so miserable for us today," said my mother. "It is so tough now but we must hope for a better tomorrow. Let us not allow our present problems to erase our hope for tomorrow. Tomorrow is a new day with new hope and life. Let's bury the dark sides of life today and hope for a brighter tomorrow because tomorrow will be a better day for us."

When the famine dragged on and on, we lost two more children and the old man who lost his sweet potato. By the time we lost the sixth person, the weather changed.

Light clouds hovered above the mountains and slowly darkened the sky. The sky got darker and heavier in the next couple of days. Then one afternoon, the winds stopped blowing altogether. The land sat still and a flash of lightning rolled across the sky and lightened up the dark sky.

The thunders came on and went off several more times before the first rains touched the mountain tops. We watched the dark skies as the rains drew closer and closer. The tall casuarina trees stood still as the land received its first rains in silence.

My mother left her fireplace and came to the door. She watched the raindrops with her arms on her cheeks. I could see fear in Konopu's eyes. She learned closer to my mother and begged her to close the door.

My mother came back to her favourite fireplace and blew the fire to life. A yellowish brown flame jumped out from the embers and lightened our faces. She smiled.

"The hard times are lifting off," said my mother.

"Mama are we going to have sweet potato again?" asked Konopu.

"Yes, child.

"But when Mama?"

"We will have to visit our dead gardens first."

Chapter 8

Two days after the rains, a gentle breeze cleared the mists and brought with it the promise of a new life. The shadow of death under which we had been living lifted. The rains revived the dead land. Weeds and sunken roots that had perished underneath the ruins sprouted to life again, turning the farmlands and the brown hillsides into their former green days.

The twin works of famine and frost hadn't killed my mother's zeal to restart life all over again. Like others, my mother was hungry to revive her gardens. She went into her room and brought out three bilums.

"We will go to Glama for sweet potato vines," said my mother. She threw two of the bilums to the girls.

My mother's village Glama was half a day's walk away. My mother's people sent word immediately after the rains for us to collect some sweet potato vines. Glama's many casuarina trees had partly preserved some sweet potato vines from the frost.

Other villages also left for distant villages in search of seeds and sweet potato vines. They left with much excitement as if the rains had promised them bountiful harvests. Some mothers removed their long-kept corn and bean seeds from above the fire and headed to their gardens.

My mother and the girls returned the next day with three bilum loads of sweet potato vines and some taro seeds. My mother also brought home two exciting treasures. She carried home a male and a female piglet on her bosom like twin babies.

"Here lies our future," said my mother smiling at the piglets and smoothing their hairs.

"They are very very young, Mama," said Kepambo.

"Yes, they are babies," said my mother. "It will take some days before they forget their mother."

"Don't worry about your mother," whispered my mother into their ears. "I will be your new mother now."

"If I were them, I wouldn't leave your side, Mama," said Konopu.

"How will we make them forget their mother?" asked Kepambo. "I'm sorry for the babies."

"I know something," said my mother. "Hold this." She gave one of the piglets to Kepambo and they carried the babies to the creek. When they returned, the babies were wet to the skin and shivered in the cold.

"Ah Mama why have you done this to the babies," complained Konopu. "Now see they are very cold. Look at this little nose." Konopu patted the little nose of one of the baby pigs playfully. "It's dying of cold."

"I have submerged them underwater," said my mother. "The creek has washed their memory away. They will no longer remember their mother. They will not die of cold because they'll live with us."

My mother then warmed the piglets over the fire and placed them inside a little enclosure near the door. She also weaved two small ropes for them that night.

"I will tie the piglets with these ropes when they get older," said my mother, who hid the ropes in her room.

Following the rains, those who had fled the village returned, some with piglets and seeds. Soon the abandoned gardens came alive with the sound of wooden spades and digging

sticks.

Koukera and his family returned from Kandep. However, her sister Pindaka was not with them.

"What happened to Pindaka?" asked my mother.

"Oh, we thought we had escaped death but how mistaken were we?" said Engaamb with tears swelling in her eyes. As the sun does not shine in one place, so was the famine. It was more fatal in Kandep."

"You mean you've lost the little one?" asked my mother.

"After we arrived in Kandep, the famine worsened," said Engaamb with tears. "We had no choice but to travel to my sister's place in the

Tsak Valley in Wapenamanda. It was during that journey when we buried our love on the way."

Engaamb stopped talking and brought her hands to her face and sobbed.

"Oh my Pindaka, how could you leave me so early?" she cried.

"We were halfway into Tsak when my little girl died on the way. We buried her under a tree near the track."

"Oh what a sad story," cried my mother. "I am so sorry you've buried our little girl in that lonely place."

"What I will never forget is this," said Engaamb, wiping her eyes. "I have buried my heart in a place I will never go back to see the cemetery. I won't even be able to clean her cemetery too.

"We took another track when we returned to Kandep. The children didn't want to see their little sister's graveyard."

It was a very sad news. We all cried. The frost not only killed our livestock and crops but also took away two dear siblings.

"We must bury the past, our sorrows and heartbreaks and look to the future," said Engaamb.

There was no way we could rise out of the famine, except through replanting and raising the pigs again like everyone else in the village. My mother distributed some of the sweet potato vines to Pepena's mother and two other women in the village. Engaamb gave us some taro seeds from her extra supply.

Sweet potato planting required the soil to be well prepared before planting. We gathered and heaped dry grasses and decayed foliage in circles in one of our old gardens. Then, with wooden saplings, we dug up the soil around the designated mounds.

The draught had hardened the soil that made our wooden spades bounce back when we attempted digging. We were about to give up but our mother said giving up was never an option.

"The only way to get out of a difficulty is to get through it," said my mother. Thus, we tilled the land day after day until the mounds took shape in the formless garden. We smashed the soil with short heavy sticks until the roots came off and the soil was loose and ready. We then covered the mounds with the soil. The sweet potato mounds reached our thighs.

My mother selected sweet potato vines in groups of three and pushed them into the mounds with her right hand, leaving their tips exposed to the sun.

After we had planted all our taro and sweet potatoes, our village fathers cleared a huge piece of forest at the foot of Mt Giluwe. We slashed all the small trees, ferns and plants. We burnt the leaves when they turned brown.

Since the new garden was rich in nutrients, the men ensured every family had a plot of land to plant their food. Each plot was demarcated by long saplings joined by their ends from one end of the garden to another.

Every morning, we uprooted all the small plants and burnt them in bonfires. We collected the unburnt branches and trunks and heaped them at the fence. When the garden was clean and ready to be planted, we young men and boys tucked our stone axes in our belts climbed the trees and slashed off the branches, leaving the trees standing branchless in the garden. For those trees we couldn't climb, we made fire at their bases. The trees lost their leaves several days later and allowed sunlight to reach the garden undisturbed.

Every day mothers and children brought out their corn and bean seeds and sowed them all day using sticks. Those families who completed their planting early, only visited the garden once in a while during the entire planting season to make sure there were no vultures around.

Following the planting, there was yet another challenge. The perished weeds that sank under the ruins threw their ugly heads everywhere and threatened to choke our young crops.

"My gardens are not for the weeds," said my mother. "They can claim the land when my strength is gone."

Just before the rains, the pandanus season kicked in. It was the pandanus that kept us alive between the planting and harvesting time. We took our pigs and went over the Kaugel River where our pandanus hut was. There we fed on both the nuts and the meat of the pandanus until our crops matured.

Nature proved supportive of our needs. The crops grew rapidly and I wondered what was causing that rapid growth. My mother said the frost had poured a natural manure that sped up plant growth and maturity.

"In your challenges, there lies some good things," said my mother one morning when we were on a hill overlooking our garden and marveling at the looming harvest.

"When a problem strikes you down, ask yourself is there something good in this problem?"

"It is true that the frost had destroyed our land", she continued. "It tested our ability to withstand hard times. But it also made us stronger and united us as a family. The hard times proved that we could live without our father, we can live through storms and come out victorious on the other side."

In the next couple of moons, the sweet potato leaves from one mound met with those of another at the base. The beans and corn became heavy and bent their stems. The beans indicated that their chase up the poles was ending.

When we harvested our taros, my father's elder brother Ponenge gathered our family together in his house and slaughtered a huge pig. He said it was fitting to celebrate our maiden harvest with a feast.

"We are fortunate to be alive," said Ponenge. "We have lived through the hard times. Now there is a reason to celebrate. We have life to celebrate."

It was a fine sunny day when we slaughtered the pig. The mothers peeled the taros and dried them in the sun while we heated the stones.

When we were placing the hot stones inside the cooking pit, the old man watched us closely. He said we should be careful as we were cooking two different foods using the same stones.

"If you are worried about the meat and put in few stones, you'll leave the taro uncooked," said Ponenge. "Likewise, if you are concerned about the taro and place more stones, you'll spoil the meat. You have to strike a balance between the two. You must apply the right amount of heat."

His statement made much sense. Taro and meat required different levels of heat to achieve the desired outcomes. Taro needed more heat to cook properly while meat was the opposite. If both were cooked separately, it would be easy to apply the appropriate heat but we were dumping them both into the same cooking pit and expected the same stones to cook them both.

"In life, you have to balance things too," said the old man when we completed the mumu and rested under a casuarina tree.

"Weigh all things first. Always think of the consequences before you make a decision.

Don't rush to make a decision. You might rush into a decision you will regret later.

The feast signified harvests and the return of many festive occasions including marriage and pig-killing ceremonies. A spirit of joy and optimism filled everyone's hearts as

we gathered together to share the food.

Ponenge cut three-quarters of the meat and shared it with us but reserved a quarter of the pig with some taro and ferns. His wife eyed the reserved meat for a while and said,

"I thought everyone here got their shares."

"Why, did I forget someone?" asked Ponenge, quite surprised.

"No, I was wondering if you were leaving that aside on purpose," said Ponenge's wife referring to the reserved meat.

"Oh, Pepena take this meat to the Kelelis family quickly before I forget. The children have seen the smoke in the morning."

The Kelelis consisted of a young mother and her three small children. They lived on the other side of the creek. Their father passed away just before the famine, leaving the children to the young mother. She never worked as hard as the rest of the mothers in the village. She had married Keleli when she was a very young girl and, ever since then, she had been leaning on him for all her needs. Her total reliance on him had made her unprepared for a life without him.

When Keleli passed away, the young mother was left incapable of raising the children on her own. She and her children continued to live in poverty even after the famine. She failed, not as a mother, but to provide for her children. She planted small sweet potato gardens but harvested them before they matured. This habit of premature harvests attracted condemnation from some of the village mothers.

"Why should we give food to that idle woman? She won't give us anything back but take, take, and take more," some of the village women would complain. "She spreads her bag in the sun and sunbaths in the mornings when we leave for the gardens. We won't waste our food on such a lazy woman."

However, our fathers never withheld anything that would go to such people. And it was their wish to see the fatherless and orphans succeed in life. They would say,

"If you neglect the poor, you are paving your own way to poverty."

Now Ponenge's wife began to complain when Pepena packed the meat and the taros inside the bilum. She spoke in low voices, more to herself than to her husband.

"We have many mouths here," she said. Her voice was low but clear enough for everyone, including Ponenge to hear.

"Woman close your mouth now," shouted Ponenge. "Who will give them when we don't? You selfish old woman."

Pepena's mother was quiet for some time and then said to herself,

"Keleli must have asked Ponenge to look after the widow for him. Maybe he will marry her someday."

Ponenge ignored her and urged Pepena to take the food away quickly before it became cold. Pepena completed packing the food but was hesitant to take it away because he knew he wouldn't escape his mother's sharp tongue later. Ponenge didn't realize that until later when he noticed his son was still there.

"Boy what are you waiting for?" shouted Ponenge. "Never mind this silly old woman.

Run to the children and give them the meat. They've seen the smokes in the morning.

They've been expecting this since morning." When Pepena left, his mother said no more of the meat. Everyone sat before a slice of taro and meat. No noise was heard except Konopu and Kepambo arguing over who could have a piece of bone. This was soon quelled when Pepena's mother threw a bone at the girls.

While everyone was eating, Ponenge wiped off the grease from his bamboo knife on some dry banana leaves.

"We are celebrating what the land has given to us after the famine," said Ponenge.

"The land hasn't given us the good harvest to console us after the famine," he continued. "No! We have worked the land hard to receive from it. The land gives according to how much one asks from it. How much one harvests from the land depends on how much effort one puts into the land.

"The land does not even favour certain people. You reap exactly what you sow into the land. I see some strong young men doing nothing with their strength. You are young only once and you will be old like me one day. Do things now while you are young. Climb the tallest tree today, chase the wildest cassowary today, fight the toughest enemy today. Use your strength today while you are young. Do things today when you are young and strong.

"Now back to the land again," paused Ponenge. "If you are thinking the land will supply you with great harvests because you own it, I'm sorry for you. You are daydreaming. You are lazy.

"Do your part. Cultivate your land and sow your seeds. Then leave the rest to the land and weather. Don't wait for the rain. Always have your land ready because rain may come in its own time. Good times come when least expected."

"If you wait for good times," added my mother, "you will wait forever."

"Yes, that is true," said Ponenge. "We don't wait for good things to come to us.

Opportunities are everywhere. If you have sharp eyes, you will be able to see opportunities.

But what do you do when you don't have opportunities?" he paused for a while but no one said anything.

"When we don't have opportunities," repeated Ponenge. "We create them. "Great things come to those who have dreams. Great things come to those who are brave enough to chase their dreams. You young men must have dreams because, without a dream, you are like a lost dog in the jungle."

We ate in silence for the rest of the afternoon. Those who had leftovers packed their food and left for their homes.

Activity rolled back to its pre-famine days. Our sow gave birth to seven piglets. The good earth restored what the famine had stolen. One harvest followed after another. My mother's workload lightened when the girls grew older and took over most of the work in the house and the gardens. Konopu and Kepambo grew into very beautiful young women and reached marriageable age.

Chapter 9

Ponenge was an old man but his wisdom never aged. I visited him once in a while to hear him.

One morning he was complaining about the rain.

"These continuous rains are spoiling my plans," said Ponenge.

I wondered what plans he could possibly have at such an age when his strength and knees were failing him.

"You couldn't be thinking of hunting, are you?" I asked him.

"Oh, son the thoughts of hunting are with me every day. My mind says, run to the forest, chase after that runaway cassowary, climb that tall tree, marry this or that beautiful young girl. All those thoughts are strong. My mind is young and fresh, the same as it was when I was young. I wish I could do any of those things my mind is telling me but you know what? Time is against me. My body is against my mind's lofty dreams."

"I've been thinking about the house lately," continued Ponenge. "It needs to be taken down."

"But I think your house is still new."

"Of course it's new but see there," he pointed towards the roof. A small hole was above the fireplace. The roof was rotting away and rainwater was wetting the floor.

"That tiny hole can be a disaster if we leave it unattended for a long time," he said. "There are few other similar holes, one each in the two rooms and another right above the doorway. We need to fix them before they become problematic."

Ponenge talked about the types of materials used in the house.

"The grass on the roof is rotting away. The wood is strong but the grass is very light.

The wind could carry it away easily.

"If we use only the strong materials, I believe the house would last longer," I commented.

"No son. That's not how we build houses. You can't build a house with wood only because the roof will collapse under the weight of the wood.

"You need grass for the roof. Grass is light but can sit comfortably well on top of the wood and can shut out the rain, wind and the sun well. Both the wood and grass play their special and distinctive roles in making the house complete.

"Now what am I saying here?" continued the old man. He took out his bamboo flute from his bag that was hanging on the wall. He blew a sad note. He played the instrument for some time and then rested it aside near him.

"Like a house," continued Ponenge, "a man has strength in some areas but weakness in other areas.

"You are young but I need to tell you something you might not learn from others.

"Although man may be famous on the ceremonial ground or on the battlefields, there are some areas where he needs a woman. She can do better in those areas than him. Looking after children, cooking and raising pigs, for example, are women's specialised areas.

"A wife is like the grass that seals the house and makes it complete. She makes sure everything inside the house is in its correct place.

"Your wife should complement you in life. She and you are the upper and lower jaws. She can build you up or break you down. If she is incapable of making gardens, looking after pigs and giving birth to children, she will drag you down. Remember when the roof rots, it spoils the entire house. Your woman is like that. If you marry a woman with beauty but without a brain, you are doomed for disaster."

I imagined how life would be like if I married a girl who was incapable of performing those tasks which were essential in building a man. How would I know which woman would be the right type? How would I know I had chosen a woman of value? I feared I might choose someone with beauty but devoid of such qualities. Looks could be deceiving.

The old man sang a song with his flute, stopped midway and said he was thinking of his young days when he was free to do whatever pleased his heart. He spoke for a little while more and then played his flute for a little while more before he placed it back on the wall again.

"If you see weakness in your woman, build her into a woman of substance," continued Ponenge. "Treasure her because when she leaves her parents, she trusts that you will take care of her well. She comes to die with you. Look after her well and she will bear you sons. Take care of her well and she will make a name for you in public. A man who does not know how to take care of his wife and children is unfit to look after his tribe.

"Remember women are not as cheap as courtship sessions. When you have a wife someday, you will work the land to feed her. Many young men these days think their woman will come to take away all the work in the garden. This is not true my son. Only after you are married, will you realise your responsibilities have increased tenfold. So, you have to learn to work now."

After he had spoken, I asked him whether he was taking the house down as he had said or he was renovating it.

"I am thinking of a new house but all the posts and rafters are still in the forest."

"When are you building then?"

"I don't know," replied Ponenge. "The work is too heavy for me these days. When I was young like you, I loved heavy work. But now, strength is no longer interested in the old. Strength favours the young."

A wave of sadness crossed the old man's wrinkled face. The heavy work in his younger days must have weighed on him. He was like a strong tree. The storms of life shook and battered him but never took him down. He must have been a very handsome young man in his prime time. I imagined how many girls were chasing after him. I said I could bring the rafters and posts back from the forest.

The old man stared at me for a while and said:

"You are bringing them home for me?"

"I'll start tomorrow."

"Son, give me your hand."

He took my right hand and squashed it with his bony fingers.

"You will look after this place when I am gone," he said. "I have some rebellious young men. I regret why I had brought them into the world. I have been talking about the house for a long time but my boys have ears that never understand the meaning of listening.

My words enter in one ear and immediately escape through the other."

The next day I rose before daybreak and brought the first bundle of rafters home.

Ponenge's boys Poi, Lip and Laipe were ashamed of themselves and brought the rest home in the next three days. Four days later, we cleared a small land near their house and drove the posts into the ground.

Ponenge watched us closely and intervened whenever his advice was needed. But his presence was enough for us to do things right.

"Make sure the posts must not rise above your shoulders," he said.

"Father what's wrong with having high posts," asked a curious Laipe.

"This is at the foot of Mt Giluwe. I don't need to tell you how cold the place is," replied the old man. "When your wall is too high, the little fire you make inside the house vanishes without leaving enough warmth behind for you."

"This will be Poi's room and that will be his wife's," joked Pepena, marking the rooms with a piece of vine.

"No, I and my wife will squeeze into the same room, the smallest room in the house," laughed Poi.

The house had two rooms, one for Ponenge and the other for Pepena's mother. The father's room was meant for the father and the boys, but it was rarely used as fathers and sons preferred the men's house over the family house. They however stored their valuables inside the room. The principal occupants in the mother's room were the very small children, girls and their mother.

Sometimes when a father had two wives living under the same roof, his house had two doors and two fireplaces. Each wife knew that one fireplace and one side of the house (including the door) belonged to her, and that must be respected. Under such a setting, not a single night would pass without a quarrel. Burning embers were the chief objects used to settle arguments. Such family feuds were only resolved once each wife got a separate home of her own. The children would take sides with their mothers when there was an argument.

There was the story of this silly little boy who set fire to his stepmother's side of the house, but when the fire spread to his mother's side, he cried and watched helplessly as the fire gutted the whole house.

Days later, the house was ready to receive the grass for the roof; vines held everything intact in their correct places; rafters hanging over the roof, walls completed with barks on the outside, blinds inside the walls and posts standing erect and firm.

Covering the roof was heavy work and thus required many hands. Other young men in the village came in to help with the roof.

We went to our abandoned gardens and bent the tall grasses (grasses taller than the height of a man) until they lay flat with the ground.

We placed heavy logs on top of the grasses and allowed the grasses to remain bent for two days. On the third day, we placed some wood underneath the grasses and chopped the grasses with stone axes until we had cut a huge area just enough to cover the whole house. The women and children then collected the grass and brought it back to the building site. This cutting alone took another whole day.

On the day of covering the roof, mothers brought sweet potatoes and cooked in hot stones outside Ponenge's home while we boys and the men worked on the roof.

Four men covered the roof in pairs, two on either side of the building. One was the assistant and the other was the specialist builder. The assistant gathered a handful of grass and handed it to the specialist builder who covered the rafters one layer on top of another. The rest of the men were on the ground, providing general advice on whether there was too much grass on a particular section or whether the builders needed to reduce the thickness on a specific spot. We boys took turns shouldering the grass up to the roof.

By the time the roof was nearly completed, it was afternoon and the place started to rain. We left two builders on the roof to put on the finishing touches. We retreated to

Ponenge's old house where Ponenge and the women were serving the sweet potatoes.

While we were eating, Ponenge thanked everyone and encouraged us to work in unity.

"We must continue to lighten one another's burdens. Let us not neglect our brother in need. If your friend is in need today and comes to you today, don't say go back and come tomorrow when you should help him today. Helping your neighbour is helping yourself."

The other elderly men also echoed similar sentiments and emphasised the importance of unity.

"Uphold unity at all times," they all said. "Where there is unity, there is greatness. Men united to fight great battles. Unity brought down strong enemies; unity accomplished great things that were far from individual efforts. Embrace unity at all times. Unity makes the impossible possible."

After the house was completed, we built a circular fireplace in the centre of the house with stones. Ponenge's wife cut some grass from the swamp and spread it on the floor.

Ponenge and his boys sharpened flat slabs of wood for the door.

When everything was completed, the family abandoned their old house and moved into their new home. The old woman said that was her final home before she died. She hugged and thanked us for giving her a beautiful new home.

Six moons later, Ponenge and his boys helped me to build our house. We wanted to remove our old house but my mother opposed it saying she wouldn't see the house my father had built with his own hands coming down.

"Let it rot and fall to the ground," said my mother.

We levelled several sweet potato mounds near our house and built a beautiful home where the girls and I grew up to be adults.

Chapter 10

It was said that when the dead had grudges against their surviving relatives, they inflicted sickness and prolonged suffering on them. Any serious sickness was attributed to the works of spirits, and the only remedy to end the suffering was to appease the spirits through animal sacrifices. Pigs were the chief sacrificial objects. Healing was granted when the amount of animal blood offered satisfied the spirits well.

One morning, Pepena came running to our house and said,

"Maya is sick. Kipingi needs our help."

"Right now?"

"Yes."

Pepena said Maya, our neighbour Kaime's son had been sick for a while and Kipingi, the village chief who ran intercession with the spirits on behalf of the sick, was needing our help urgently.

Maya's mother rested the sick child on a pandanus mat and was sobbing. Kipingi and Kaime stood over the boy with their hands behind them and were discussing the possible causes of the sickness.

Maya was tall and light-skinned. He was the last in the family. The Kaimes first was a girl who was married to Puluwe. They lost their second child, a boy about the same age as

Maya in the same sickness. The family offered two pigs to the spirits but that couldn't save their boy. When Maya was born, his mother chopped off the small finger on his left hand to chase the spirits away.

The two moons that he had been sick had reduced Maya's flesh to the bones. His mother called his name from time to time, but the child remained motionless. She brought the child to her heart and wept.

"Look," said the boy's father, "we have lost his elder brother in the same disease or curse or whatever. I don't know. Maya has been struggling to breathe for days. His breathing improved yesterday and when we thought he had recovered, the attacks are coming back again. The spirits have intensified their work on the child last night and made his legs useless. He cannot walk. His breath has slowed to the point where it might stop anytime. Things don't happen to children like this for nothing. The dead are attacking my boy."

Kipingi took Maya into his arms and examined the child's eyes and felt his heartbeat. He ran the inside of his palm gently across his forehead and placed his right ear closer to the child's heart and heard its pulse.

"It's true. The spirits of the dead are attacking this child," said Kipingi.

"What are we going to do now?" pleaded Maya's mother with tears rolling down her cheeks.

Kipingi said nothing. He handed Maya back to his mother without taking his eyes off the child. The child's hands dropped to its side. So weak was he that Maya was incapable of using his limbs again.

"Please save my child. I cannot lose yet another boy," said Maya's mother.

"We need to appease the spirits quickly or else we'll lose him too," said Kipingi.

Kaime hesitated for a moment. The child's mother looked at him with impatient eyes. Kaime remained quiet for some time and then slipped off to his pig pen. He returned a while later with a black pig. His wife's face brightened up a little. At least there was hope for her sick child.

"This is all we have," said Kaime, handing the rope over to Kipingi. "If the spirits attack my boy again, I don't have a choice. They'll have to kill me too."

The crying mother held the sick boy in her hands and the father watched with fading hopes as we took away the family's only possession to the spirit house. Spirits never played any role in raising pigs but whenever there was an illness in a family, they must have been smiling because a family in illness would give anything away to save their loved one. Kaime had no choice but to give away the family's last pig to the spirits as the young boy's recovery hung precariously on the pig.

The spirit house stood at the end of the village under the foot of a mountain. It was separated from the village by a small fast-flowing creek. A small track led into it. Ancient casuarina trees stood at either side of the track with their tops shooting straight into the cloudless sky. Sloping vines and lush ferns obscured the huge trunks at the base, creating a ditch-like track.

When we approached the spirit house, a gentle breeze shook the branches and shed some of the needle-like leaves. Some of the flying leaves settled on the blue lake opposite the spirit house, but a noiseless wave swept them further away into the deepest parts of the lake.

The track narrowed as we neared the spirit house until it admitted us into a small clearing, like a small ceremonial ground. It was shaped in the likeness of a heart and was fenced around all corners with fens of various types. The spirit house sat facing the clearing.

Kipingi tied the pig in the middle of the clearing and searched with his feet among the dead foliage. He uncovered a large stick, about the size of a man's hand and pushed it to me with his toes.

"Clean this one," said Kipingi and walked away to the spirit house with his head bowed and hands folded behind him.

Pushing away the dry banana leaves at the door, Kipingi disappeared into the spirit house. The leaves closed behind him as if some invisible hands were manning the door and were keeping everything inside secret.

The stick was small but heavy enough to kill any pig regardless of size and strength. Perhaps it had killed many pigs and saved many people. I did not know how long our forefathers had been consulting the spirits but the aged casuarina trees indicated that the practice was as old as the casuarina trees because the trees were as old as the village. Our ancestors had the habit of planting casuarina trees as soon as they settled on land. The practice of offering sacrifice was as old as the village. It was inbuilt and was passed on from one generation to another, from father to son.

Now heavy smoke rose inside the spirit house and some escaped through the door. Later when the smoke cleared away, Kipingi emerged at the door and waved the banana leaves away.

"Kill the pig and collect the blood in these," said Kipingi and handed two containers to Pepena.

When Pepena turned to leave, Kipingi warned us, "Do not spill a drop. It's difficult to look for an additional pig."

After we killed the pig, Pepena and I collected the blood as it seeped out of the fractured nose and mouth. Now the fire produced a lot of smoke as if it was sensing the blood. We couldn't see Kipingi for some time until after the smoke cleared away when he was standing at the doorway, looking across the heart like clearing.

He walked quietly over and snatched the two containers away from Pepena's hands as if they were in the wrong hands. Perhaps he needed to quench the spirits' thirst without the slightest delay, probably because the spirits couldn't hold their patience in the sight of blood.

After greeting the containers with some esoteric language, Kipingi raised them to the heavens and lowered them slowly.

"Pour this one into the lake for Ola Yemo," said Kipingi, handing one of the containers to Pepena. He said Kuru Piamu would receive half the blood because he issued great harvests when he was happy or could strike the land with famine if he was angry.

Ola Yemo was the great spirit that lived in the blue lake where it met the cliff. The water around that part of the lake was green and deep. When one talked, the voice floated across the lake and Kuru Piamu would send the echo back from the cave.

After Pepena poured the blood into the lake and returned, Kipingi indicated with his head for us to follow him into the spirit house. Pepena and I lifted the lifeless pig by its limbs and brought it in after Kipingi.

The spirit house was triangular shaped with its roof covered with decayed leaves. All its sides were walled with a special brown bark used in building houses. It was dark inside but when Kipingi pushed aside the banana leaves at the door, light entered.

Two fleshless skulls were sitting on a small flat form below the roof on top of some dried ferns. One was large and the other was slightly smaller with its upper jawbones toothless. Both skulls were positioned in such a way that upon entering, one would see them staring at you.

Each tribe built a spirit house and kept their skulls. Whenever there was an illness, they offered sacrifices to the skulls. The spirit houses were revered throughout the land because they held the healing for the sick.

The highly venerated skulls were those of perished chiefs and great warriors. When such men died, the corpse was buried except the head, which was left exposed from the neck up. The skull was detached and was taken to the spirit house after the flesh decayed and fell off the bones.

The sacrificial fireplace was positioned in the middle of the hut. It was made of stones stacked one on top of another. The stones were blackened by animal fats which ran freely down the sides. Figures of eagles and flying pigs were engraved on the stones but most of them were obscured or rather erased by the congealed fat which smothered the stones. A little fire was flickering weakly on the fireplace, sending out golden flames.

Kipingi stood near the fire and raised the bamboo container to the roof. When the base of the container neared the flame, he turned the container upside down and poured the blood over to the flame. He was careful not to pour out too much as doing so would stump out the flames.

Now as soon as the blood left the container, the flame leapt to the blood as if the blood had grown wings for it to climb the rafters. The flame rose higher and higher when more blood was poured. When the last drop left the container, Kipingi cleaned the mouth of the containers with his tongue and placed the empty containers back on the roof. Then he produced a sharp bamboo knife from the rafters, ripped the heart out and placed it on a newly cut banana leaf.

"Hold this up," he said, holding the bloody heart in his two hands and handing it over to me. The heart was raw and fresh. Kipingi disturbed the fire with a thong and removed two round stones from the charcoal. Although the stones had been heating there, I didn't see them until then.

We took the heart out to a small place near the heart like clearing and Kipingi cooked it inside some banana leaves with the hot stones.

As the smell ascended to the skies, Kipingi enquired with the spirits whether Maya's spirit had arrived in the spirit world.

A light breeze rose from the treetops and shook the trees gently. It was like someone whispering through the treetops. Then a voice spoke somewhere far above the treetops:

"Molg oh," said the voice and nothing more was said.

Kipingi watched the skies and meditated for some time until the stone cooled and the steam disappeared.

"The spirits have accepted the offer," said Kipingi. "The child's spirit has not yet gone to the spirit world. Maya's paternal grandmother's spirit has been causing the illness because his mother had failed to look after her when she was sick. The boy will be well again because the spirits are satisfied with our offer. Ola Yemo says he will chase the boy's spirit back if he nears the spirit world."

Kipingi said his prayers again and after he cut the half-cooked heart, we ate it. We also cut out the ribs and roasted them over the fire and cooked the remaining pork inside a pit in the heart like clearing.

We gave some of the meat to the Kaimes and distributed the rest among ourselves.

"You must never share with others what has happened here today," said Kipingi when we left the spirit house.

Kipingi said he had chosen Pepena and me because he said we were brave young men.

Maya's health improved gradually until he recovered after a moon.

I visited the spirit house two or three more times before our enemies burnt it down later.

Chapter 11

Young people from different villages would gather at a central location once in a while for a courtship session called Ambo Konane.

I observed the occasion once a long time ago when our young men came to our house to court three girls from my mother's village. The event was a success. Yare hooked one of the girls with his sweet love songs that she refused to go back when the other two returned to their village. The girl's people arrived a moon later to receive her bride price.

Ambo Konane became a joy when I grew up. Our elder brothers would allow us to accompany them whenever they went out for a courtship season in another village.

My first time to court a young girl was in Piambil during a courtship session. I didn't know I would marry that Piambil beauty many moons later after I almost lost her to another man.

While we were on our way to Piambil, the boys talked much about a young woman named Piambil Ambo Mopune. Many of them agreed that Pepena would court her but when the winds of love blew her to me, I did not wait for the same winds to blow her away.

Piambil, the land between the Pawenda and Aliponga rivers was the land of dreams. Piambil was famous for its endless supply of beautiful girls whom our young men affectionately referred to as 'The Tonan beauties' after the largest tribe in Piambil. Our fathers and grandfathers had been courting the Tonan beauties for ages. No one doubted the success of such visits because over a quarter of the women married to our village spoke the Tonan language.

"Imagine if you take her home," said Koukera to Pepena when we neared Piambil.

"He would be very lucky if he owned her," added Poi and patted Pepena on the shoulder. Pepena smiled and said nothing.

I had never heard of the Piambil beauty nor had I ever seen her before. The boys must have met her from their previous meetings with the Piambil girls. I guessed she was of stunning beauty to attract such lofty comments, wishes and widespread admiration. However, I collected some information on her on our way to Piambil.

Piambil Ambo Mopune was Chief Kole Yaldo's daughter. Her father was famous for marrying fifteen wives. Toropo, his tenth wife hanged herself when she was forced to marry the old man. Toropo's father had prearranged the marriage with Kole Yaldo. He had accepted a large amount of bride price for his daughter when she was still young. When the first signs of breast developed in Toropo, she was taken away from her mother and was given to the old man Kole Yaldo. Unable to cope with life's challenges at that tender age, Toropo found a quick escape. It was just before she reached her fifth moon of pregnancy when her lifeless body was found hanging on a tree in an abandoned garden near the forest. Oh, what a sad story, dear Toropo!

When we arrived at Piambil, the sun set on the horizon. The village was empty as people were still in their gardens. A group of small boys were playing with mud near the road but they were so busy building a house or a tree that they failed to notice us when we approached them. An older boy cast curious looks over us but said nothing as visitors were not a new sight in the village.

We crossed a fast-flowing stream and reached their village ceremonial ground and met three beautiful girls who had been waiting for us. They said they had been tasked by their elder sisters to receive us when we arrived. We shyly exchanged quick handshakes with them. One of the girls, who I thought was the prettiest of the three, giggled when Pepena held her hand a little longer and then released it.

The girls led us to a large house belonging to an elderly woman where the courtship would take place. Two girls were in the house helping the elderly woman to cook sweet potatoes.

"Boys please feel free here," said the elderly woman with a smile. "This is not the first time nor the last time you Yanos are coming to Piambil. You will only stop coming here when Piambil has no girl for the courtship seasons. Your girls will join us soon."

Piambil had a natural tendency to replenish the Tonan beauties when the older ones were singled out for marriage.

It was at dusk when young girls began to arrive one by one. Some of the latecomers searched for places to sit. They were all lovely and beautiful.

The courtship season was beginning soon and I wondered which of those beautiful girls I would court that night.

Among us, we had a bachelor named Paraka. Paraka's age group had three or four children but he remained unmarried.

Short in stature and having few wrinkles on his cheeks, Paraka was unable to attract even a single girl in numerous past courtship seasons. Whenever Paraka approached a girl in a courtship session, girls would ignore him. Every courtship session thus ended in humiliation for Paraka. That night I decided to take him under my wing. Pepena said he would also help Paraka get a girl. Pepena said if he didn't succeed, they would use our love magic Malke Lopalopa.

Malke Lopalopa was our tribe's love magic used to win a young woman's heart by those who longed to have a girl but she appeared out of reach for them. It was a small plant that had been found near a lake in Mt Giluwe. An old man was in charge of it. He had brought the plant home and had planted it near a pool in the forest at the hillside. In the night, the plant would glow and one would see clearly from the village. Whoever wanted to use the love magic approached the old man. Five of our mothers said they wouldn't have married our fathers had it not been for the Malke Lopalopa. They cursed the love magic.

Now just before the courtship session started, three more young women entered the house quietly. One of them was so tall that she lowered her head to enter the door.

The first two girls squashed in a small space against the wall but the elderly woman (whose chief task appeared to keep the fire always burning) offered the tall girl a space near her. The tall girl quietly sat beside the elderly lady with her head slightly bowed. She had a striking beauty that commanded undivided attention. She had a long sharp nose perfectly carved out between her two beautiful white eyes. Her long black hair fell back to her shoulders and complemented her beautiful light-skinned face. I believed everything she beheld melted away. She was the type of girl who would make heads turn. When she entered the house, everyone raised their eyes to the door. The top of the doorway only reached her chest. She looked in my direction once.

"Do you see that girl?" whispered Paraka into my ear.

"The tall girl with long hair?

"Yes that is Piambil Ambo Mopune."

"Ah, how do you know she is her?"

"Oh it's very easy," said Paraka. "It isn't that hard to remember a girl of your dreams.

I did not know how Paraka knew the names but such was he. He had a unique memory for remembering names.

I caught Piambil Ambo Mopune casting her powerful eyes on me, but she quickly turned her face away when I caught hers with mine.

Now when all the girls arrived, the elderly lady announced that the courtship was starting.

"Since my girls are the hosts, they'll choose whom they'll be courting tonight," said the elderly woman.

This was the least we were expecting. Every young man had a girl fixed in his mind but when the power of choice shifted to the girls, he knew he was not at liberty to select the girl of his dreams. We had no choice but to accept whoever chose us. We all knew that was contrary to our cultural norms where men made major decisions, including choosing a girl in courtship sessions. Now it was clear that we would be chosen, instead of to choose. And for the girls, the most handsome ones were their first choice. They waited no more to choose their boys as soon as the power of choice was handed over to them. Each girl hesitantly stepped over to the young man of her choice.

Several girls threw their eyes on me but before anyone else selected me, Piambil Ambo Mopune walked straight to me.

I had a different sensation in me when the most beautiful girl in the house, probably in the whole land, sat near me. Some wild emotions ran mad inside me. I imagined touching those beautiful lips with mine but she was too far from me although she was so near to me. The courtship would bring her closer to me.

The other girls, who had been eying me withdrew their eyes. They knew whoever Piambil Ambo Mopune chose would not even think of them. The boys shot sharp glances at Pepena when Piambil Ambo Mopune walked over to me and sat beside me.

I guessed Pepena was envious when Piambil Ambo Mopune evaded him, but he smiled because Perai Wenepo chose him. Perai Wenepo was equal in beauty and built with Piambil Ambo Mopune physique but she was slightly shorter than Piambil Ambo Mopune and a little darker in complexion. Perai Wenepo must have liked Pepena so much that she also shot across to Pepena before the other girls grabbed him.

Pepena was a lofty young man with broad shoulders and a thick beard. His white teeth brightened up his face beautifully when he smiled. Our mothers often joked, and it was probably true too, that Pepena's smile even attracted married women. His grandmother, whose favourite grandchild was Pepena, said Pepena would continue to take wives up to the time when he picked up the walking stick. She said if she was still alive, she would stand with her grandson if he chose to take home all those ladies chasing after him.

Piambil Ambo Mopune threw secret glances at me whenever I was not looking at her, but I pretended to avoid her eyes because I wanted more of those side views. One time I caught her staring at me from out of the corner of her eyes. She smiled when I caught her white eyes. That rare smile had all her beauty inside. And the rumours I had heard of her beauty were only half true, and the other half was never told. And it was true that the boys were not mistaken when they desired her. My love for Piambil Ambo Mopune surged like a tide at first sight.

Now the pairs were fixed. We had a girl each, but Paraka sat with his head bowed in a little corner. He stared at the flames as thoughts of rejection rose and fell like the flames inside his mind.

How could we enjoy the courtship session with the girls while one of ours was rejected? How long should girls shun him? Paraka always found himself in the pit of rejection in every courtship season. His sorry state moved me with compassion.

Now Pepena and the elderly lady gave out the tunes of the courtship songs. However, none of the three remaining girls chose Paraka. This made me mad. I had to help Paraka out of his sad situation.

"We cannot start now," I said.

"What do you mean?" asked a surprised Perai Wenepo.

"We still have one of ours without a girl. If none of you three girls are choosing him, I am leaving this house."

"Oh no please," said Piambil Ambo Mopune softly. No one had prepared for such a shock interruption.

"He is right," said Pepena and looked at the girls. "Why don't one of you girls choose our boy just for the night? Oh, is he going to bite you?"

The three girls threw a glance at Paraka and looked away. A moment of silence ensued.

Leaving Piambil Ambo Mopune behind, I made for the door. I knew my decision to help Paraka would cost me dearly but I didn't have a choice. I had to leave Piambil Ambo Mopune behind.

"I am also leaving," said Pepena and followed me out to the door. We stepped further away from the house and met under a group of casuarina trees.

There was total silence back in the house. It appeared as if everyone had lost their voices. Then voices came up again, more sharply.

"Why don't one of you three court him," rose Perai Wenepo's clear and sharp voice.

"Why have you come here if you don't want to take part? Did you come to watch? Eh?

"Before I break this firewood on your heads, leave this house at once," she shouted.

Again, there was total silence. We were expecting a bang or something but nothing of that happened. Instead, a soft and clear voice cut through the still night.

"Please call the young men in. I will court the gentleman first."

We later found out it was Piambil Ambo Mopune's voice.

When Piambil Ambo Mopune's voice was gone, a light emerged at the door and one of the young girls threw her head out of the door and called us in.

"Thank goodness you are still here," said Perai Wenepo when we re-entered the house. "Please take your places, quick."

"Let me court the young man for a while," Piambil Ambo Mopune whispered into my ears. I wholeheartedly consented and later thanked Piambil Ambo Mopune for her condescension and selflessness. I moved to the fireplace and kept the fire burning while Piambil Ambo Mopune walked over to Paraka and sat beside him. Paraka must have been over the moon. He smiled at me from time to time.

Now the numbers were fixed and the young people waited now to begin the event they had almost lost. Being seated in pairs, and facing each other, they shook their heads sideways as they chanted the courtship songs. They touched each other's forehead once after a count of seven.

After several more songs, Piambil Ambo Mopune politely asked if Paraka would allow me to court 'his girlfriend'. Paraka smiled and moved away to the fireplace.

I had the chance to touch Piambil Ambo Mopune's beautiful purple lips but with some initial unsuccessful attempts. Every time I neared her mouth, she turned her face away. But I did not back away from her. How could I be so close to Piambil Ambo Mopune yet far from her lips? I wanted to make the most out of that opportunity. After several attempts, I managed to touch those coveted lips four or five times before the courtship session ended.

We were lost in our little world we created in pairs that we didn't know it was past midnight. What an awesome night!

Before the girls left, Piambil Ambo Mopune whispered into my ears,

"Please…don't leave forever. Come back for me someday. I can't wait to see you again."

That whisper concluded the night. No, that whisper ignited a fire in my heart, a fire that would burn for a lifetime.

Pepena and I established our superiority that night. I was pleased. If I hadn't taken that risk, the girls would have turned the event to their advantage. Our boys were pleased with us afterwards for our courage to stand up for our brother.

The girls left after the courtship season ended. I couldn't remember any sleep that night. Piambil Ambo Mopune was in my mind all night. She stayed in my imagination. Her beautiful smooth voice, the smell of her soft body, that long black hair, that great shape of her body, I could not stop imagining- all kept coming back to me again and again until the first morning birds cried.

Chapter 12

After our visit to Piambil, we courted girls in the neighbouring villages. I enjoyed meeting those girls but when more girls fought among themselves to befriend me, it became a problem for me as I didn't want to be the center of their arguments.

My mother must have learnt of an incident where two girls fought over me. She warned me of the dangers of attracting many girls.

"Son, I see eyes are coming to you from all directions. You are a colourful butterfly," she said. "You have taken the likeness of your father. I know how girls would react to such a stunning beauty. You are much taller than your father. You know how I married your father? It was a matrimonial suicide. Your father came to our village once and that one sight of him was just enough for me to run away with him. You can easily cause problems for women."

She also warned me of married women.

"Remember beauty can attract both good and bad. Beauty can steal a wife despite bride price or husband. You have to be extra careful with women because your father who defended this house is gone."

In another courtship season, I met a beautiful and talkative girl from the Tendepo tribe named Ambuwape. She was beautiful like Piambil Ambo but Ambuwape became angry over little matters and often put up fights with other girls whom she suspected of befriending me. She was aggressive. She wouldn't tolerate any nonsense. A moon after I met her, she had a fistfight with another girl from the nearby village whom she suspected of befriending me.

Despite meeting those girls, my love for Piambil Ambo Mopune never stopped growing. It got deeper and deeper every day. It was so special that I thought my fathers had never experienced such love before.

Piambil Ambo Mopune and I craved each other so much that not even a single day slipped by without us thinking of each other. Pepena's love for Perai Wenepo also blossomed. Pepena said we needed to visit the girls often in their village to deepen our relationship.

Cold weather and flooded rivers were nothing to us. We didn't even care when we had to travel through our enemy lands to meet the Tonan beauties. Distance means nothing when one is insanely in love.

The more our love for the girls grew, the more frequent our visits became and soon the villagers said the four of us were meant for each other.

Whenever I visited her, Piambil Ambo Mopune would greet me with open arms and tears swimming in her beautiful white eyes. All her love for me was wrapped inside those tears. She never talked much. I wished she talked more but she would say one or two words, not twice, but once, and that was all, leaving her tears to speak the rest, leaving me yearning and longing for her sweet voice. If I were asked to give away my ears, I would give both to my Piambil Ambo Mopune's voice. Her soft voice was pleasing and sweet to my ears.

In one such meeting when Pepena and I were leaving Piambil, someone whistled and ran down the hill on the other side of the Aliponga River.

"Oh, that is Perai Wenepo," said a confused Pepena.

She waved her hands for us to wait for her. She crossed the river in a hurry and reached us, exhausted and short of breath. Sweat was all over her face. We were surprised to find her without her bilum.

"What happened? Has someone been chasing you?" I asked her.

"No. I am running away with you," said Perai Wenepo, wiping away the sweat on her face with the back of her right hand.

"Why? asked Pepena.

"Why, why?" said Perai Wenepo. "Why have you come to Piambil?

Perai Wenepo stopped talking for a while. I was unsure whether she just came to see us off or whether she had come to follow us to Malke.

"Oh, I couldn't stay back and watch your backs disappear behind the hill," said Perai Wenepo and broke down in tears.

Perai Wenepo looked back to see if her people were pursuing her but nothing happened. We walked on until we reached an old couple's house at the wayside. Perai Wenepo said she had to speak with the old couple.

"Let me leave a message with the old woman," said Perai Wenepo and called the old woman's name. Luckily, they were present when we arrived.

"If anyone comes looking for me here, tell them to go back," said Perai Wenepo. "Tell them that I am going to Malke with my boyfriend. We will announce a time for them to come and see the bride price."

"How could you say that to the old people? I am not ready for a bride price," said Pepena to Perai Wenepo when we were out of Piambil.

"Never mind about that," said Perai Wenepo. "Assuring them of bride price would stop them coming after me."

I believed Pepena's striking beauty swept Perai Wenepo off her feet that she ran away with us. That may have been true too but Perai Wenepo said she was running away from her cruel father. She said her father had been arranging for her to marry a man from the other side of Mt Ialibu. Perai Wenepo said she didn't like to go there.

Two days later when our village chiefs learned that a beautiful young woman had followed Pepena home, they called everyone together for a meeting.

"She has come to us," said Kipingi to our people. "If we had gone to her father for her hands, do you think her father would accept your little kina shells and pigs? She has made everything easy for us. She is part of us now. Bring whatever you have and let's buy her hands."

The chiefs gave us a moon to gather items for the bride price but Perai Wenepo's infectious smile and striking beauty caused our people to contribute the items in less than a moon.

Although the bride price didn't satisfy her people, Perai Wenepo said it was not her concern whether her people accepted the bride price or not. They took the bride price away and gave nothing in exchange, except three pigs and two kina shells.

Two moons after Perai Wenepo came to Malke, our village hosted a great show called singsing. It was a tribal event that required concerted efforts of the entire tribe. Everyone was excited about the singsing because it was a rare event that took place once in a while.

All other activities in the village were suspended and everyone was assigned a task to prepare for the great singsing.

We erected huts along the edges of our long ceremonial ground to dry firewood for the great pig killing after the show. We also split firewood from many logs and dried it in the huts. All tribes in Kaugel Valley and beyond were attending the great occasion.

Pepena and I were so caught up in the tasks that we missed our usual visit to Piambil. Even after he married Perai Wenepo, Pepena continued to accompany me every time I visited Piambil Ambo Mopune.

Now when the preparations dragged into another moon due to bad weather, questions began to hit my unsettled mind. Is she Okay? Has someone taken her away? I couldn't keep on delaying the visits that long. I was already missing Piambil Ambo Mopune so much. When your love is near, you forget time but when she is far away, days become moons.

Three days before the singsing, my worries and concerns over Piambil Ambo Mopune were over when she sent word that she was attending the singsing. That was her first time to come to the village.

At length, our great day arrived. The kundu drums bit in the distance. Spectators from places far and wide flooded into our ceremonial ground in numbers.

Skilled painters brought their decoration items (feathers of many colours, furs, pigtails, armbands) out in the parcels and displayed them in the sun. Pepena and those of us who had to be decorated for the singsing sat on logs and the painters dipped their small painting sticks into the vials and applied red, gold and black colours on our faces. They kept painting our faces until the coloured patterns obscured our faces.

Pepena's mother was known for her exceptional face-painting skills. Anything her painting stick touched caught fire. Her talented hands would carve out unmatched beauty when met with paints. That morning, she painted Pepena and my faces. She would stop and admire her painting from time to time and comment as if it were someone else's work. "This is the first time I am painting you," she said, running the tip of her painting stick along my nose, "but I haven't seen such a glowing beauty as I see in this painting from all my previous paintings."

When she was done with the face painting, she added feathers of various colours to my headdress and fitted two brand-new armbands on both my hands.

"You look exactly like your father with that thick beard and tall build," commented my mother who had just arrived at the venue. "From a distance, I thought I was seeing your father."

My mother was happy to see me fully dressed for the occasion but there was sadness in her eyes. She was probably missing my father that day.

"I can remember a great singsing here," continued my mother. "I did a crazy thing. I fought with another girl to be your father's girlfriend although we knew he had two wives."

"Why did you fight to befriend him when he already had two wives?" I asked.

"Oh son, I couldn't stand your father's stunning beauty. His sharp eyes were too good to be ignored."

"Yes, Amboama is correct," said Pepena's mother who was older than my mother.

"Engaamb and another woman came to your father's house at the same time to be his second wife. However, Engaamb was so determined to marry him that she chased the other woman away and became your father's second wife. Even your grandmother was concerned about an influx of women to your father's house. One time she chased your father out of the house with a thong because she was tired of women fighting over her handsome son every now and then."

"Beauty blinded us," laughed my mother. "We fought to claim someone else's husband."

When she was done with the face painting, Pepena's mother repacked her decoration items and placed them inside her bilum. She and my mother held me and Pepena's hands and led us into the ceremonial grounds. Other decorated men also converged for the great singsing.

Heads turned when we walked past the crowd. Girls whispered among themselves, some in pairs. Many were reluctant to take their eyes off us.

"You are a standout here because no man here is nearly as tall as the two of you," commented Pepena's mother before she and my mother left us with the men.

Young girls stood along the edges to steal a glance. Piambil Ambo Mopune was leaning her back against a casuarina tree with Perai Wenepo and Kenenga, another girl from Piambil. The girls had left Piambil the previous day and overnighted with Piambil Ambo

Mopune's aunty at Kondopi before coming to Malke. They informed Pepena and me earlier that they would hang around the ceremonial ground after the singsing for the waipa.

The decorations made us all look alike. Our faces were lost behind the uniform red, gold, black and white colours and our hairs were hidden underneath the brightly coloured red geltemba caps. Young girls however were very quick to single out their lovers among the uniformed dancers. One could not question the accuracy of their eyes. Those sharp objects never gave their owners a false impression. They were sharper than those of the eagles that ruled the skies of Mt Hagen.

Now we stood with our hands clasped in each other's hands and formed a horizontal line with five men in front and five at the back. There were about five lines of men, all decorated in the same fashion.

We marched around the ceremonial ground, chanting warlike songs. The spectators watched with awe from the start of the singsing to the end. Whenever we neared their corners, young people smiled with admiration while elders nodded and commented among themselves. We stopped at intervals to rest our legs and pull in some air.

The marches continued throughout the day and ended at sunset.

And when the singsing ended, young spectators, who had been waiting all day poured into the ceremonial ground for the long-awaited waipa or dance around the circle. It was their time.

Waipa held the greatest excitement for young people. Some married men also enjoyed the event but with some strong restraint from their wives. This was because Waipa offered endless chances for men to hold hands with as many young women as they wished. Some wives, especially those suspicious ones who had very crazy minds saw waipa as something that would pull their husbands away by younger women. The crazy women saw every girl who held hands with their husbands as a potential wife. They were not always wrong with their suspicions. We had stories of some of our mothers following our fathers home after a waipa session.

That evening, Yare's wife Wanis lashed out angry words at a young woman who was holding hands with her husband. When Yare said it was just a Waipa and that he was not taking the girl home, Wanis snapped back angrily.

"Only a waipa? Yes, I know, it's only a waipa," she said, "but there is no free hand here."

When everyone rushed to waipa, a mother and an old man from my father's maternal village placed two strings on my fingers and congratulated me for putting up a great singsing.

The mother hugged me and cried tears of joy.

"Grandchild I am so happy," he said. "You have grown so tall and big like your father that I couldn't recognise you at first. I can't believe you've grown so fine young man." The old man also expressed his shock at seeing me change so much. I asked them both to come to the singsing feast when the singsing ended.

"Son now you go and waipa with the girls. I think I've wasted enough of your time," said the old man.

Now I rushed off to join hands with Piambil Ambo Mopune. She had been waiting impatiently at the side of the ceremonial ground, resisting many eyes.

With hands joined from shoulder to shoulder, we danced up and down and around a circle following the rhythm of a song. Pepena came in after me and joined hands with Piambil Ambo Mopune and me. Kenenga, the young woman from Piambil held hands with us but left to waipa with Poi in another waipa circle.

As more participants joined hands, the circle swelled and expanded to the edges of the ceremonial ground, forcing some of the hands to break loose and form new circles. The circles multiplied as more hands broke away.

New entrants joined the waipa circle by tapping on the arms of the person with whom they desired to hold hands. However, some young girls refused a hand, especially when the young man she was holding hands was handsome. Such denials often instigated altercations and fights amongst girls when a girl felt that her right to waipa with a handsome man was denied.

When the waipa song ended, the waipa came to a stop. Yare never ran out of songs. He was the first one to get the line moving again with a new song.

Now the setting sun dried my neck. I left Piambil Ambo Mopune with Kenenga and went away for a drink at the creek.

Many girls smiled at me when I left the waipa circle for the drink. They would probably hold hands with me but Piambil Ambo Mopune and Kenenga never left my side.

Ambuwape, the Tendepo girl was in another waipa circle. She stared at Piambil Ambo Mopune and me for some time but Piambil Ambo Mopune didn't see her.

When I returned from the creek, two groups of women were standing at a respectable distance from each other and voices rose and fell.

Ambuwape and her girls gathered on one side of the ceremonial ground while Piambil Ambo Mopune, Perai Wenepo (who had joined the girls) and Kenenga were on the other side with those who supported the Piambil girls. They were shouting insults at each other.

Perai Wenepo was raising Piambil Ambo Mopune by the hand. Piambil Ambo

Mopune's long hair had been disarrayed and blood was oozing out from a cut above her left eye. On the other side was Ambuwape with her face covered in blood. She was wiping blood from her nose and mouth. Her voice was the loudest and most dominating.

"What happened here?" I asked Kenenga who was exchanging harsh words with Ambuwape.

"No, that good-for-nothing girl over there thinks she owns you," said Kenenga staring at Ambuwape.

Ambuwape, being driven by hatred and jealousy, had attacked Piambil Ambo Mopune at the waipa circle. She knocked her down and dragged her in the mud by her long hair before

Kenenga approached Ambuwape from the back and landed a tight fist on Ambuwape's nose. Like Piambil Ambo Mopune, Ambuwape held her bloody nose and crouched down with blood leaking out of her fingers.

"You said I was your only one," said Piambil Ambo Mopune with tears swimming in her eyes. "That woman says she had married you."

"She is lying. When did you marry him?" shouted Perai Wenepo to Ambuwape.

"It's okay. I'll go back to my Piambil now," said Piambil Ambo Mopune softly. "I won't come here again tomorrow."

Ambuwape now began to pour her anger over to Piambil Ambo Mopune and the girls again.

"Shame on you girls," shouted Ambuwape. "Why don't you choose the others here?

Losers!"

More bad words rolled out of Ambuwape's untamed tongue like a rush of water down a mountain. She had a mouth which spilt words before she even had time to think. When her voice dropped a little, Kenenga's voice rose.

"Where have you been, you fool?" said Kenenga. "Have you just woken from your sleep? Let me tell you straight now. You will never have him because his heart is mine. Sorry sister, his heart belongs to the Piambil girls."

"I'm going to knock your eyes out," said Ambuwape

"If you don't knock my eyes out then, you'll be here," said Kenenga, giving the middle finger to Ambuwape.

"Hi come on. Let me break your mouth," said Ambuwape and took a step towards Kenenga but stopped again.

"What's stopping you then, you fool?" said Kenenga. "Come on, be quick. Come here now. Let me tear that bad mouth of yours."

"I'll kill you," said Ambuwape and approached Kenenga with her hands on her hips. Her girls stood behind her but none followed

Ambuwape to the Piambil girls. Kenenga observed Ambuwape's every movement from the toes to the head. Perai Wenepo also left the group and stood side by side with Kenenga.

Such was how girls took sides and stood up for each other. Whenever two girls argued over a man, it quickly evolved into a women's matter. Like men, they wouldn't watch one of theirs being insulted, spat upon or even crunched by words.

Ambuwape took a few more steps closer to the girls. In front of her were Kenenga, Perai Wenepo and two other girls from our village. Sensing the group was too much for her, she confronted me instead.

"How many men are you? One or two?" said Ambuwape, fixing her eyes on me.

"Can you just shut up and leave?" I said.

"Me, leaving? Are you telling me to leave? Eh, no way."

"You are a fool," I said. "In which ceremonial ground did I pay you bride price and marry you? You are out of your senses."

Ambuwape flew to me and swung her right fist. It bounced on my chest. If it was aimed at Piambil Ambo Mopune, it would damage her beautiful eyes. She then swung another fist but I caught it and pushed her away. She jumped up and scratched my face with her sharp fingernails, leaving lines of blood across the forehead. I grabbed her hands and slapped her left ear twice and pushed her away.

"He blew my ears off," she cried.

Some of her brothers who were at the waipa ground rushed at me. Our boys joined me and a fistfight ensued. The fight continued for a while before some Kulumidi and Yap boys intervened and separated us.

Meanwhile, Piambil Ambo Mopune, Kenena and the girls had left while we were fighting.

Chapter 13

Aday after the singsing ended, we pulled our pigs into the ceremonial ground and slaughtered them. I killed two pigs and gave the spines to the two old people who had placed strings on my fingers.

Everyone including the visitors enjoyed the feast. However, for me, the feast ended with concern.

Piambil Ambo Mopune was absent amid the excitement. She didn't attended the show over the next two days. Her brief presence in the village appeared like a dream to me. How am I going to see her again? Should I allow the incident to delay my visits further? These questions knocked against each other inside my head.

Pepena said we should visit Piambil Ambo Mopune as soon as possible.

"Maybe we can visit her sometime next moon," I said.

"No, we need to propose the marriage as soon as possible," said Pepena. "Do you think she'll be waiting for us in Piambil when we keep delaying? We have to grab her now or else we'll lose her to someone else."

"But we don't have enough bride price," I said to delay the visit. I had lost all courage to face Piambil Ambo Mopune's father Kole Yaldo. He was a famous leader who was also known for his harshness.

"That is beside the point," said Pepena. "We have to bring her here."

"But Kole Yaldo?"

"I'll deal with him," said Pepena.

"Pepena are you sure they'll accept our proposal?"

"That's not ours to decide. We cannot expect Piambil Ambo Mopune to show up here. If you really want to marry her, you have to go after her at all costs. Things don't come to people when they expect things and do nothing. If you want something, chase it until you get it.

"Remember we have been befriending the young woman for too long. Oh, have you been courting her to be taken away by someone else?" He stopped and stared at me.

"Ah man, you are speaking as if Piambil Ambo Mopune is going away tomorrow," I said laughing.

"My brother, you don't know about this," said Pepena. "Women have broken many hearts. Some young men like us wake up in shock when they realise the girl they thought they owned has been taken away.

"We have to propose the marriage now or else we won't have her. Will you blame the incident if she goes away? She is a young girl. She is up for grabs by anyone. Perhaps the first man who shows up with a bride price might take her away. Problems are problems. The incident has happened already. We cannot reverse things. We have to make our move now."

A day after the feast, Pepena and I took a quarter of a pig and left for Piambil.

Questions still disturbed my mind as we left home. What are Mopune's parents going to say about the incident? Will they chase us out of their home? Such questions kept pouring into my mind one after another.

We arrived in Piambil at sunset. We had been away for several moons and the place appeared strange to us.

Once we reached the ceremonial ground, a group of small boys were playing hide and seek at the shoulder-high grasses. Piambil Ambo Mopune's small brother ran to us and threw himself into my arms.

"Is Piambil Ambo Mopune at home?" I asked the little boy.

"She just returned from the garden with mother."

"Who else is at home?"

"Mother and the baby."

"Ok run and tell her we have come."

The little boy left his playmates and sprinted away. Moments later, Piambil Ambo Mopune shot out of the house with her hands on her face. She threw her arms around my neck and sobbed.

"Oh …. oh…, I… missed you so much," she said, releasing.

"Oh no please, don't cry like that."

"Oh, my dear I thought you wouldn't come back for me again."

"Why? Why should I not come back here?"

"Will you not marry that Tendepo girl?" she said, wiping her tears.

"Is that what you've been thinking?" Piambul Ambo Mopune nodded.

"Oh forget about her," I said. "She is no way near you." Piambil Ambo Mopune smiled and hugged me.

"Oh I thought I would miss you forever," she said, smiling at me.

Piambil Ambo Mopune's love for me was in her sweet voice. I could sense it swelling and swelling in her heart too. She had the most beautiful heart a woman could ever have. Her heart knew no wrongs, a heart full of pure love and kindness, kindness that sprung out like a spring.

"Oh I thought I would never see you again," said Piambil Ambo Mopune again smiling at me. "I did not sleep for the last few nights."

Standing there with her white eyes staring at me was a different feeling. It was the most beautiful feeling I had ever had. I felt like staying with Piambil Ambo Mopune all night.

Pepena was right. I should take the Piambil beauty home immediately.

"I'm so sorry for what has happened," I said.

"Oh I have forgotten everything that happened at Malke," said Piambil Ambo

Mopune. I was worrying whether I would ever see you again. I regretted why I had left early."

Her wound had dried but a tiny scar was visible at a closer look above her right eye.

"It was late. How did you get back here?" I asked her.

"It was dark when we reached Yawere so we had to overnight at Kondipi with my aunty."

Now the cicadas gave out their final cries in a hurry. A few spaces away, a family had returned home late. The father was rushing to break firewood in the fading light. The fire in the opposite house got brighter as the daylight began to disappear. The meeting of light and darkness happened so quickly that before Piambil Ambo Mopune and I realised, the darkness stamped out the remaining daylight and dissolved the smoke that was floating above the rooftops.

"I curse this darkness," said Piambil Ambo Mopune. "Why didn't you come early?"

At this moment, Piambil Ambo Mopune's mother sent her little boy out to check us out.

"Mother says tell the two young people to come in," said the little boy. He stood at the door and delivered the message with a shout exactly the way his mother had told him and returned to the house quickly as if someone would steal the meat.

As we were about to enter the house, Piambil Ambo Mopune grabbed my hands and pulled me further away from the house. Her face turned pale. The smile on her face died and tears swelled in her eyes. I sensed something wasn't right.

"Wait," she said, searching around with her eyes. She even looked towards the door to make sure no one was listening. When she was satisfied that there was no one near, she said,

"Some people from Mendi came to take me away but they ----"

"Take you away?"

"But they left yesterday when my father said the bride price wasn't enough."

She continued talking for a while but when tears drowned her words, she rested her arms on my neck.

"Oh, my dearest. I don't want anything to separate you from me," she said. "I could have been taken away had my father accepted the bride price."

"Are they coming back again?"

"My father said they could only return if they have more than twenty pigs and ten kina shells. They said they won't take their bride price elsewhere."

"You know how much I love you," said Piambil Ambo Mopune, drying her eyes. "I will do anything to make sure we are together. If anything happens, I'll let you know."

"No, you have to assure me now," I said.

"I won't let you down. But remember as a girl, I have my limits. If anything happens, this is what I will do. I will send words for you and Pepena. As soon as you receive my words, come to the mountain and make a huge fire on the mountain. I will be watching for the smoke all day. I'll run away to the mountain."

When we entered the house, Pepena was helping Piambil Ambo Mopune's mother to cook the meat inside the cooking pit near the door. Nothing was said about the incident. That provided some relief for us but I was still worried about Kole Yaldo. He was still out.

A few moments later, Piambil Ambo Mopune's mother handed two hot sweet potatoes each to us. She mentioned nothing about the fight. Kole Yaldo entered moments later but also said nothing of the incident. However, I feared for my Piambil Ambo Mopune and what could happen to her. The chances of marrying girls whose fathers had a natural tendency to add one wife after another relied on the bride price. Such fathers gave their daughters away to anyone so long as a huge bride price was paid.

Piambil Ambo Mopune's father never turned his eyes away from a fair young girl when he had the means to acquire her. Half of the wealth Kole Yaldo used for bride price for his last four wives was said to have been made possible by his three daughters. None of his three daughters he gave away during that time were for free. Piambil Ambo Mopune said the bride price her father was asking for her from the Mendi people was twice the one her father had received for one of her stepsisters five moons ago.

Now the family removed the pork from the mumu and brought it out before the fireplace on the cooked leaves. Kole Yaldo sent for his children and wives. Eight of his wives came in. He had married fifteen but five passed away at old age and one, the young Toropo, hanged herself.

After all the wives and children arrived, he waited for a little while more then enquired for his wife from Jika.

"Where is Melpa Ambo," he asked.

"Mother just returned from the garden. She says she is very tired," replied a little girl.

Kole Yaldo cut the pork and when he distributed it to his wives, he addressed them as the mother of the name of her first-born son. When the wife had only daughters, he would refer to her by her tribe of origin. He called his latest wife Engowal Ambo because she was from the Engowal tribe of Mondike. To the Engowal Ambo, he said, "Engowal Ambo here is your pork."

Kole Yaldo's wives and those children who represented their mother including Melpa Ambo's little girl, left for their houses after receiving their shares. Some of the children remained with their father. He cut the remaining pork into smaller pieces for them. No noise was heard from the children until the meat was gone.

Piambil Ambo Mopune didn't eat much. She was beside her mother with her head bowed.

Piambil Ambo Mopune was the second-born child. The firstborn was a young man who was away in Iombi in one of his friend's wife's places. Kole Yaldo lived with Piambil

Ambo Mopune's mother, who was the thirteenth wife. The fourteenth was Melpa Ambo and the fifteenth was Engowal Ambo. Four moons ago, Kole Yaldo had added another wife, a young girl. He had built a house for her but she preferred to live with the sixth wife who was advanced in age. Kole Yaldo had built a house for his latest wife but he rarely visited her because the young wife was always said to be in the sixth wife's house. The sixth wife loved her as her daughter because all her daughters had married elsewhere. She rarely allowed the young wife to live alone in her new home. Kole Yaldo was said to have once been very disappointed when he found his latest wife not at her home one night soon after he married her. He sent for her but when the young wife arrived late at night, he bashed her up. Some boys said he hit her out of impatience. The young woman could not leave him because Kole Yaldo had bought her with ten pigs and seven kina shells.

Apart from his string of wives, Kole Yaldo was also famous for his moka and pig killings. He wore a long bracelet made of twenty-four small bamboos knitted together by strings. He displayed his object of fame proudly on his chest with its end reaching down to his belly. Each single piece was the size of a finger and represented a moka or a pig killing he had made. Every time he threw a pig killing or made a moka, he added one bamboo which he arranged horizontally across his chest. He saw each pig killing or Moka as an opportunity to lengthen his bracelet and thus his wealth and popularity. He included his wives in his record of wealth but needed nothing to represent them on his breast because women were there. He still had some good times ahead to see this bracelet reaching his knees, and probably more women to replace those who had passed on.

It was quite a wonder how such an old man like him could continue to acquire wives even at old age. In his younger days, Kole Yaldo was said to be a fierce warrior who made women fall for him. But his addition of wives at this late age was a wonder. Some said he had received a love magic like our Malke Lopalopa from a great lake in Mt Giluwe which enabled him to attract those women even in old age.

When everyone had left, Pepena said we had come to propose Piambil Ambo Mopune.

"We will collect a few more pigs and will come back for her in two moons' time," said Pepena.

Piambil Ambo Mopune's mother smiled but Kole Yaldo remained silent for some time before he spoke.

"You are welcome here so long as she remains unmarried. Piambil Ambo Mopune is a young woman. Whoever comes here first takes her away."

My chances of having Piambil Ambo Mopune rested on a precarious situation. We had seven pigs and a cassowary but that wasn't enough for the bride's price. We didn't know how the two moons would solve the issue of bride price. We however gave them time. When we gave them time, it gave us breathing space to secure the bride price but that also gave others enough time to take Piambil Ambo Mopune away.

Since a part of the bride price went to the mother's side of the family, a bride price was expected to satisfy both sides of the family. It was paid to a young woman's family to appreciate her family for raising their daughter. The acceptability of it rested heavily on the most influential member of the bride's family. If your bride price was below their expectations, you would lose your girl regardless of how deep your love and affection for her was. Bride price also determined where a young woman's bones would be laid to rest when she died.

It was not always a guarantee that a young man would marry his love. One couldn't tell whether a young woman would still be waiting, whoever approached her father first with a reasonable bride price had a huge chance of taking her away.

I spent the night devising a plan to take my Piambil Ambo Mopune away but no workable solution settled in my mind. The same thought, 'Maip you won't have Piambil Ambo Mopune' kept coming back to me again and again, chasing the sleep and peace away. Piambil Ambo Mopune was out of reach for me. I was awake until the morning birds cried.

Next morning when Pepena and I were leaving, Piambil Ambo Mopune accompanied us to the ceremonial ground and saw us off at the creek.

She waved at us for a moment and then covered her face with her hands when we disappeared behind the mountains.

Chapter 14

Konopu and Kepambo were the village beauties when they reached marriageable age.

They were our tribe's pride. The village boasted of having them.

Konopu had taken the likeness of my father. She was very tall with long black hair.

Her striking beauty reached distant villages even before she fully developed her breasts. Kepambo was also beautiful like Konopu. Their beauty glowed like a bright light so that marriage proposals flooded in from all corners of the land.

One morning three men and two women from the Tekep tribe arrived at our house to propose Konopu for their chief.

The Tekeps were one of our former enemy tribes who lived on the other side of the Kaugel River. My fathers fought with them when my father was a small boy. In recent times, intermarriages and frequent moka exchanges between the two tribes fostered peace. Our fathers however warned us to be wary of them.

"When enemies want to kill you," warned our fathers, "they won't come right up to you, take their poison out and kill you right away. They'll do everything to win your heart first. The Tekeps are experts in using poison so you should be careful with them."

The visitors said their chief had two wives and wished to add a third.

"The first wife is barren and the second has two daughters," said one of the women to my mother. "We have been searching the whole land until we heard of your daughter. Our chief is preparing to pay twenty kina shells and twenty-five pigs for bride price."

"Not only the bride price," added one of the men. "We would like to use this marriage to strengthen our tribe's relationship with yours."

The visitors rested their eyes on my mother but she said nothing. Konopu was beside my mother twisting some ropes for my mother's bilum. She did not even have a slight interest in the conversation.

When the Tekeps completed their speech, we excused the visitors and once we were outside, my mother asked Konopu for her thoughts on the proposal.

"Mama, I don't want to go. I don't like the idea of marrying a man of many wives."

The Tekeps returned to their land that afternoon.

"I'm glad you've rejected the proposal," said my mother after the Tekeps left.

"I know what it means to marry a man of many wives," continued my mother. "When I was young and in my father's house, my mother would say to me." "Daughter, if you court a married man, you are digging your own way to the grave. The moment you start courting him, you will give him all the rights to have you, and not long, you will be one of his wives. The worst is he might leave you with a baby and marry another wife."

"You might be thinking. His wife is not seeing me. His looks and talks are so sweet. That is wrong my daughter. Behind those sweet talks lay the danger."

"Do you think the wives of that Tekep Chief will accept you in his family? No."

"You are a woman of value. Don't throw your life away like that to the dogs. That man is another woman's husband. Don't force yourself to be part of someone's life. Remember, you will not only break a marriage, you will be a constant source of trouble to the mother and her innocent children."

"Even if he had been your boyfriend, don't choose him if he wants to marry you on top of another wife. Has he not chosen another woman over you?"

"You don't know what it is like to court or even marry a married man. Once you start courting a married man, let me tell you this straight; your life will be a misery. You will be at the mercy of his first wife or wives. You will try your very best to hide this relationship from the public. What will you feel like when someone steals your husband?" my mother paused.

"Ah I will kill that woman," said both girls at the same time.

"Mind me, when his first wife finds out you are courting her husband, she will not have a second thought to break your head. She will knock your eyes out and shame you in public. She will ruin your reputation in public."

"So my daughters, never set your eyes on a married man. If you do, let me warn you again. You will invite an axe for your head or a knife for your heart. So avoid giving your ear to a married man. His words will be sweet, innocent, and caring. He knows how to use the power of his words to seduce a woman. He knows how to twist his words to make a woman fall for him. Once you incline your ears to a married man, you will be drowned in a pit of pain you will create with your own choice."

"So don't jump into the turmoil of double marriage and expect a magical hand to bail you out. You cannot jump into a flooded river, expecting it not to drown you. If you have created a problem, you are not free of its consequences. You will still face it sooner or later."

"Therefore, my daughters, marry a single young man. Build him up and enjoy life with him. Sail through life's challenges and problems with him."

"Don't steal another woman's husband. A curse will follow you around like a puppy everywhere you go."

"When you realise you have fallen prey to his deceptions, tears will soak your pillow every night. Thoughts of regrets and guilt of cheating will drown your mind. Regrets will haunt you every night."

"If you get into a polygamous marriage, you will lose your peace and ruin your reputation with such a poorly thought-out decision."

"You will compete to get his favour, love, resources and affection because you will not be his ONLY one. You'll be ONE of his many wives."

"I have made a mistake when I married your father. I was too young then to weigh things out properly. I just accepted when your father proposed to me. I was a very beautiful young girl then. Your father had to marry me before someone else grabbed me. He paid a huge bride price to secure me. I couldn't resist him also because he was a very handsome young man. But I have experienced a lot of ill-treatment from his wives, especially his second wife Engaamb."

"When I came here, your father was living with Engaamb. She didn't want to share her husband with me. She said I was a thief who sneaked in and stole her husband. It was a real nightmare for me. When problems started kicking in, I remembered what my mother had told me which I am sharing some with you now."

"I don't want you girls to experience the same pain as me. I don't want you to repeat the same mistake I made. I want you to be happy and marry happily."

She paused and wiped away the tears that streamed in her eyes. My mother was a very understanding mother. She wanted us to be happy. She said our happiness was her joy. And she believed marrying happily was crucial for a happy life.

Both Konopu and Kepambo shed hot tears that afternoon. They reflected on how our mother had brought us up despite all the challenges she had faced. They were sorry to leave her behind because they both were in the ripe age for marriage. They both agreed that they would get married once I found a wife.

"I wish you marry in the same place and coexist like thunder and lightning," said my mother. "I don't want distance and loneliness to separate the two of you. It's heartbreaking for a mother to see her child going away to start a new family in another tribe."

She knew the girls were marrying soon because having daughters who had reached marriageable age but remained unmarried became subjects of gossip.

"You don't know what it means to bring up children single-handed," continued my mother. "If only you were a single mother, you would know exactly what I mean."

I remembered how our mother fought life's challenges to raise us. Her struggles started as soon as my father passed away. She fended off life's challenges and brought us up by herself. Three men wanted to marry my mother and support us after our father died but she rejected them all. She said, "When my children grow up, they'll be able to look after me."

The same Tekep people tuned up a few days later for the second time. This time the Tekep chief sent two of his most trusted men. They said the whole tribe was preparing for a huge bride price.

"We have contributed five more pigs and the chief himself had added another seven more kina shells for the bride price," said the men.

After the Tekeps had spoken, my mother sent for Uncle Ponenge, my father's elder brother. When Ponenge arrived, we excused the visitors and consulted among ourselves at the back of the house. My mother briefed him about the visitors.

"They have come to us when we are in great need of pigs and kina shells," said Ponenge. "Maip is getting married soon. We will be needing the huge bride price they are promising. As far as I can remember, no girl here has received such a huge bride price. We married our women with seven or eight pigs and a few kina shells. This is a great opportunity for us to receive this huge bride price. I am glad my daughter will make a name for me in the ceremonial ground."

He then paused and asked my mother.

"Who is the man again? Did you say Tekep Nondigomo?"

When my mother nodded in the affirmative, Ponenge shook his head and said,

"No, my daughter is not marrying that man. His father killed my father's last-born brother. She will marry into a curse."

"Oh thank you, Papa," said Konopu and hugged Ponenge.

"Don't worry my daughter," said Ponenge, releasing Konopu slowly. "You are a beautiful young woman, the finest of women. I am very proud of you, my dear. You are my pride. You are a woman of value. Though we may have needs, we cannot throw you away to the old and the wealthy. Young girls are not commodities to be traded for pigs and kina shells."

Ponenge thanked the two men for coming and politely informed them that Konopu was not going with them. They left without saying a word. They, however, returned for the third time a few days later with their chief.

The chief was bald and had scars all over his body and one deep axe scar on his right shoulder. Our response was the same.

"Ok we'll see what kind of man you will give your daughter," said one of the men to my mother as they walked out of the fence.

The chief however stopped at the wayside and added,

"I'll make sure you won't receive any bride price for your daughter. What Tekep Nondigomo says, Nondigomo does."

Chapter 15

Now the time for showing the bride price for Piambil Ambo Mopune was a moon away. Konopu's rejection of the Tekep proposal didn't help us either. Pepena and Perai Wenepo were looking after two pigs for me and my uncle Kimembo Wak had given me two pigs. We had ten pigs but how could Kole Yaldo accept our bride price if he had already turned away twenty-five pigs and ten kina shells?

One afternoon Piambil Ambo Mopune sent words via an old man for Pepena and me to go to the mountain. The old man's grandson said his grandpa had arrived late the day before from Piambil.

"Grandpa says you must go to the mountain now," said the little boy and went away.

"Why would she want us at the mountain?" asked Pepena.

After I had explained to Pepena why Piambil Ambo Mopune wanted us to go to the mountain, Pepena shook his head and said:

"We must leave now." We reached the mountain at midday. Piambil was sitting still in the cloudless morning. Several clouds of smoke were rising at the mountainsides beyond the villages where the gardens were.

We found an abandoned garden hut further up the mountain away from the track.

"We will make the fire here in the open space so that the smoke can catch Piambil Ambo Mopune's eyes easily," said Pepena.

Pepena brought the fire-making objects out of his bilum and spilt them on the ground in front of the hut. It consisted of a strong dry vine and a short stick like a piece of middle-sized bamboo that had been split, but halfway through to the middle.

Placing the stick on top of some dry grasses and mosses, Pepena placed the rope underneath the stick and on top of the moss. Holding the two ends of the rope in his hands, he stepped on the stick with his foot and pulled and released the rope against the stick until a thin blue smoke formed in the gap in the middle of the stick. He continued to pull and release the rope until the smoke grew bigger and thicker until a tiny red flint was formed in the moss. Pepena brought the moss close to his mouth and blew the smoke into flames.

We added twigs onto the fire until we built a huge fire. Pepena slashed off some low-lying branches and heaped onto the fire to produce more smoke.

The fire blew out a huge cloud of smoke which rushed straight to the sky and floated above the treetops like low-lying clouds.

"I'll check how the smoke is seen," said Pepena and ran down the mountain and up again on the other side of the valley. He returned a while later and said the smoke was big enough for Piambil Ambo Mopune to see.

Since the mountain wasn't too far from Piambil, we expected her to turn up within moments but there was no sign of her even after the fire exhausted and the smoke faded.

"She wouldn't send the message if she wasn't at home. By now she would have seen the smoke," observed Pepena.

"She wouldn't take this long to reach us," I said.

"Let's go back home now," said Pepena. "She won't come here. We'll send Perai Wenepo and the girls to take Piambil Ambo Mopune home tomorrow."

By the time we arrived at home, it was midnight. Next morning, Perai Wenepo and Kepambo went to Piambil to check Piambil Ambo Mopune. They only returned the following day to inform that Piambil Ambo Mopune had been given away for marriage.

We learnt later that the old man who brought the message from Piambil Ambo Mopune had spent a night at Kiripia, halfway from Piambil before he returned home. The bride price was paid a day before we made the fire.

"She was forced to marry the man," said Perai Wenepo, sobbing. "Her father couldn't let go a huge bride price. I was looking forward for my sister to follow me here but she's gone."

The news shattered my dreams of marrying Piambil Ambo Mopune. The wind of wealth blew her away to a stranger, to a strange land.

The thought of Piambil Ambo Mopune being given away to another man produced a different sensation in me. My whole skin burned with a sudden rush of heat. My blood boiled with anger. Piambil Ambo Mopune was the only woman I loved. Our love for each other blossomed like a tender flower. She watered it with her tears and I treasured it with my love.

She not only took away my heart, she took all of me away. What does love matter when wealth gets in its way?

"We gave her father our word but he acted in his best interest," said Pepena. "That's how the world works. It works in puzzles and twists."

Pepena assured me I would be all right. But I didn't know how I would recover from this shock. I couldn't think of a way out of that nightmare. The world came crashing down hard on me.

Now the sun was already up. Pepena was splitting a log with his stone axe outside the house while I rolled a smoke and allowed the smoke to carry my thoughts away. Pepena enquired about several girls who were interested in me, including Ambuwape the Tendepo girl but I had no interest in them.

"Isn't Ambuwape equally beautiful as Piambil Ambo Mopune?" asked Pepena. "There are many women out there you can choose. You are a butterfly. They are flowers. You can choose to sit on any one of them. You can go to the next when the nectar is dry. Why thinking so much of a single woman? If she isn't meant for us, we should move on in life."

"I can choose Ambuwape or any other girl but none of them is as dear as Piambil Ambo Mopune. She was the only one I had."

Pepena rested his axe at the side and gathered the small pieces of broken wood with his feet. Then he spread the newly split firewood on the bare earth for the sun to dry. Resting his back against the wall, he spoke again. He spoke as if it was a small thing for Piambil Ambo Mopune to go away.

"Breaking a man's heart is not a new thing," said Pepena, without looking at me. "Women have broken many hearts since the beginning of time. Many young men find themselves stripped of the woman they loved dearly. I know what it feels like to lose someone you love so much. The pain of love will hurt you deeply but I assure you that time heals everything. Just give it some time. You will eventually recover."

I doubted whether time would heal the wound in my heart as Pepena said. If it healed, I didn't know how long it would take for me to forget her. I realized, for the first time, that women were immune to the pain of love. They quickly forget those poor young hearts that love and cherish them.

"Maybe I should go to Piambil tomorrow and confirm the story myself," said Pepena.

"Man, you are speaking as if she is still in Piambil."

Pepena said nothing

Chapter 16

When I woke up the next morning, the golden rays of the sun were already painting the peaks of Mt Giluwe. The clear sky brought the tops of Mt Ialibu, the great mountain behind Piambil closer to me. Piambil Ambo Mopune was no longer waiting for me under the mountain. She only left her fond memories behind that would haunt me for ages.

The silent memories of my lost love flooded my mind and the fire of anger within me burned me to death. I would do anything to take my Piambil Ambo Mopune back. I realised I had made a mistake by giving all my love to her. I couldn't take that love back. The depth of the loss was equal to the depth of love I had for her. I knew she loved me so much too but what else could she do to protect that love? Forces of wealth and family influence were too strong for such a helpless young woman to resist.

To shed off those recurring reminiscences, I decided to go hunting for the day. I went over to Pepena again but he had left for Piambil. There was no point in him going to Piambil but he went anyway.

I called up our two dogs, got my bows and arrows and aimed for the forest. When I reached the creek behind the ceremonial ground, I met Paraka who was returning from the forest. He rested his firewood at the wayside to have a chat with me.

"Are you still here?" said Paraka, taking out a dry bundle of tobacco from his broad bark belt. He smashed the tobacco onto a dry leaf and made a thick roll, about the size of his thump and set the tip of it alight. He placed the tobacco in his mouth and swayed the tobacco to the right and then to the left as if he allowing the tobacco to find its right position on the lips. Eventually, when the tobacco rested on his lips, Paraka inhaled a great amount of smoke and trapped it inside for a long time and released a cloud of smoke with relief. He meditated on the effect the smoke produced on him.

"Ah the tobacco is so sweet especially when you skip it in the morning," he said, taking another puff again.

"Where do you suppose me to go?" I asked him.

"Kipingi was looking for you yesterday evening. He wanted you to accompany him to Kandep today."

"Has he left already?"

"Ah let me think," he said and looked at the sun. It was hitting our faces and began to become painful on the skin. He looked at the thick forest beyond the Kaugel River where the track led to Kandep.

"Kipingi and Yare left at daybreak so I think they must be somewhere behind the mountains."

That was a great adventure for me to forget my Piambil Ambo Mopune. I rushed back to the house and after chasing the dogs away, I picked up a kina shell and went after the men.

The kina shell was one of the three we had been keeping for the bride price but I wasn't interested in marriage. Piambil Ambo Mopune had taken my interest to marry away with her. My mother suggested to me to take home one of those beautiful girls who were fighting for me but I was not interested in any of them. I couldn't keep Konopu and Kepambo waiting that long. Marriage proposals were flooding in from all corners of the land for both girls.

By the time I reached the mountain beyond Kagul River, the sun was directly above the treetops. The great river rested in the valley below. Fresh memories of the deaths flooded my thoughts. The cold afternoon when they were swept away was like yesterday. A new bridge was pulled over on the same spot but I hadn't used the bridge after the deaths except once when I went to Kandep to exchange kina shells for salt. That was a long time ago.

I had difficulty remembering the track well. In certain places, the track disappeared where the rainwaters had created new paths. In other low ground, the track branched into two where travelers had marked out an alternate path to avoid knee-deep mud.

The sun was sliding past the trees when I reached the top of the highest mountain where two huge Karape trees stood reaching for the skies. I remembered this place well because it was where my father and I rested before we continued our journey to Kandep. The trees grew so tall that we could even see their tops from our village. You wouldn't see four men standing on the other side of the trees. Some said the trees were planted in ancient times by our great, great grandfathers while others said they germinated out of birds' droppings.

This, I remembered, was halfway to Kandep. As I left the mountain and reached a creek, footprints began to appear wet and recent. I quickened my walk to catch up with the men before they disappeared into one of the huge villages in Kandep. Still, I could not see their back. I climbed a tall tree and called across the valley. The echoes floated above the treetops and brought back Yare's familiar whistle.

I sprinted for some time until I caught up with them. They were resting near a creek.

"We have heard your whistle," said the men.

Kipingi was pleased I had come but even happier when I gave him the kina shell.

"Very good. We will get some more salt with this," said Kipingi and placed the kina shell inside his bilum.

Now the sun floated past the trees and its rays failed to reach the forest floor. The winds began to pick up speed and shook the leaves. Above us, flocks of birds rose from the treetops and flapped their wings across the sky. The flowering season in that part of the forest was ending and the birds were migrating away elsewhere in search of food. There were fallen flowers laying everywhere on the track and in the bush.

The birds appeared happy as they whistled across the open sky. They had nothing to worry about. They laboured not for food but migrated to where there was food. They knew the seasons very well; they knew where to get their food; they knew how to survive without labour. They were carefree but humans had many things to worry about; hunger, death, a brokenheart, rejections and family and cultural obligations. I imagined how life would turn out to be like if we lived like birds singing joyous songs every morning and feeding from tree to tree. Would life be meaningful without care and challenges?

We travelled on until we reached the mountain overlooking Kandep. The sun shed its final rays over the Kandep valley and painted the hillsides brown. The houses spread out in the valley like some small pools in a wide swamp. The village had pushed the tree line further up to the mountainsides to accommodate the increasing need for houses and gardens.

We descended to a small valley and arrived at a creek where a rushing stream had been brought out to the track through long bamboo trunks joined at their ends. Ferns and leaves decorated the waterfall, giving out a fresh scent.

After having a drink, we continued our journey and arrived at the village ceremonial ground. We were received warmly and well accommodated with plenty of food. Such was the way they treated their visitors.

Our host was Kipingi's brother-in-law. He assumed Wane's leadership when the latter died. They belonged to the same clan.

We talked about many things all night. First, it was about the latest battles in Tambul and Kandep. Then stories of pig killings and moka exchanges in both lands took us up to midnight. Sometimes when a subject became more interesting, we allowed it to drag on longer and when things became worrying, we went to the next. Towards midnight, the Kandep chief took on a new topic. It was about a rumour that was spreading like a bushfire in their land.

"I'm not sure whether this is true but there is this talk all over the land," said the Kandep chief. "I've heard that some of our dead ancestors have come back in a different form. They have been spotted in places like Porgera." "Did they look like those we hear in the legends? Those with long ears like that of pigs and tongues that drape down to the breast?" asked a curious Kipingi.

"Nothing like that," cut in the chief's son. "I've seen two in Porgera. And you know what? They were normal people just like us but they were very tall. Their skins were bright and smooth like the kina shells."

"I guess their skins are so smooth that flies would slip over and injure their tiny legs," laughed his father.

His son continued after a good laugh.

"Both men had their feet covered with a pair of objects which stuck to their feet." "Did they appear like real people, like talking or something?" asked Yare.

"Maybe they must have whistled like the spirits," observed the Kandep chief.

"No, they never whistled," said his son. "They talked like us but in a strange language. We couldn't understand anything of what they were saying."

"What were they talking about? Did they come back to take more of your men to the ancestors?" asked Kipingi.

"That I'm not sure," said the young man, "but they were searching the creeks and the rivers for a precious stone. We even helped them to scoop up mud and pebbles using a shiny object which they said would help them to locate the stone."

"Are they still in Porgera?" asked his father.

"They have gone back to Mt Hagen where they came from. They must be the ancestors of the Hagen people."

"I don't think so," laughed his father. "Hagen people are no different than us. They don't look like the people you are describing."

"Neither of the two men were similar to people I know here in Kandep or elsewhere," continued the young man.

The thoughts of the strange men and Piambil Ambo Mopune occupied my mind until I dozed off to sleep.

The next morning, we waited for a little while for the sun to rise and as soon as the sun spread over the valley, we walked over to the salt ponds. The place was a good distance away from where we slept so by the time we arrived; it was midmorning.

There were several small ponds where salt was extracted. The bushes near the salt ponds had been cleared. Dry logs were piled up in groups along the shores ready to be burned. Ashes and fragments of half-burned ambers were scattered everywhere at the lakes.

Logs had been cut and submerged inside the ponds for several moons to collect salt. Once the logs absorbed sufficient salt, they were removed and dried along the shores before being burned in bonfires.

The salt ponds were owned by two tribes that lived nearby. Ownership of the ponds had been passed on from one generation to another. The salt ponds also served as the trading spot for different tribes. Whenever traders came to exchange salt, they brought with them stone axes, kina shells and even pigs for the landowners and also traded among themselves.

Our men exchanged kina shells for stone axes which the men in Kandep obtained from another faraway land beyond the mountains. In that faraway land, the men selected a strong stone from a river and rubbed it hard against another stone until it got the desired shape. They then attached a handle to the axe head. The stone axes taken from that land were highly valued because they were so strong. They were used to fell trees and even sharpen house posts. Our men also got a black rubbing oil which was also found in that faraway land.

We used the oil in body decorations in singsings. When we arrived at the ponds, Kipingi walked over to a pile of logs. He stood with his hands behind him and looked at the dry logs as if he were counting them. Then he broke off a young tree and dusted the dust away from the pile of logs.

"This is ours," said Kipingi and untied the logs.

Kipingi had cut the logs some moons ago, submerged them underwater and asked a young boy to dry them for him. The boy waited for some moons for the logs to absorb enough salt. It was only a few days ago when he removed the logs and heaped them at the side of the lake. Kipingi brought a kina shell as a token of appreciation for the boy. He was very happy and took it away to his father.

We built a fire with twigs and heaped all the logs onto it. While the logs were burning, Kipingi retired under a shade to have his sweet potato and tobacco. Yare and I explored the other ponds and came across an old man and two young boys at the far end of the salt ponds. They said they had arrived from Karel in Upper Mendi a day earlier. The old man was chopping some logs and the boys were placing them inside the pond. They said they would come back another time to burn their logs but in the meantime, they had brought two kina shells to obtain some rubbing oil.

"Were your tracks clear when you came?" asked the old man.

"We don't have any enemy along the way," said Yare.

"Oh, that is very good," said the old man. "At least you don't have to worry about your back. We have some enemies along the way but we all have a common understanding that trade is essential for survival. We allow each other to pass freely through each other's lands for trade purposes."

It was at sunset when all the woods were burnt out. We sprinkled fire onto the ashes and left the ashes to cool off for some time.

Moments later when everything cooled, we collected the brownish salt and packed them in huge leaves and attached the parcels on some sticks with ropes. Kipingi said he would exchange his salt with some Kaupena people for kina shells in three days' time. Yare said he would give all his salt to a man from Gia who had given him a pig. I didn't know what to do with my salt.

Next morning, we left Kandep before daybreak. The journey home was long but we managed to come home at sunset as there was no rain and we left Kandep much earlier.

My mother was in the house roasting some corn. Konopu and Kepambo were in the pigpen. Kepambo was chopping some raw sweet potato for the pigs while Konopu struggled to remove a rope which had cut through one of the pig's left arms. She removed the rope and placed it on its right arm.

"Have you seen Pepena?" I asked the girls.

"We haven't seen him for a few days now," said Konopu.

I thought of checking Pepena out but was too tired to even take a few steps to his house. I rolled a tobacco instead and smoked away. A cloud of smoke rose to the skies. Soon a gentle wind blew some away. It appeared that the smoke was reluctant to leave me but the winds forced its way in and swept the smoke away. The same thing had happened to Piambil Ambo Mopune. The power of kina shells and pigs carried my love away against her wishes. I recalled her beautiful smile and charming heart. The smoke resurrected every thought of my Piambil Ambo Mopune. Although life moved on, memories lingered. Sorry oh my Piambil Ambo Mopune.

Chapter 17

Next morning when I was about to check out Pepena in his home, he came looking for me. He said he had been to Piambil while I was away in Kandep. He confirmed it was true that Piambil Ambo Mopune had been give away after a huge bride price was paid. That news erased every hope of seeing my Piambil Ambo Mopune again.

Seeing my heart deeply troubled Pepena said we shouldn't be thinking hard on something we couldn't help. However, it was hard for me to let Piambil Ambo Mopune out of my mind. She was more than a woman to me. She and I had been building our friendship on trust and mutual affection. Our love for each other had been glowing like a fire at dusk.

Her sudden departure put a knife in my heart.

"Come," said Pepena. "Mother is cooking some sweet potatoes. Let's check it out."

Pepena's house was warm from the morning fires. His mother was removing the sweet potatoes from the exhausted ashes and Perai Wenepo was opposite her weaving a bilum. Another young woman was beside Perai Wenepo with her head slightly bowed. I couldn't tell who she was because the house was quite dark inside.

I went straight into the house to take a seat next to Pepena's mother when Pepena, who was entering the house behind me, asked me to take the place at the raised flat form behind the fire.

"Hi, Maip you are here. I thought you were still in Kandep," said Pepena's mother.

As soon as she mentioned my name, the young woman near Perai Wenepo raised her head towards the door. Then our eyes met.

We stared at each other with tears swimming in our eyes. She and I were speechless. Standing face to face with me was she. The familiar atmosphere, the touch of her presence, the smell of her beautiful body, all thrown there right in front of me. The world suddenly turned upside down for us. She rose, and my heart rose to my neck.

The house stood still as every longing and loneliness parted ways with me, with her.

The pain of love I had been nursing inside my heart knocked the walls of my heart away and fled. We could not say anything, for we knew nothing to say.

How could she be here? This must be her ghost for I could not believe the impression my eyes were giving me. I rubbed my eyes again and again to confirm if this was not a dream. Yes, it was her, and she was there right in front of me, and there for me.

Pepena and Perai Wenepo laughed till tears ran down their eyes as Piambil Ambo Mopune and I embraced each other crying and smiling at the same time. How could Pepena take Piambil Ambo Mopune out of the hands of the Mondikes? Did he kill the man? Did he steal her?

I couldn't reward him much. I led Pepena to our pig pen that day and asked him to choose one of the two large pigs.

"Why should I take the pig?"

"This is the least I could do."

"You don't need to thank me." "Why?" I insisted.

"Piambil Ambo Mopune was meant for you. It was my responsibility to reunite the two of you. I want the two of you to live happily together."

"I'm going to give you both pigs if you keep on denying this. I mean it."

"Keep both pigs," he said. "I guess the Mondikes will be coming here to demand back their bride price. I have stolen Piambil Ambo Mopune from them."

My mother crossed Kepambo and Konopu when they brought Piambil Ambo Mopune home.

"Son how could you possibly bring this woman here?" said my mother that afternoon.

"You have brought a curse into this house."

I didn't mind what the Mondikes could do or the curse that would follow thereafter. I had Piambil Ambo Mopune.

Pepena was so brave to pluck Piambil Ambo Mopune out of Kundaka. He had brought her home the previous night but kept her secretly in the house. When I thought he went to Piambil, Pepena went over to Alkina where Piambil Ambo Mopune was taken.

"I did not know how to locate her house," said Pepena when we asked him how he managed to get her out of the Mondike's land, Alkina.

"Fortunately a small boy helped me. He was struggling to fix his bowstring onto his bow when I arrived at Alkina in the afternoon. While helping him I enquired if he had heard of any young woman married there lately.

'That's her house,' pointed the boy to Piambil Ambo Mopune's house.

Pepena said he spent the entire afternoon planning how to take Piambil Ambo

Mopune back.

Pepena said he met her very early the next morning when she came out to the tracks to 'awake the birds'.

Awaking the bird was a practice whereby a newly married woman consulted a certain bird in a secluded spot at dawn. The woman would ask questions and the bird, possessed by the spirits of the dead, would provide answers to the questions. The questions were about anything of interest including the future of the couple to the cause of the death of a close relative.

"When I said I had come to take her home, she broke down in tears right there," laughed Pepena.

"Honestly I couldn't believe I was seeing you," said Piambil Ambo Mopune. "I thought I was dreaming. When Pepena said he had come to take me home, tears swallowed my eyes. I embraced his legs and sobbed right there. He rescued me from the pain of love that tormented me for days."

Pepena smiled away as if it was fun to just walk through the land of the Mondikes and steal Piambil Ambo Mopune away.

They arrived at Malke without being detected. No one in the village knew she had come except Pepena's mother.

In the morning when Pepena and I went to his house, Piambil Ambo Mopune was looking worried. She wasn't expecting me because Pepena had informed her that I would be in Kandep for several more days. When we met inside Pepena's house, she couldn't believe her eyes. She flew to me, rested her arms around my neck and sobbed like a child, which made everyone laugh.

There was this confusion about her whereabouts that delayed an immediate search. The Mondikes thought Piambil Ambo Mopune had gone back to her people in Piambil and her people in Piambil never expected her to be elsewhere. Several days elapsed without us receiving any news or threats from Alkina.

When the Mondikes found out later, they threatened us and demanded their bride price back. However, Pepena and our leaders sent word back that we were pleased to repay their things on the battlefield.

Since the Mondikes were our enemies, they did not press their demand further. They knew the strength of our tribe and how we had successfully driven back a coalition of enemies that invaded our village. In my grandfather's time, our tribe invaded the Yap tribe and got their land. They also chased two other powerful tribes out and seized their lands as well. The Mondikes knew any tribe that waged battle against us was playing with fire so they were reluctant to invade us. They instead sought an alternate means to demand their things back. They threatened the Piambil people to repay their things.

Pressed by the huge demands, Piambil Ambo Mopune's uncle, her father's younger brother, showed up at the house one morning shortly after Piambil Ambo Mopune had come to Malke.

"Why did you run away like this? You foolish girl," he shouted at Piambil Ambo Mopune. "Didn't you realise you've put our necks on the arrow? "Your father is going crazy. He will cut your mother's neck if you stay here forever."

Piambil Ambo Mopune sat beside my mother, sobbing quietly. If she was a child, her uncle would beat her up.

"Have you forgotten the Mondikes are our enemies?" continued her uncle. "Haven't you realised you have revived this enmity between us?"

Pepena, Ponenge and several other men entered the house moments after Mopune's uncle had arrived. They shook hands with him and Pepena took a seat near my mother. When Piambil Ambo Mopune's uncle completed pouring his anger over her, Pepena cleared his throat.

"We didn't expect things to end like this," said Pepena. "When things didn't work out the way I expected, I had to change my approach to bring the girl over here. We gave you our word. We said we were coming but I was disappointed you gave her away to another man."

Piambil Ambo Mopune's uncle never said a word. He stared at the fire and shook his head continuously. Piambil Ambo Mopune told me later that she was worrying she would be taken away forcefully and be reunited with the Mondike man. If her father was well enough to come to our village, he would show up with an axe to demand her girl back. However, such an attempt was only a wish because Kole Yaldo's bad knees wouldn't support such an urgent journey. However, his brother was as mad as him and was determined to take his niece back.

"We know you have received a huge bride price from the Mondikes," continued Pepena. "We have heard they are threatening you to repay their things. We understand you are concerned that this issue would revive this hostility. But I'm sorry to say that Piambil Ambo Mopune is not going back with you. Her bones will now be buried here."

Pepena spoke like a man with a wealth of experience. Despite his tender age, he was becoming an excellent orator, the essential attribute of a great leader. He knew all the aspects of public speaking. He knew what to say and when to say it and how much to say. People said he was outdoing his father in terms of public speaking.

"Now, you must be thinking Piambil Ambo Mopune is the cause of the problem," continued Pepena. "The young woman is innocent. She is innocent. I went to Alkina and took her out of the Mondikes myself."

Piambil Ambo Mopune's uncle cast doubtful eyes on Pepena. He must probably have been thinking about how Pepena could snatch his niece out of the Mondikes' hands.

"I cannot say I am sorry for what I have done," continued Pepena. "I am very happy that I have taken the risk, and it paid off very well.

"Now that she is here, she will bear me sons. Tomorrow Piambil Ambo Mopune will bear my sons who will look after me when I walk on three legs. She will bear me sons who will protect and defend this land in battles."

"No, I will take her away," said Piambil Ambo Mopune's uncle with a stern voice.

"We have received many things from them. You haven't paid anything for her. You are a thief. You have no right to keep her here. I have to take the girl away right away and restore her to her husband. Her father wants the girl restored to her rightful husband, the man who paid her bride price, not a thief like you."

"Piambil Ambo Mopune was meant to come here," said Pepena. "I have not been befriending her all those times for another man to just sneak in and take her away with some bride price. I swear in my grandfather's name. I won't let her go away to our enemies and bear sons who will fight us. Piambil Ambo Mopune will be mine from now onwards. If they want a wife, let them look elsewhere. I won't give what is mine to my enemy. Piambil Ambo

Mopune's bones will be buried here."

Piambil Ambo Mopune's uncle didn't utter a word for a while. Perhaps Pepena's words convinced him that Pepena was not playing games here. He probably admired Pepena's bravery but must have been worrying about how his brother would react if he returned without her.

"Leave the Mondikes to me," said Pepena. "I will deal with them if they come here. For now, tell Kole Yaldo that Piambil Ambo Mopune's new home will be Malke. Tell him not to worry about the Mondikes. They won't harm you. They know our strength and what we can do on the battlefield."

Ponenge and our men also threw their support behind Pepena. They all agreed that Piambil Ambo Mopune was not going back again.

When Piambil Ambo Mopune's uncle realised that none of our men and even some of his sisters who were married to our village supported him, he cleared his voice and said to Pepena;

"Seems that you've been brave enough to take my daughter and bring her here. Likewise, be brave to defend whoever comes here. Also, look after my daughter well."

Now Piambil Ambo Mopune's uncle and the other man rose to leave but Ponenge said it was getting late.

"I'll grab some sugarcane for you," said Ponenge and went back to his house. He asked my mother to follow him.

While they were gone, Piambil Ambo Mopune's uncle said he was resting everything on our hands.

"I don't think the old man has anything left to deal with the Mondikes. He has used up all his share of the bride price in a moka two days after we received it. Should there be any issue arising hereafter, you'll be responsible."

"It should be okay," said Kipingi who had just entered the house when he heard the two Piambil men had arrived. "If they threaten you, let us know. Otherwise, will take care of them."

My mother and Ponenge returned with a huge pig. We killed the pig for the Piambil men that afternoon. Kipingi asked them to come back again after five days.

"We will put together a few pigs for you to sort out the issue with the Mondikes," said Kipingi.

The entire tribe contributed a pig, kina shell or salt to my bride price. They said my father had done so much for the tribe and that they were obliged not only to pay the bride price for me but to defend the tribe from any forthcoming attacks.

The bride price was more than half less than that paid by the Mondikes but that was just enough to pacify the Piambils and the Mondikes.

Chapter 18

A moon after Piambil Ambo Mopune came, two men from Birop turned up at our house to ask for Konopu's hand in marriage. One was a middle-aged man with a few grey

hairs while the other was a tall handsome young man.

"We have been sent by our chief Koropa to find a wife for his youngest son," said the elderly man.

"Oh, is Koropa still alive?" asked my mother.

"Yes, he's a very old man now," said the elderly man. "He has been searching for a suitable wife for his son until lately he learnt your late husband Karimbi had a young girl. The old man enquired after your daughter and was pleased with the girl.

"The old man said, 'In case the young woman refuses to come with you, take my son with you'.

"So here we came. His son and me." The young man put his head down.

"Chief Koropa said Karimbi was not only a famed chief but one of his closest friends. Thus, the old man is very keen to revive this relationship with Karimbi's house."

"Oh, I would love to see him again. My husband and I attended one of his pig killings before," said my mother.

"Koropa said he would come here himself but he is now walking on three. His last wish of old age is to see his son get a good wife. Look this," continued the man, raising his left hand. There was a small string tied at the end of the small finger. "See this is how desperate the old man is to marry your daughter for his son. Despite my assurances that

I would deliver his words, the old man tied this rope for you to see as proof that he had sent me."

The old man's rope was something I couldn't forget. It signified the old chief's urgency, desperation and desire to secure Konopu for his son before he died.

The young man was the first and only child of Koropa's last wife and his father was hanging his heart on his child in old age.

When the man completed his talk, no one spoke for a while. My mother said nothing and eyed Konopu for an answer. Konopu sat beside my mother, weaving a bilum. Tears were already forming in her eyes. She looked away and then dried her eyes.

I remembered Koropa sometime back. He was one of the visitors we received often. My father would even go away and spend several days in Birop with him. He was strong and tough like my father. It was sad to learn that he was no longer the tough man I knew. Strength had forsaken him and youth, which glowed like a bright star in him had faded with time.

"We are pleased that you've remembered your old friend," I said. "Unfortunately, the friendship Koropa had with my father ceased when my father died. It is this saying that when you see smoke, there is a fire somewhere below. Likewise, friendships thrive on the backs of men. When there is man, there is activity. It is an unfortunate thing that every good thing must come to an end.

"As for the girl, several men had come to take her away but she refused them all. I don't know why she rejected the proposals. Perhaps this could be her time to go away. My sister will decide for herself, but thank you for coming a long way."

Konopu said nothing for a while. She cleaned her eyes several times. She must have been sad to leave behind Mother or maybe she was moved by the story of the old man who was unable to come with his youngest son.

"Mother I don't know their place or the people," said Konopu. "I don't even know the old man but his message on the finger is too much for me. Mama, I am sorry. I think I am leaving you."

"I am very happy that you are accepting our proposal," said the elderly man. "You are making a great honour to my old man. Your decision tonight is forging and strengthening the connection between our Yakumbu and your Yano tribes.

"I can't wait to go back to Birop with the good news. I would leave right now to deliver the good news to my old man if it was daylight. He will be excited about this good news. Let his blessings and favour be upon you, young woman. The bride price is ready but we will give a few days for others in the village to contribute."

Everything was settled that night. The bride price was fixed in several days. Kepambo would accompany Konopu to Birop and stay with Konopu until the day of the bride price.

The two men went back to Birop the next day. Meanwhile, the girls would go over to my mother's village Glama. My mother's brother had said to slaughter two pigs for the girls to take with them to Birop.

Before the girls left the next morning, my mother went into her room and brought out two grass skirts. "I've been waiting for this day for so long," said my mother and stressed the skirts in the morning sunlight.

My mother had made the skirts from the tall grass that grew in the swamps and had been hiding them in her room since the girls were small. She never showed them to anyone nor did she mention the skirts to the girls. When the time finally arrived, she called the girls over and handed the skirts to them. "Try one each and see if it fits you well," said my mother.

Konopu tied the two ends of her skirt around her waist and stretched it down from her waist until the tips of her long skirt floated just below her knees. She was however dissatisfied with the skirt.

"Mama it is not long enough to cover my legs fully," said Konopu, removing the skirt from her hips.

"Oh my dear I didn't know you would grow this tall," said my mother, taking the skirt from Konopu.

"Then give that to Kepambo. She can try mine," said Piambil Ambo Mopune.

Piambil Ambo Mopune slipped into her room and brought out her grass skirt and gave it to Konopu. Konopu hugged her and brought the skirt to the door where the sunlight was bright. She clapped the dust away hurriedly and stretched the skirt from her waist down to her legs. Then she brought the two ends of the skirt around her waist together and smiled.

"Konopu and Piambil Ambo Mopune are of the same height," said my mother. "The skirt is fitting Konopu perfectly well."

"Wait Konopu. Let me see," said Piambil Ambo Mopune. "Oh, oh I see. Turn your waist around. Now loose the rope a little."

"Like this? Is it okay now?" said Konopu, relaxing the rope that she had tied at her waist.

"Relax it more, some more," said Piambil Ambo Mopune. "It's too tight. Your waist is bigger than mine."

"Let Piambil Ambo Mopune help you out," said my mother.

Piambil Ambo Mopune untied the ropes and relaxed the rope a little. Konopu smiled down at Piambil Ambo Mopune.

"Now I think it will work," said Piambil Ambo Mopune, fitting the skirt again on Konopu's waist. This time there was nothing more to adjust. Konopu smiled. Kepambo also put on her skirt. They both fit the girls perfectly well.

Now both Konopu and Kepambo had their grass skirts on, bilums on their heads and digging sticks in their hands, all good to leave. Piambil Ambo Mopune was so emotional.

"I thought you would stay with me for a little longer before you go. I'm very sad to see you leaving me too soon," said Piambil Ambo Mopune and sobbed.

"It is a terrible thing to raise a daughter and give her away to another tribe," said my mother wiping her eyes. "It won't be long when Kepambo will leave us like this too."

My mother raised us herself in both good and bad times. We were a small family travelling life's challenges together, and here a part of our small family, part of our little world was tearing away.

My mother and Konopu, lost in each other's arms, cried a lot for the last time. It reminded me of the moment when Konopu threw her arms around my mother and cried when Koukera broke her little nose. The feeling that morning was overly-sentimental.

Now as they were about to leave, Engaamb stormed into the house.

"Why didn't you notify me earlier?" she said. "Am I not her mother? I should be the first one to know this. I will talk to you people later."

She cried for a while and rushed back to her house. She returned moments later with a highly prized bilum woven with black and white cuscus furs.

"Daughter take this one with you to your new village," said Engaamb and gave the

bilum to Konopu. She hugged her and they cried for a long time before Konopu left.

It was a little after midmorning when the girls left for my mother's village Glama.

Konopu's would-be village Birop was beyond the great mountain ranges that bordered Kandep to the east and Hagen to the west. From Glama, the girls would walk for half a day to reach Birop.

My mother saw the girls off the other side of the creek and came back crying. She watched the hills until the girls disappeared beyond the hills. Konopu's footprints were in the mud near the house. She saw the gardens Konopu had planted. She came into the house and saw Konopu's empty room. The place was void of life, only shadows and footprints were the remains of Konopu. Everything in and around the house had lost their liveliness without Konopu. An air of emptiness clouded my mother's world. She broke down in tears.

"Oh, my daughter," cried my mother. "I never thought I would miss you this much."

Others in the village were excited that Konopu was getting married but they were also sad to see her go because she was like a fire that kept the village warm.

Konopu was the pride of the clan. Her beauty stunned whoever beheld her. Whenever an old woman was making a sweet potato garden, she would stop and help her. She even helped carry firewood for the old people. People said she was the carbon copy of my father and could take my father's place if she was a man. Some mothers cried with my mother when Konopu went away to Birop. The elders predicted she had a great future ahead of her. One of the old men even complained about why she was a girl.

"I hate the idea of my daughter going away. I wish she was a boy. She would make a great leader," said the old man.

Two days passed and we didn't receive any news from Birop. Usually, the groom's family would confirm the date of the bride price one or two days after the bride went to the groom's village.

Hoping to catch some news from travellers, my mother visited the ceremonial ground every afternoon for two days, but she came back worried.

Long-distant messages were delivered via a traveller. Sometimes an active young boy was dispatched to relay a message when it needed immediate delivery. If the message was urgent and important, the sender would tie a rope on the messenger's last finger lest the messenger forgot to deliver.

On the third day, a young boy from my mother's village Glama came back to check if the girls had returned to our village.

"The girls left Glama two days ago but we received word that they haven't arrived in

Birop," said the boy.

We discussed at length in the night and concluded that if the girls were not in Birop, they could either be in Kuma, just across the Tongo River at my step-sister's place or in Konopu's best friend's home in Ekari. But why would they go to those places? They went away to marry and not to visit friends. Besides Konopu had gladly accepted the proposal. We decided to confirm with my uncle the next morning.

When we arrived in Glama the next day my uncle confirmed that the girls never reached Birop.

"We just found out yesterday from a Tendepo woman who came from Birop that the girls did not arrive. That's why I have sent the young boy to check whether they had come back to Malke."

While we were talking, two young men arrived from Birop to find out why the girls were not arriving.

"The old man sent us back to check for the girl," they said.

They couldn't get lost along the way because the track was familiar to them. The main track ran through the thick forests before cutting through a swampy land. There was only one river in the Nemarep valley formed by the confluence of several little streams that ran into it but it didn't require a bridge to cross.

We immediately searched the entire village and the surrounding forests. Different search groups went out to the various tracks along the riverbeds and forest floors to trace the footprints.

The search continued after midday without any success. The sun disappeared beyond the black clouds and rain started to fall. The rains increased and complicated the foot tracing.

My uncle said we would continue the search in the morning.

Everyone began to leave the forest. Now when we were some good distance away from the Nemarep River, a faint cry floated across the trees like an echo.

We rushed to the scene. There was no noise, except murmurs and sobs. Some mothers and several of the searchers had gathered around her. Pepena was on his knees and was lifting

Konopu's head which was resting against the root of a huge tree. Two fist-sized stones rested beside her head, both painted with blood stains. She had bruises all over her body. Her long black hair was draped with blood and some loosely covered her face, and some fell back and served as a pillow. Her face had turned purple.

Pepena lifted her head and checked for signs of life. Her body was white and cold. Her heart must have given up a long time ago. There was blood everywhere, on her head, on her chest, ears and forehead and even on the roots of the tree against which she lay. The blood on her forehead and around her neck had dried.

We found Kepambo further down the river. Her left leg was bleeding heavily from an axe wound. She had fragments of torn green and brown leaves on her rough hair. She must have been dragged along the forest. Kepambo's heart was still beating weakly.

We quickly placed the two on stretchers and hurried them to my uncle's house. Kepambo recovered from the wounds but we could do nothing to save my little sister Konopu as she was already dead when we found her. We had a funeral in Malke the next day and buried our beloved sister and daughter two days after we found her.

Both my father's and my mother's people gathered as well as the surrounding tribes to mourn the loss. Everyone was enraged by the manner in which the defenceless girls were attacked. They condemned the attackers with the strongest words.

Kepambo remained bedridden for days. She couldn't talk nor could she move her limbs. The women washed the wound on her leg every day with warm water and applied pig fat to soothe the pain. They also heated a leaf and wiped it around the wound so that the warmth could slowly soothe away the pain.

Our men and boys were impatient for Kepambo to recover her health. She stayed in bed for the next few days as the wounds were still fresh and wet. The blackness in her eyes gradually faded. She required support to get out of the house and come back.

Three days after we found her, Kepambo's voice came back. Everyone gathered in the house to learn how the tragedy had transpired.

Chapter 19

"The incident happened at the Glond River," said Kepambo.

"Three men emerged from the bushes near the river and two seized Konopu while the other wrapped his arms around my neck to strangle me."

"Did you see their faces?" asked Pepena.

"I only identified one of them but the other two had their faces painted with charcoal."

"Did you recognise his face?" asked Kipingi

"Yes, it was the Tekep chief."

"Oh, he had kept his word," cried my mother.

"They knocked us down with heavy fists and dragged us away towards the river," said Kepambo.

Kepambo said when they were only a few spaces away from the track, there was noise at the track. They feared that they would be caught so they quickly chopped the girls and left them at the banks either for the floods to carry them away or for them to bleed to death.

"What happened next? How did they escape?" asked Pepena.

"I don't know how they escaped, said Kepambo "The last thing I remembered was a sharp axe on my leg. I lost consciousness after that. If you had arrived a day earlier, my sister would have died in your hands."

"How could strong men attack the weak and the innocent?" said our village chief

Yopai. "I want all men to meet at the men's house right away."

That afternoon we explored several options and settled on two. We agreed to give the Tekeps a three-day ultimatum for compensation and if the ultimatum failed, we would declare a battle.

"We will demand a compensation. If the Tekeps deny the murder, we will consider revenge," said Kipingi.

There was a silence in the house. No one spoke for a while. The younger men put their heads down.

"Will compensation bring my daughter's life back? Or will it heal the pain in my heart?" said Yopai. "We will not accept compensation. The Tekeps had poisoned our young man Nomash six moons ago. Now they've killed my daughter. What is this? What kind of cruelty is this? What have I done to receive all this pain? Are we their killing ground? Are we women? Don't we have hands to defend our weak and dependents?"

Kipingi who had earlier preferred compensation over battle changed his mind.

"I had never seen such a thing like this before," said Kipingi. "I have never seen women being slaughtered like this. Even when we fought, we only killed men. We never killed women or children. How could one kill a woman? We can't fight with women. If you are attacking women then you are not a real man. Women are weak and defenceless. We men are supposed to fight for our women. Men are supposed to protect the women. Real men don't test their strength against women and the weak."

"When I was young," continued Kipingi, "Testing a man's spear was my joy. Tasting blood was my game. Now that I am old, the Tekeps think the sight of their spear will terrify me. I fear no man. I fear no spear."

Kipingi's talks rekindled a fire in our hearts. We unanimously agreed to battle but Kipingi said we would first issue the Tekeps the ultimatum.

"They must show some remorse. They must admit and own this murder," said Kipingi.

Next morning, we dispatched two active young boys to deliver the ultimatum to the Tekeps.

When the boys were gone, Yopai said it was unlikely that the Tekeps would accept our ultimatum.

"Three of our four past attempts to strike peace deals with them had failed," said Yopai. "We should prepare for battle."

We went back to our houses and brought our best bows and arrows to the men's house and polished them with pig grease. Some fixed their bowstrings to the bows while others oiled their arrows and wiped off the dust with moss.

I brought out my father's bow and arrows which had been concealed between the house posts in the old house. The bow was made of a strong black wood from the Kutubu area and the arrows were made from the same tree which had been split into small long portions. Sharp bones were affixed at the tips of the arrows. My father got his two spears from some gifted weapon makers in Kutubu during one of his trips there to get black rubbing oil.

My father used the weapons to fight the same enemies when he was my age. I had no idea how many men he killed. He was a humble person who preferred to keep his achievements to himself. When he died others commended him for his bravery and achievements on the battlefields.

Over time when peace ruled in the land, my father used the weapons to hunt cassowaries and large tree kangaroos that roamed our jungles but when he died, the weapons relapsed into a lengthy period of inactivity. The last time I had a practical use of the spears was during a hunting trip when I brought the hunting dogs to a standstill when one of the spears pierced the heart of a runaway cassowary. Since then, the village chiefs learnt of the use of the spears and restricted their use.

"You will degrade the lethal power of the weapons if you consistently apply their use to the animals," they warned me.

I grabbed my weapons and strolled out of the house with my arrows hanging in a quiver. It appeared as if the quiver had been restraining the arrows for ages from attacking the enemies.

Now the sun was over our heads. All the men and boys were at the men's house, polishing their weapons with pig grease and fixing their bowstrings to the bows, and oiling their arrows and wiping away the dust with moss. They were excited to use the spears and arrows if the ultimatum failed.

I examined my weapons and to ascertain if they were all perfect; bowstrings intact, arrows perfectly constructed and the spear properly polished. We did not have a slight fear for our enemies. It appeared that the spear and the arrows would advance the enemy lines and shoot the enemies by themselves. My mind was focused on the ten arrows I had in my quiver and how I could use them to their maximum effect. Ten arrows meant ten lives if successfully used.

It was at sunset when the two boys arrived at sunset.

"They threatened to spear us. We delivered the message via a shout," said the boys.

"What did they say," asked Yopai, resting his polished spear against the wall.

"They laughed at us and said, 'Have your fathers sent you to negotiate compensation for the death of a simple girl? If you want compensation, give us time, more time. But if you want to sort it out on the battlefield, we are very very happy to meet you there.'"

"Doesn't a woman's life matter?" cried Yopai. "They can't slaughter our people like this and get away. We can't watch innocent lives being lost in the hands of cruelty. How could we allow this evil to dwell among us and infest this land with its poison? This evil needs to be purged out immediately before it spoils the entire land."

"Take up your weapons," said Kipingi. "Can't you imagine how long it takes to raise a man? Lives lost aren't for genuine reasons. We have to weed out this evil."

It was before daybreak the next morning when we made for the enemy land. A full moon shone upon us and shed enough light when we crossed the vast area of grassland between our land and the enemy land. It was still dark when we crossed the one-log bridge at the great Kagul River that separated us from our enemies.

The darkness gradually lifted and a faint light spilled thinly over the highest tops of Mt Giluwe as we ascended the other riverbank towards the enemy village. Moments later, the first rays of the sun kissed the highest tops of Mt Giluwe and chased away the stars that hung so close over the skyline. We left the riverbank quickly and by the time we reached the enemy land, the sun was already floating out of the sky unimpeded.

We made a huge fire at the enemy land and warmed our hands for a while. One of the young boys was concerned the fire would alert our enemies of our presence.

"We should attack them while they are asleep," said the boy. "If we alert them, they will attack us."

"No son. We don't fight like that," replied Kipingi. "To be a real fighter, you must give your enemy a chance to defend himself. Your enemy must challenge you in battle. If you attack your enemy when he is unaware, you are not a real warrior."

Now the smoke rose to the skies and the sun began to spread throughout the valley.

We weren't aware the enemies were alert and ready to face us. They shouted war cries just a short distance away when they saw the smoke.

Pepena climbed a decaying trunk to get a good view. He said they were behind a huge tree just next to us.

"Hand in your leader so we can repay his debts," said Pepena.

The enemies replied with war cries and shouts. Verbal confrontations erupted between us and them. Soon men with painted faces pushed through the shoulder-high grasses and were approaching us. They pounded the earth hard with huge sticks and caused the place to shake. Their men outnumbered us and swamped us. We found out later that three of our former enemies joined hands with the Tekeps to drive us out completely.

"Get your weapons ready," advised Pepena. "They are moving towards us rapidly."

Suddenly, there went a bang! The enemies shot a sharp arrow and it landed on Pepena's bark shield. Three more arrows flew to Pepena in quick succession, one after another and the last one took him down. He let go of the shield and stumbled backwards.

When Pepena fell, Paraka flew in for his rescue. Paraka knew what to expect and how to react under such circumstances. Although he was unattractive in the eyes of girls, he was a man of war. He shot out an arrow before he leaned over to help Pepena to his feet. The arrow flew across like a wind and brought down one of the strong men in the enemy's frontline. The enemy stumbled forward with the spear's end protruding his back. This single shot sent everyone on the enemy side backwards. Paraka sprinted in and raised Pepena by the hand.

The rest of our men pursued them down to the stream and Yopai plunged his spear at the right rib of Tekep Nondigomo, the one who killed my sister. The old chief screamed for help with the spear hanging on his side. The enemies rushed up to rescue their wounded but we responded with several quick shots which brought another three down. Realising that they could not stand against us, they abandoned their injured men and retreated to the creek.

By this time, Pepena picked up his stone axe and went straight to the fallen leader and slashed his head off after several repeated heavy blows. The head rolled off the cliff while the headless body made turns and twists before it followed the fleeing head down the cliff. Within a short moment, our men closed up on the headless body and mutilated the corpse beyond recognition.

The enemies went away to the other side of the creek but came back again a while later, much stronger and more determined. They stood their ground and retaliated. A full-scale arrow fight ensued. The fight continued until midday.

We killed four men, including their chief. We tore up their flesh without granting them a quick death despite their pleadings and begging to preserve their lives. And they killed Kaime, Maya's father and wounded several of our men.

After midday when black clouds were gathering above us, the enemies made their war fires just on the other side of the creek. Although we were close to each other, we couldn't shoot each other because the gulf was too wide for us to shoot each other. We swallowed our anger and employed ourselves in the rest of the afternoon cursing and insulting each other with war cries until the sun kicked out its final rays for the day.

A gloomy cloud overshadowed the valley. The coolness of the night settled in and rain began to fall. We carried the wounded and the dead home and buried the dead that same night. The wounded were taken to the men's house and were treated under the light of the night fires.

The three-footed arrow smashed Pepena's left arm against the bark shield. The wound was equal to the size of the arrow that attacked him. Fortunately, none of the bones broke. We washed the wound with warm water and applied pig fat in and around the wound. Paraka had his left leg pierced with an arrowhead. Lip sustained a massive cut in his right thigh from a flying arrow. The arrowhead was still inside the flesh and caused excruciating pain. We pressed him flat against the floor and poured hot water into the wounds. Dead brownish blood and dirt came out and dripped down at the side of his thigh as the hot water worked its way into the wound. Lip screamed and punched me right across my chest when we released him. Fortunately, I was expecting such a blow, so I avoided his fist.

The battle continued with renewed intensity and momentum in the next few days, with both factions recording heavy casualties. In every battle, one or two of our men fell and several more were injured. We were either sad or happy when we returned home depending on how well we had spent the day on the battlefield. When the battle turned out in our favour, we returned home shouting and singing, but when it didn't turn go the way we expected, we returned quietly with some of our men groaning and limping while one or two hanged lifeless on the stretchers.

When the fighting intensified in the next few days, we destroyed some houses and chopped their casuarina trees but we still had more grounds to acquire, more lives to take, and more gardens to destroy. We yearned for more and more fights after the day ended but the women must not have been happy with the fights.

Piambil Ambo Mopune pulled me aside one morning and said I was not going out that day. She stared right into my eyes with her arms folded around my neck. Tears swam in her eyes. There was fear, concern and uncertainty all mixed up in her eyes. Perhaps she was worried about the unborn child inside her.

"I don't want to lose you like the others," she sobbed.

I gently took her arms away and assured her that I would return home safely. She slowly released me but she was unable to control her emotions. Her pregnancy made her so oversentimental that she crouched on her knees and sobbed. Kepambo and Pepena's mother comforted her as I left her to join the others in battle.

On the battlefield that day, my mind shifted back and forth to Piambil Ambo Mopune. The picture of her sorry state that morning kept repeating in my mind. I felt like going back to her. I had to fight both battles, one physical and the other mental. Pepena and a few other elder boys understood my situation and were sympathetic that day.

"You can take the back line but be careful of the spears we avoid," they said. "An avoided spear is very dangerous because you won't be able to see it coming."

Casualties continued to pile up as the battle continued. The smell of blood was everywhere and the air was filled with pain and agony. The excitement that accompanied the battle in the mornings faltered in the afternoon.

When the battles went past a moon, we received word that two more tribes had joined the Tekeps and were planning a massive invasion of our land in the next few days.

After receiving this news, our leaders ordered for the women and children to be evacuated to the caves under the foot of Mt Giluwe.

The caves had been the place of refuge for our people in battles. The last time the caves were used was only for storing our valuables for a short while when our tribe had a battle with our brother tribe, the Yaps during my grandfather's time. Our men burned all their houses, chased the Yaps out of their land and took possession of their land. Since then, more land has given us more power and influence, more women and more sons. No other tribes beat us thereafter.

Everyone moved into the caves one night with their possessions. Ours consisted of two medium-sized pigs for my mother and a large pig for Piambil Ambo Mopune, and the tribe's Kina shell.

This kina shell was the tribe's treasure we kept on behalf of the whole tribe. It was called Koka Maldi, meaning highly prized. We hid Koka Maldi in between two house posts in my room. Its fame spread throughout the entire Tambul valley and it became a product of curiosity in the whole land and a target for our enemies. Even young girls were enticed and attracted to my clan because the clan owned the beautiful kina shell. Some moons ago, there was a young girl from Balg in Togoba, who refused to marry a young man in our village. When the girl's tribe heard that my tribe owned the precious item, she was forced to accept the young man's marriage proposal. Her people expected us to pay Koka Maldi but when we didn't give away our treasure, they were disappointed. How could throw away our treasure to another tribe?

When my father died, the tribe agreed unanimously, out of respect for my father, that I should keep the kina shell. So, the priceless object needed to be kept secured. Our other hoardings consisted of two stone axes, a special black body oil and a clay pot my father had exchanged with the Chimbu people.

We deposited our things inside the caves and the women and the children proceeded inside to occupy the small spaces inside the caves.

There were eight caves, dotted along the mountainside. One cave could accommodate up to three families if it was not too small.

My mother Engaamb and all of my father's family occupied the furthest end of the cave. Piambil Ambo Mopune, however, refused to enter the caves or even go closer to the mouth of the cave where our family resided. She had a quick look at the sides of the caves and then glanced in and around the caves as if she were recollecting her thoughts. It was as if she had been to the caves before and now trying to confirm whether this was the place she had visited earlier.

"Maip, I am afraid of getting inside," she said.

"What are you afraid of?"

"I have heard of a legend about the caves from women back in Piambil which frightens me."

She said many years ago, a group of people went to gather pandanus in the forest surrounding Mt Giluwe. They decided to spend the night in a huge cave at the foot of the mountain. They left their belongings and went out to cut the pandanus nuts. Among them was a young girl pregnant with her first child. Because she was heavy with child, people left her in the cave and went away looking for the nuts. She went under a huge tree where the sun spilt its rays through a broken canopy. There she spread her pandanus mat and slept. Just a little while after noon, a mighty wind shook the place so much that the young woman grabbed her mat and walked towards the entrance. Now as she was about to enter the cave, something fell in front of her, just above the mouth of the cave. To her surprise, a piece of the rock above the cave broke off and landed, missing her face narrowly. Then another, a larger one broke off and dropped on the same spot. This time, the fear of the falling rocks was greater than the fear of the wind. She took several steps away from the cave, still with her eyes fixed on the falling rocks and walked back under the tree and watched from a distance.

Slowly the stones began to break loose one by one and slid leisurely to the cave and blocked the entrance. Then, the rocks stopped cracking and with a heavy crush, the mouth of the cave descended and closed the cave. The young woman stood petrified in fear. She did not know what to do or where to seek solace for her frightening heart which had already died within her. The cave remained closed for some time and opened up a little while later.

The pieces of rocks that fell out flew back to their original places and re-joined the mother rock. With fear closing in upon her, the young woman cried and cried until her eyes had nothing to shed.

The young woman related everything that happened during the day to them. She persuaded the people not to spend the night inside the cave, warning them that they might meet the same fate in the night. However, no one believed her. No one trusted the superstitious talk of a young woman. The men rebuked her saying,

"Our ancestors have hunted this forest and taken shelter in this cave. Now we are using the cave. When we are dead and gone, our sons will use the same cave. We haven't heard anything of such stories. Nothing bad has ever happened during our ancestors' times and during our time. Woman you came yesterday. Don't presume to tell us you know something. You know nothing."

Seeing that the people could not believe her, the young woman dissuaded her husband from spending the night in the caves. They spent the night out in the forest in a makeshift shelter her husband quickly constructed in the fading light of the day.

In the night the young woman did not sleep. The young man kept his pregnant wife company during her fearful night. They made a fire and stayed awake. Just before daybreak when the place was getting darker, a strange noise descended and enveloped the place as if a storm had arrived. Then the cave closed up exactly as the way the young woman had seen during the day. The couple expected the cave to open again but it remained closed for many moons. And when it opened again, only bones remained inside. All the eight women and the eleven men and their five children perished in the caves. Piambil Ambo Mopune concluded the tale with a more determined mind never to enter the cave.

"Oh, those were only legends," I assured her.

Even when I assured her that what she had heard was untrue, she couldn't believe me.

It was only after my mother and Kepambo threw in their support after me that Piambil Ambo Mopune agreed to enter the caves, but she occupied the space near the doorway, saying it would be easy for her to escape unhurt if the cave closed its mouth. She stayed awake most nights watching the cave in case the mouth closed.

Chapter 20

A few days after we moved into the caves, we roasted a huge pig one night which Pepena had speared in the enemy land during a raid earlier that day. It was a fitting celebration because we killed two of our enemies and burned down several of their homes.

We sent two men to the village to guard the village entrance at the creek while we enjoyed the meal at the caves. It was after midnight when Kipingi called for an urgent meeting.

"This is an emergency meeting," he said. "The enemies have entered the village in the night."

We grabbed our weapons and rushed down to the village. Upon arriving, we learnt that the enemies had entered our land under cover of the darkness and were camping near the village, ready to attack us anytime.

Panic seized Yopai and the leaders but they remained calm and confident as any display of fear or weakness in public would erode the confidence people had in a chief. They knew they had to be strong in the face of adversity to defend and lead their tribe. They had a brief discussion among themselves and then addressed us.

"By morning, we will know whether we will keep our land or we will exist in the legends," said Kipingi. "The time has come for us to defend our land. The enemies are here to test the strength of our hands. If we don't defend our land, we don't have a land. If we don't have a land, we don't have a future. Should we allow our enemies to deprive us of the good of our land? No. We must fight.

"We must fight for our land. We must fight for our people. We must protect our innocent and the weak for they are inside our shield of protection. We must protect with our blood."

Turning to the sleeping guards, Kipingi said,

"When you are given an important responsibility, do not neglect. You are the eyes of your people. You are your brothers' keepers. Do not let your brother down through negligence. Now we must not dwell in the past. The enemies have already arrived. I will let Yopai brief you on what we are going to do before we face our enemies."

"We will go out as a team," said Yopai. He was younger than Kipingi and talked less but whenever he spoke, he instilled confidence and hope in the men.

"But firstly, before we face our enemies, we'll check ourselves. We have underestimated our enemies in our past battles and as a result, we have lost our men. We have also failed to check ourselves. I want us to shake off anything that will hold us back. We must be free to take the battlefield. We'll have to go back to our past and check where we have gone wrong."

"The enemy's arrows have eyes," continued Yopai. "The arrows go to where there is a wrong. If you've done something bad against your brother, you must confess it today or else you will be the first one to fall on the battlefield."

"When a wrong is confessed, it no longer attracts the enemy's arrows," continued Yopai. "A hidden wrong attracts defeat and destruction. If you are hiding a wrong, you'll be held accountable if the tribe loses the battle."

"Confess and save your neck, save your tribe. Confess and be a free man," added Kipingi. "I know it isn't that easy to confess something shameful or serious. However, living under the veil of guilt won't help you either. My sons and brothers, you don't have a choice now. You have to confess your wrongs. When a wrong becomes a known crime, it no longer attracts curses. Any wrongdoing that remained buried under the veil of guilt surely shows itself on the battlefield."

Now the enemies shouted war cries as the darkness began to roll away.

We had no choice but to reveal. Every man's secret remained no longer a secret that morning. It was shocking to learn of the secret deeds but Kipingi and the leaders said that was the best thing one could do before he faced his enemies.

Pepena said he had an affair with Kipingi's niece who was married to Ialibu but was with us after her husband chased her away with two kids. Poi admitted he had killed Yopai's pig which went missing seven moons ago. Yopai's face turned red and his mouth quivered.

When there was nothing more to share, Kipingi commended everyone for their selflessness and courage.

"You are doing the right thing by putting the tribe's interest ahead of yourselves," he said.

"The one standing near you is your brother," he continued. "We don't have any enemy here. Our common enemies are the Tekeps. If one of us here has done something bad against each other, forgive him now. Let not hatred and unforgiveness hang on your shoulder like a disease. Let the past go. Shake off the past. You have already done that and I am proud of you. You are the true sons of Yano."

"Now you are a free man to take the battlefield. We will go out as a team. We will go out as one. We'll embrace unity to fight our enemies. Forget whatever you've just heard. We are burying the past here today. I don't want you to even talk about it even after the battle. I don't want you to take these bad feelings to the battlefield too. No one fights his enemy with ropes tied to his limbs. We are free men now to take the battlefield. We are now ready to seek revenge and make right the wrong."

When there was nothing more to reveal we approached our enemies. However, before we even shot an arrow, the enemies set alight the first three houses near the creek including ours. The heavy smoke spread over the village and reduced visibility. They quickly set fire to the next few houses. In no time all the houses near the ceremonial ground were burnt down.

We retaliated and arrows and spears flew like flying foxes in the smoke-filled sky. Some landed on the shields, others missed the targets. Some well-aimed spears accomplished their purposes.

We slowly forced the enemies out of the village and towards the creek, but we paid a high price to defend our tribe. We lost more than half of our homes and three men to their hands. We killed only one of their men in return. The feeling of revenge shot up once again.

Despite the loss and injuries, Kipingi and our leaders never stopped encouraging us to fight in the next few days.

"We can nurse the wounds on the battlefield," said Kipingi when some of the boys turned up with their injured limbs and when injuries clouded our prospect of winning the battle.

"If your leg is wounded," he said, "don't worry. You are not yet dead. You still have your hands to fight.

"We will fight in the grasslands. We will fight in the mountains. We will fight in the valleys. We will fight until we drive this evil out of the land.

"We will continue to fight and protect our land. We won't surrender, we won't retreat. They have burned down our houses. They have destroyed our prized casuarina trees. They have raided our land. But you know what? They haven't taken our land yet. They haven't killed us all yet. We will fight to the last breath."

Several days after the enemies attacked our village, we left for the enemy land when it was still dark. We planned to reach the enemy land undetected. It was very cold so we heated stones and brought with us in barks to keep our hands warm.

The day broke open with clear weather. We were glad that we would have a great day to revenge on our enemies. However, little did we know that the enemies were guiding over the single-log bridge at the Kaugel River. They made a huge fire near the bridge and were on full alert. Since the bridge was the only access to their land, we couldn't reach their land.

We sent Maya, the young boy who was saved from the spirit attacks up a tree to check the enemies.

"Five men are guiding the mouth of the bridge," he said shaking his head in disbelief. "Many others are sitting around the fire, fitting their bows and arrows and smoking tobacco."

"Where exactly are they? Are they on our side?" asked Yopai.

"No, they are all on their side of the bridge," replied Maya.

"We still have some chance," said Yopai.

Kipingi and Yopai discussed how we could access the enemy land.

"Pepena can shoot across the bridge," said Poi.

"Then we check with him," said Yopai.

Now the sun was already up and was spreading over the valley. Kipingi asked Pepena if he could shoot across the bridge and take the guards down. Pepena was our top shooter. His targets were accurate. His arrows or spears could reach the furthest but he thought for a while. He lifted his spear and swung it from left to right without throwing it. Then he rested it at his side and said "My spear is heavy. I think it will only reach the middle of the river. I can shoot my arrows but I don't think they'll reach the target as it's too wide."

"Our chance of success is low," said Kipingi. "We have two choices. We either have to fight today or return home. If we go back from here, we are defeated. We have lost our houses, trees, and food gardens. We have lost our men in their hands. Now we are only a bridge away from our enemies. Just look across. They still have their casuarina trees; they still have their houses. We are so close to our targets. If we don't fight them today, I don't think there's a better time coming for us to take revenge. Our enemies are already at the bridge. We are so close to them. We are seeing them now."

The urge to fight swelled inside everyone's blood but no one put forward a way to reach the enemy.

Paraka was very quiet all this time. He was fixing his bowstring into his bow and was sorting his arrows. He was selecting his best arrows and placing them on his right and others inside his quiver. When he completed sorting out his arrows, he cleared his voice and said "If we are thinking of a better time to avenge our enemies, I don't think a better time is coming. My father once told me that a single decision on the battlefield determined a tribe's destiny.'

"Most of you have wives and children to take care of. You have promising futures ahead of you. Some of you have just got married and have been looking forward to starting your family when the fight broke out. I know you will bear many sons who will replace me, me this old bachelor.

"My chances of having a wife and children are over. You have wives, you have children. You see I have nothing to worry about. Is that right?" he paused.

"You might be thinking this poor bachelor has nothing in the village, no wife no children, nothing to fight for. But let me tell you this. I am the richest man in the land." How could he be the richest? I thought. As far as we knew, he owned nothing, no kina shells, no pigs and nothing of value to prove what he claimed to be. But what he said next won all our hearts.

"I am the richest because I have the tribe, I have you, you and you," he pointed his finger to each one of us.

"If you could cut open my heart, you would see yourselves and all our people inside me because I have all of you inside my heart.

"I don't have sons of my own. That is true but that is not a problem because your sons are mine. Your pigs and kina shells are mine. I take pride when you become successful. I celebrate when one of you kills a pig. I shout with joy when one of you makes a moka.

"I sing with happiness when a woman marries into our village. That is because I know she comes to bear me sons. I am overjoyed when a mother gives birth to a son because a son is added to my tribe. I count every child born into the village. I count every young woman who marries into the tribe. I am happy for her because she would make gardens, bear children and look after my brothers and sons. My land and my people, you are my treasure and that's why I said I am the richest person in the entire land.

"Now listen. This is what I am going to do." He picked up his spear and his shield.

"I will walk across the bridge and will run straight to the enemies. You take advantage when the enemies focus on me."

Saying that Paraka headed downhill towards the bridge. We tiptoed after him. In a few moments, we were at the end of the bridge on our side.

Paraka shouted and walked across the bridge while we hid in the bushes.

"Come out and face me if you are man enough to fight me," said Paraka to the Tekeps. He stepped on the log bridge and quickly walked across with his shield in front of him. He was already halfway through the bridge. Seeing him, the enemies picked up their arrows and stood on their feet. They must probably have been surprised to see a single brave enemy challenging them.

The five guards at the end of the bridge shot their arrows one after another at Paraka.

Soon others at the fireside joined in the attacks.

Paraka continued to walk towards them. While the spears and arrows were focused on Paraka's shield, we stepped on the bridge after him.

The enemies continued to shoot arrows at Paraka but when they realised that five of our men were on the bridge, they shot several arrows at Paraka quickly and some of the enemies retired to the end of the bridge to shake and dislocate the bridge. Meanwhile, Paraka now was nearly on the other side of the bridge.

They tried to roll the bridge into the river but they couldn't because the bridge had been firmly rooted in the ground.

They quickly left the bridge and took up their arrows and began to shoot again. This time they were shooting more vigorously. One of the strong spears split Paraka's shield from top to bottom. At the same time, Pepena and I shot out two arrows at the enemy and brought one of them down. The enemies retaliated. Two more spears that were aimed at us caught Paraka's shield and destroyed it completely, leaving Paraka exposed to the enemies' arrows.

Paraka continued to sway from side to side until one arrow caught him on his right shoulder and another on his chest. He broke the arrow on his chest in an attempt to pull it out. The arrowhead remained buried inside his chest. The other on his shoulder was hanging with blood pouring out of the wound. He did not stop for us to pull the arrows out nor did he look back for help. He was in constant motion, always moving, always shooting arrows.

Before more arrows met him, Paraka threw his damaged shield away and shot his last spear across the enemies. The arrow took one of the enemies' front men down with it. The man fell off the cliff and slid rapidly into the river. Paraka wasted no time this time. He ran straight into the enemy but before his feet came off the bridge, a flood of arrows and a spear combined and forced him to the bottom of the river. The next wave of spears took the man immediately behind Paraka down as well.

While the enemies were focused on the two men, we crossed the bridge quickly. The enemy shot arrows at us but we kept pushing to the other side, exchanging arrows and spears on our way to the enemy land until they vacated the bridge.

All our men joined us and the battle continued until sunset. We completed our successful invasion that day by killing five of their men. We also burnt down half of their houses and fell their prized casuarina trees on the ceremonial ground. We lost two men and sustained many injuries.

In the next few days, the battle continued. We attacked them and they retaliated. We kept pushing towards the centre of their village until days later when we burned down all their houses and occupied the land along the river banks. This meant we would attack them whenever we felt like.

Each morning was a joy for us because we loved the sight of blood spilling everywhere and enjoyed seeing our enemy crying out in pain. Warfare was an exciting thing. We forgot death, we forgot wounds. The prospect of facing our enemy dismantled the fears of death. Exchanging spears and avoiding arrows became an exciting game. It became something like a hunting game we enjoyed so much.

Although we were gaining new ground and slaughtering our enemy, we realised we were not fighting with dead men. Every night after the battle, a young woman was left a widow or a son was snatched away from his beloved mother.

Several more deaths brought a change in our men's minds. The first was when Maya, the young boy saved from the spirit's attacks, was killed by the enemy in one of the fights. His poor mother lamented for him. She smeared ash and clay all over her body and wailed day and night. Two other mothers and several young women who had lost their husbands were also against the fight as well.

"You are saying you are winning your battles but I'm not seeing any winners," cried Maya's mother. "I have lost my husband, now my son. If you are saying you are winning your battles, I don't see any areas you are winning. I have been counting all our men killed since the start of the battle. Every day the number is going up by one or two. We have lost thirteen men so far. I think we are losing this battle."

Despite this outcry for the battle to be called off, the battle dragged on and on for many moons. We enjoyed visiting the battlefield. The fading away of another day only increased our impatience and yearning for another day of battle.

However, when hunger chased us day and night and when our people's health deteriorated, our interest in fighting cooled off a little. Most of our mothers and children lost weight. Piambil Ambo Mopune was losing her weight and form gradually. She was six moons pregnant with our first child.

The excitement that was building up before the battle now began to falter off. We not only lost our men in the fights but the battles destroyed our land and ripped off the good of the land. It snatched away our freedom, peace of mind and good night's sleep. Instead of hunting in the forest or killing pigs and organizing great singsings, we were constantly out on watch for our enemies or nursing wounds. And pains of loss and revenge piled up day after day and casualties continued to afflict us day and night.

Tired of women's complaints and the problems of warfare, our leaders agreed to call off the battle. They advised the Tekeps that all their land we had conquered in the battle was ours. They on their part must also have been tired of being strangers in their land like us. They agreed to our terms. We both realised that there was no winner in a battle. At length, the fighting ceased after many moons.

Chapter 21

My stepbrothers Koukera and Paraka were among the ones we lost in the great battle. Many of our men received permanent injuries and more than half of our prized casuarina trees which were planted by our ancestors were levelled to the ground.

We left the caves only to return to a land already claimed by weeds and bushes.

Shoulder-high grasses had replaced our gardens and houses.

A heavy work of reparation waited for us. We dusted the ruins away and embarked on a long journey to set up our houses again in their former locations.

Piambil Ambo Mopune was heavy with child when the battle ended.

I had to build our family house before the birth and other worries kicked in.

Those of us who had distant relatives were fortunate enough to receive help. Piambil Ambo Mopune's three brothers and two men from Piambil came as soon as they heard the battle had ended. They brought the rafters and posts down from the forest and cleared the ruins where our former house had stood. Our house was one of the first three to take shape in the desolate land.

We never forgot the widows, the old and those who lost their sons in the great battle.

We stood as a family to lift one another's burdens in times of need. The battle reinforced our spirit of unity and our love and compassion for each other. Our unity which first gained prominence on the battlefield was now solidified in our reparation efforts. The widows, the old and the unfortunate dropped tears of joy and hugged us when they moved in to occupy their new houses we had built.

Piambil Ambo Mopune's brothers gave us a huge pig to kill when we completed our house. They also cut down a huge garden for us to start life after the battle.

I built a small 'birth house' for Piambil Ambo Mopune some spaces away from our house, which she would use during her labour also and in her 'unclean days' when she had

her periods.

The menstrual blood and birth fluids were equal to poison. Those women who had their periods observed a period of abstinence. They would refrain from touching food as that would contaminate the food. They also didn't come near men, as doing so would inflict sickness on men and make men weak in battle. Sometimes as a child, I would wonder when my mother disappeared for three or four days. I later found out she was living in isolation during her periods.

When Piambil Ambo Mopune went into labour, she moved into the birth house one afternoon to bear the pain of childbearing in solitary confinement. My mother and Pepena's mother accompanied her to the birth house to assist with the delivery.

The labour extended to the next morning and through to the second night. I feared she would die of birth complications because it was common for mothers to die during and after childbirth. But every concern was over after the second day when my mother informed me that Piambil Ambo Mopune had delivered a baby boy.

I couldn't hold the child in my arms because I had to wait for two more days before the child was brought home.

My mother placed the child in a bilum made of cuscus furs. There was nothing inside the bilum except some soft dry leaves which were used as the child's bed.

I took the bilum into my hands and spied the baby. Oh, what a beautiful little boy he was! He had the likeness of his mother. Like Piambil Ambo Mopune, the child had two tiny dimples on both cheeks and a little sharp nose. His eyes were the whitest I had ever beheld. I kissed his tiny hands and handed him over to my mother. She placed the baby near Piambil Ambo Mopune as she rested at the fireside.

Everyone in the village was happy with our little boy. He was born when we had lost many young men in the battle. Women brought sweet potatoes, beans and leafy vegetables for Piambil Ambo Mopune to eat and feed the child well. Piambil Ambo Mopune's mother arrived from Piambil several days later with a quarter of the pig.

"Oh you have taken the likeness of your mother," said Piambil Ambo Mopune's mother, opening the bilum and exposing the child's face. She gently pushed aside the dry leaves that covered the child's face and caressed its little fingers. After planting a kiss on the little forehead, she smiled and commented again and again how beautiful the baby was.

"Look at this long sharp nose," she said. "Piambil Ambo Mopune was exactly like this when I found her."

We killed a pig two days later and gave half to Piambil Ambo Mopune's mother and shared the rest with the villagers. Piambil Ambo Mopune's mother took her share back to Piambil.

In the days and moons that followed, my mother encouraged Piambil Ambo Mopune to rest a lot and feed the baby well.

"You don't have to work as hard as you used to do," said my mother. "When you work a lot, you won't feed my child well."

"We will wean him shortly. He can follow you around the gardens," said Piambil Ambo Mopune to my mother.

"Ah don't be foolish like Pepena and Perai Wenepo," replied my mother.

"Look at them. Perai Wenepo is pregnant again with her third child when their little boy is barely walking."

My mother's comment reminded me of what an old man said in the men's house a long time ago. He said:

'When you see your child playing outside and running around the house, when you see your child taking the container to the creek, you can consider visiting your wife again'.

The old man said children should be well-spaced. But how could one wait that long when he had people around him to take care of children? How could I spend days in the men's house while I had my beautiful wife at home? Things would become complicated for me.

We showered the little boy with unconditional love that he grew up like a flower. Piambil Ambo Mopune would hang him on a branch in the gardens inside a string bag when she worked. She would only stop to feed him when he cried. When he grew up, the child floated in the hands of my mother, his mother and Kepambo. One of them would take care of him while the other two worked in the garden.

It was not long after the child started walking when Piambil Ambo Mopune fell pregnant again. At this time, Kepambo married a Jika man near Mt Hagen.

Back in the men's house, the fire blinked lazily on the remains of the two logs we added the previous night. Most of the men were still out, either hunting or in their gardens. It was not a strict rule that all men should sleep in the men's house, but when a man was absent for days, it raised questions in the men's minds. Our elders said men should be with men.

"What are you going to learn from women?" they would say. "You should spend your days with men because that's where you get everything."

Laipe and Anis brought in a live cuscus and started plucking the furs out and placed it on a leaf for the women to make bilums. The cuscus cried in pain but they turned a blind eye to it because the furs came off easily when the cuscus was alive.

Now the men arrived one by one and gathered around the fire. Those who had stories talked as we listened. Our conversations were usually on various subjects like hunting, warfare, mokas and how to dress for a great singsing but that night, Lip returned from his wife's home with a different story which kept us discussing till midnight.

"It's the latest that reached Tambul," he said.

"What's that?" asked Pepena who had joined us a while ago. He spread his icy hands over the flames for each of his ten fingers. Laipe who had been near the fire moved away to make space for Pepena to warm himself.

"The story is the talk of the land," continued Lip. "Two brothers of the strange men who visited Porgera have come to live in Pabrabuk."

"How could that be possible?" asked Ponenge.

"Oh it's their soft-hearted chief," said Lip. "The foolish Pabrabuk chief has thrown away the tribe's best land to the strangers. He moved his people up to the mountainsides. The chief also tied a huge pig to the strangers to welcome them to his tribe. The strangers are called missionaries. They are now living with the people in Pabrabuk."

"What good have the strangers brought with them? "How could the chief cast their land away like that?" asked Pepena.

"I don't know but the missionaries are said to have brought something called their

God with them."

"What is God?" asked Pepena.

"He is a powerful spirit the missionaries are carrying around with them," said Lip.

"What happened?" asked Poi. "Did the locals kill the strangers when they found out they had brought their spirit with them?"

"One of the two strangers is already in Tambul," said Lip.

"What? Is he in Tambul?" asked a surprised Ponenge.

"He must have escaped from Pabrabuk," said Pepena.

"No. It was Kengelga Karoma who lured the poor man to Tambul. They arrived five days ago."

"Have you seen him?" asked Pepena.

"The stranger? No. I was told he is very cold so he is staying indoors all day after he arrived from Pabrabuk."

"How could Kengelga Karoma trick the white man into Tambul?" asked Pepena. "I heard those people are very very clever. You can't deceive them."

"It was a great lie," said Lip. "Kengelga Karoma lied to the stranger that the best pineapples and juicy bananas were in Tambul."

"Ah sorry for the poor white man," said Poi. "He was deceived to come to the land where the soil had never smelled any pineapple or banana seed."

"Karoma would not have deceived the white man for nothing," observed Pepena.

"Maybe he must have seen something others failed to see in the missionaries," said Anis.

"I don't think so," Laughed Poi. "Perhaps he is interested in the God the missionaries had brought to Pabrabuk."

"That, I doubt," replied Lip. "We have our ancestors' gods. So long as we have our gods, there isn't any need for anyone to bring their gods to Tambul.

"Some of the white man's brothers are in Mt Hagen too," said Genemba who had been away in Mt Hagen with Kepambo. Genemba was Poi's last born brother.

"They are exploring the Kuta Ranges and some have gone up to Porgera to look for a rare stone called Gold. Others have cleared land in Mt Hagen near Kepambo's village to settle among the Jikas and the Mokas. These men claim that they've been sent by their leader called the government to live in Mt Hagen."

"This man government must be a great warrior," said Yopai. "He must be a powerful man to send his men to foreign lands to build their homes and settle."

"This couldn't be true because you know how the Jikas and Mokas value their land," said Ponenge. "They hold their land very close to their heart like us. Imagine it would be hard for someone to convince such people to give away their land to foreigners. The government must be a very clever man to secure the land for his men."

"If the government has successfully secured land for his people in Hagen, I'm afraid," said Anis. "He might as well extend his hand to our land."

"That will never happen on my land, never," said Yopai with clenched fists. "I have fought hard to preserve my land from the Tekeps. Government let me remind you now. I will test the strength of your arrows."

The rumour was confirmed days later. The missionary was allowed to settle in Tambul and a house was built for him on the grassland where pigs roamed during the day.

Another white man soon followed his brother to Tambul.

One day when I returned from the garden at sunset, a group of people had gathered at the village ceremonial ground. Genemba was speaking to them. Genemba raised a white substance in a parcel.

"This is different from the one we get from Kandep," he said, holding the white thing up.

"Come, taste it and see how sweet it is. This is the white man's salt."

"Not only the salt," he said, taking something like our stone axe out of his bag. A short handle was attached to it.

"I got this from the white men in Tambul. I'll show you how it works. Bring me a piece of wood here, quick."

A young boy brought in a small log and placed it in front of Genemba.

"Move away from me, move," said Genemba, lifting the axe into the space as if he was going to chop everyone there.

We watched from a distance when he brought the axe down with a massive bang on the wood. The axe sank halfway into the wood and remained buried there. Genemba pulled it out and hit the log again, forcing the wood to split in two.

"If this thing has come to stay, we need to throw away all our stone axes," said Yopai.

"Go to Tambul if you want to get an axe like this or salt," said Genemba. "Take your sweet potatoes and pig manure to the white men and they'll give you these things in exchange."

The next morning, Piambil Ambo Mopune and other women got the best sweet potatoes in their gardens and went to Tambul. Piambil

Ambo Mopune returned in the afternoon with a sack of salt and two pieces of smooth things to protect the baby from the cold. We learnt moons later that the smooth things were called cloth.

Since then, we supplied pig manure, charcoal and raw sweet potatoes to the white men and they gave us axes, salt and clothes. Sometimes they paid us with something called money which we exchanged with some new food called tinned meat and rice from their little storehouse in Tambul. The white men used the manure to grow a tiny red fruit called strawberry.

We no longer used the salt from Kandep but we continued to take and give women and attended pig killings in each other's land.

Chapter 22

Since the white men arrived in Mt Hagen, they began to make demands on the villages and often intervened in people's everyday lives.

The government led by the white men went to Nebilyer and stopped a fight when the two tribes only just began to enjoy the fights. The tribes were mad because they hadn't fully avenged each other when they were stopped. The white men were said to possess a magical stick that could kill them easily at long distances if the tribes defied the white men's orders. After the fights were stopped, two white men convinced several tribes in Nebilyer to give them a huge portion of their land. The white men planted the land with a small tree which bore a tiny red fruit called coffee. The tribes were paid instead to cut the grasses around the coffee trees and pick the ripe fruits.

One evening, we were asked to gather at the village ceremonial ground. I wondered why the meeting was called at the ceremonial ground because important meetings were held in the men's house. When all the people were present, Yopai cleared his throat and said,

"We are seeing the influence of the white men spreading like bushfire. Their presence is being felt even in small villages like Malke. The government, influenced by the white men is beginning to make demands on us.

"We have called this meeting to inform you that there is a white man in Tomba who wants all men. He represents the government. You all know how strong the government is becoming, don't you?"

The men nodded in agreement, some in confusion.

"They are coming up with all sorts of rules to control people. The white man has sent word out for every village to send their men to Tomba tomorrow. Come here very early in the morning and we will leave for Tomba."

"What is in there for us?" shouted Poi.

"I am a simple man," said Yopai. "I don't know many things about the white men. I don't know why we are going there. The white man is needing us for a special work that will require the strength of all men in the land."

That night I kept thinking of what those rapid changes meant for us. It was not long ago when we came out of a bloody battle. We had not fully recovered when strange things were happening in puzzles - first the treasure seekers in Porgera, the arrival of missionaries in

Pabarabuk and later in Tambul, the planters in Nebilyer and the introduction of white men's food and tools. Now we were being called in for more confusion.

The dawn of a new day began slower than ever before. A cry of an early bird indicated that the half-moon that crawled out late in the night would no longer be needed. Then another bird followed the first cry, others joined in to farewell the night with a quick joyous song. As the darkness lifted away, the moon lost its significance and bowed out for the sun to take over. A new day slowly pushed its way out over the horizon. As the light spread over the valley, the smoke of the morning fires clouded above the treetops- some old people had risen before the birds to warm up their fireplaces. A newly married couple's house was still without smoke even after everyone else awoke.

Now it was not only the dawn of a new day. It was the dawn of a new era, an era of confusion and uncertainty.

Several shouts brought the men out to the ceremonial ground before the sun touched the treetops. We left Malke at sunrise and arrived at Tomba at midmorning. Men kept pouring in until the small ceremonial ground was crowded with men, both young and old. I thought we were gathering for a big singsing.

The white man asked us to fell two big casuarina trees and strip their branches. We placed the trees parallel to each other and made crossings with the branches by tying the branches onto the trees with vines. The thing we had constructed looked something like a huge stretcher.

"What are we going to carry in the stretcher?" I asked Pepena.

"I don't know," he said, rolling his eyes from one end of the stretcher to another.

"Maybe we are carrying some white men who are unable to walk."

"I think you are right," I said. "Look at their skins. Isn't it so soft like that of babies? I don't think their soft legs will be able to carry them up the mountains."

"Yes, these soft people are weak like babies," agreed Pepena. "I can knock them down with a single fist."

Now the sun was above our heads and began to burn strongly on the skin. Some men went to the nearest creek to drink while others remained at the ceremonial ground and greeted each other.

A little while after midday, a strange thundering noise rose and fell from the direction of Mt Hagen. It appeared as if a roaring pig was climbing the mountains and falling flat into the valleys.

The noise grew louder and louder. The more we waited, the more the fear of invasion increased. We were not prepared for a fight. We had no weapon, except the axes we used to chop the trees. Then as if it was happening in a dream, a four-footed beast crawled into the ceremonial ground through what appeared to be a huge pig track. The beast left behind two long tracks and a line of smoke. It had four round identical limbs, two in front and two at the back. The limbs were as black as charcoal and all looked alike. The two back limbs were chasing the two in front.

Those few who had either seen or heard of the beast only stood and watched while the rest fled to the bushes for cover. The noise now thundered above all voices and swallowed even the screams of the runaway men. Its echoes reflected along the tree lines in the mountainsides. We were yodeled in after a while when the great noise subsided.

The beast crawled around the ceremonial ground two times and then came to a complete stop near the stretcher. It remained quiet for a little while before it opened its mouth and discharged a white man. We wondered how the white man managed to kill the beast without any visible combat.

The white man went straight to the white man of Tomba, and after the two spoke for a while, the white man of Tomba briefed us through an interpreter.

"You will take the truck to Mendi. Do you understand?" So, the beast was called truck!

"Is the truck taking us to Mendi?" asked an excited old man from Poika.

"No. You will carry the truck on your shoulders," said the white man.

"Can we break the truck into its parts and take it to Mendi?" asked Yopai. I didn't know where Yopai got the idea but he asked anyway. The white man's face turned red with anger. He came over to Yopai and slapped the old man across the face with his right hand. Yopai lost his balance and fell into the mud. A furious anger leapt up in my heart like a flame chasing dry grass.

"I have lost men in the battle. Ok," I said and snatched a thick branch. However, before I made a move, Pepena came from the back and snatched the branch out of my hands.

"You cannot hit the white man and get away," warned Pepena.

"You are a fool. How could you watch your father being knocked down before your eyes? Have you lost your senses?"

"You can't play with fire, Maip. I warn you again. You will be kissing the ground before you even hit the white man. He has his stick with him. He points his stick to you and you are a dead man."

I later found out the 'stick' Pepena referred to was called 'gun'. The gun was used by the whites and the government to threaten warriors and stop tribal fights in Nebilyer and Buiyer. It was a killing stick. The ability of the gun to kill was displayed in Tambul one afternoon when we were building a road after our trip to Tomba.

The white man in charge of the road building demonstrated the gun's use on a pig when two young men rebelled against orders and escaped work. He ordered everyone to gather at the clearing. Then the white man pointed his gun at a live pig (which was tied to a sapling) and asked his ancestors to strike down the pig with thunder. Within a moment, his ancestors sent fire down from the heavens and stroke the pig dead instantly. The small stick's target and precision were more accurate than our spears and arrows combined. It hit the pig in between its eyes, leaving the poor pig in its blood. The white man achieved both silence and obedience simultaneously with only a simple display of the gun.

It was after midday when we tied the truck against the two trunks with strong vines and lifted it onto our shoulders. Our long journey to Mendi began at sunset. Mendi was a long way and we had to pass through our village and the lands of many powerful tribes.

Some men cleared and widened the track ahead while others took turns carrying the truck.

There were so many of us that the huge truck floated like a dry leaf on the shoulders. Each tribe took turns shouldering the truck for a marked distance. We cheered on as the truck floated on the shoulders through the forest up the hills and across the valleys.

By the time we reached the top of Murmur Pass, it was dark. We left the truck on the mountain and returned to our different villages.

We picked up the truck again the next day and continued our journey. After three nights, we reached our village Malke and crossed the Glond River which was in the middle of the forest where no tribe lived. But as we passed through Komia, Kerenda, Kuma, Karel and Enep villages, the men poured out in numbers and offered their shoulders.

The truck floated from one shoulder to another until we reached Mendi one afternoon.

A crowd had gathered at a small clearing to see the truck. We were told that they had been waiting since dawn.

As we dismounted the truck and placed it in the middle of the clearing, the crowd was wild with mixed feelings of fear and curiosity. They cast doubtful eyes from a respectable distance but none came any closer to the truck. Then moments later, a few brave young men slowly edged closer to the truck and felt its surface and limbs with the tips of their fingers. They removed their hands quickly as if they had touched live charcoal. An old man stared at the truck for a while and cried out in shock, "I can see my ghost in this thing's ears." Saying that, he hurried away. He was never seen again.

Now the white man jumped into its belly and brought the truck back to life again, just like the way he did in Tomba. The truck roared and spurted out heavy clouds of smoke to the skies and crawled around the clearing. Everyone fled the scene. A little boy who was watching at the end of the clearing jumped into the nearby creek and broke his arm on the rocks.

The truck went around the clearing two more times before it came to a complete stop and the white man jumped out of the truck.

"Now listen," said the white man, "Go back to your villages and organise your people. We are building a big road for the truck to run from Hagen to Mendi by itself. We will not carry the truck."

The white man said everyone should build the road because it would bring immense benefits in the future.

A few days after our trip to Mendi, each tribal chiefs organised their people and the road construction began.

The road began at Tomba and slowly stretched its way up the mountains towards Tambul. Trees were slashed and flattened, trunks were uprooted and pushed away to the cliffs, grasses were slashed and burnt, and giant roots and chunks of earth were cut out off the cliffs and cleared away each day.

Along either side of the road, we dug up two tranches to receive the runaway rainwater. We spread the freshly cut earth over the cleared road for the sun to dry. Then collected heaps of stones from the creeks and spread them over the road.

With the feet of countless men, women and children, we stamped the surface of the road until the stones sunk into the soft earth and remained solid. We left the surface to dry in the sun and moved on to cut out a new road. The road surface dried and hardened.

As the road cut through each village, more hands joined and the flattening of hills and raising of the low places continued day after day. The road wound up the mountains and across the valleys like a snake. One standing at the Taraliwaru mountain would think a giant snake had dragged itself along the Tambul valley, leaving behind a smooth path like a river.

After many moons, we reached a land jointly owned by the two largest tribes in Upper Mendi, the Yakopas and the Yakumbus. The two tribes argued over whose land the road should cut through.

They had been lifelong enemies. The tribes had been attacking each other for ages and had been trying their best to destroy each other's ceremonial ground for a long time but their attempts were unsuccessful as they each defended their ceremonial ground well. Now that the road was cutting through, they viewed it as a weapon to destroy each other's ceremonial ground.

The Yakumbus insisted the road should run through the heart of Komia Pena, the

Yakopas ceremonial ground, while the latter said the road should cut through the Yakumbu's ceremonial ground. Both ceremonial grounds were beautified with ancient casuarina trees and were famed for hosting great events of pig killing and moka.

Neither of the tribes wanted their ceremonial ground to be destroyed because whenever a tribe's ceremonial ground was destroyed, it revealed one's weakness and inability to defend his tribe. It also exposed a tribe's susceptibility to future attacks.

The white men who supervised the road wanted the road to reach Mendi quickly, and he wanted the road to cut through the Yakumbus' land which was the shortest way to Mendi.

However, the Yakumbus couldn't see a better way to destroy their enemy than the road. Yakumbus had one of their men working with the white men. Since he was quite influential, he directed that the road should cut through the heart of Komea Pena, their enemy's ceremonial ground. He convinced the white men that that was the easiest way to reach Mendi. The Yakopas saw this as a direct attack by their enemy, but how could they retaliate?

They could do nothing to save their ceremonial ground with all its prized casuarina trees.

They feared the white men's guns more than their enemy if they stopped the work for no good reason.

It was a fine morning when the road cut through the Komea Pena. The Yakumbus led the construction team, slashing and burning the aged casuarina trees, even those far from the road, and dug through the ceremonial ground. The Yakopas folded their arms and some wept as their prized trees came crashing down to the ground.

The Yakopas were planning to attack the Yakumbus after the road was completed but that did not eventuate because soon they realised that it was a good thing for them to allow the road to pass through their village. The Yakumbus on the other hand, admitted to having made a mistake when they directed the road out of their village. They said they would miss out on the benefits the road would offer.

The white men and the locals also cleared a huge land near Mt Hagen. A huge bird was said to be visiting Mt Hagen once in a while.

Chapter 23

Many moons after the road was completed, we received some men from Hagen who came to select some men to work in a faraway garden called the 'coast'.

We were told that only grown-up men would go to the coast but the younger boys were also interested in going.

In the next few days, the interest to go to the coast increased. Every young man wanted to go. We were told that we would earn money to buy axes, salt and cloth. We were also told that we would go to a place full of beautiful girls with long hair.

"Why can't I go as well?" asked Laipe, as we gathered around the night fires under the moonless sky one night.

He was Pepena's younger brother who liked to run around with grown-up men. He joined the men's house when he was still a young child.

"It's because the work is tough and only strong hands are needed," said Pepena.

Laipe's demeanour slumped. Tears stood in his eyes. He pleaded with me to help him go to the coast.

Days later, a team arrived from Mt Hagen to recruit men. Young men and boys were yodelled to the ceremonial ground.

Laipe ran to the house and informed me that the recruiters were collecting names.

"They denied Tepu. He was the first one to turn up this morning, but was rejected because they said he was too young to go."

Tepu was Kipingi's youngest child and was of Laipe's age.

"Do you really want to go?" I asked him.

Laipe stared at me with tears streaming in his young eyes. He wished his mother had born him before Pepena. Pepena's mother had two unsuccessful births after Pepena before Laipe was born. Pepena was already married when his brother was still a boy.

"You can stay back and look after your mother when we leave," I said.

"I will set the house on fire if you leave without me," he said, raising his voice.

I advised him to collect some congealed liquid from a plant (like a tapioca tree whose leaves were used for cooking food in the earthen oven).

When he brought it back, we heated it over the fire. Then we trimmed off some of his hair at the back of his head and stuck them on his face with the liquid. Moments later, Laipe was a grown-up man with a childish face.

It was past midmorning and the young men were in a long queue when we arrived. A fat stocky man was writing down names roughly on a piece of paper which was half empty with names and another, a middle-aged man with a moustache, was selecting the men with a stick.

We joined the end of the line with Laipe in front of me. When they came to Laipe, the man with the stick looked at Laipe straight in the eyes and said,

"He looks young. Anyway, put his name down."

The man with the paper blindly put his name down and then mine. They moved to the next.

If they were not in a hurry, Laipe's fake beard would reveal his true identity. Perhaps they must have been fooled by Laipe's huge size. They also failed to have a closer look at him. Looks can be deceiving.

Six of us, including Anis and Laipe, were chosen to go to a place called Rabaul while a few others were selected to go to another place called Madang. We were told that we would work in huge gardens called plantations. We were further advised that a huge bird called plane would pick us up in Mt Hagen in a few days' time.

The old and the very young were rejected.

My mind was heavily disturbed to leave my young family behind. Piambil Ambo Mopune was pregnant with our second child and our first child was only a boy when she fell pregnant. The little boy cried and clung to me. A few mothers and two young wives also cried when we left for Mt Hagen one morning.

After spending the night in Kepambo's home near Mt Hagen, we walked over to where the plane would arrive and waited inside a small building. In front of us was a long narrow runway where the plane would descend from the skies.

I had never seen a plane before except once a long time ago when a tiny plane like a bird floated over the Sugarloaf mountains. It was so small that I couldn't make out whether it was a bird or a plane.

It was after midmorning when our plane descended with a thundering noise. We were guided into its huge belly. Then the plane's narrow door slid shut and we sped down the runway. My heart doubled its beat when the plane lifted off the ground and soared high in the sky like an eagle. We were flying!

Now everything below us disappeared from view as we rose higher and higher from the ground. The mountains were levelled with the trees.

Although the plane was flying at an unimaginable speed, the journey appeared endless. The land stressed more and more to infinity. I couldn't believe the land was that wide. I had no idea whether those great lands were inhabited. We spotted one or two hunting fires in the middle of the thick forest.

After some time, we flew over some huge rainforests which were marked by great rivers that branched out in several places and met again after meandering for many spaces. It was a mystery how the plane could sustain itself in the skies that long. When you throw something up, it falls back to the earth irrespective of how high from the ground you throw. The plane defied that order. Nothing on earth was strong enough to pull the plane down. I wondered how the white men made the plane fly forever in the air without falling.

After a long time, Laipe cried out, "Look at that blue land! That blue land over there!" "That's not land. That's the salt water," shouted Pepena.

I had never seen such a huge lake. I couldn't draw any likeness or comparison with Lake Ekari in Mogol or Lake Pakelem in Kandep. Those lakes would disappear like raindrops in the great salt water.

The plane appeared not to be flying at all above the sea. Its voice changed to that of some lonely old man in want of company. I was sad how the plane would get out of the sea and onto land safely again.

After flying in the clouds for a long time a mountain appeared on the horizon. Now the plane descended and Rabaul town appeared on the horizon. The town sat still under the tall mountain. The mountain's shadow fell lazily on the beautiful shiny houses near the sea.

We were exhausted but relieved to set foot on land again. The warm weather of the coast greeted us as we stepped out of the plane. We were immediately ushered onto a waiting truck and the truck pulled out.

It was at dusk when we arrived at the plantation. The plantation was a forest of its own with tall coconut trees planted in rows and separated by straight narrow roads. Each block boasted a great many coconut trees that reached to the sky. Towards the end of the plantation were the living quarters for the workers. We were given the one at the end of the plantation where the trees met the seas.

The next morning, we were called in for a briefing at the meeting ground in the middle of the living quarters. We were issued with grass knives, plates and clothes, and two blankets each.

We left our supplies and went straight to the huge coconut fields. The first day of work was terrible. I could not withstand the blazing heat of the merciless sun. It burned my feet. The sand and the soil were like burning ashes on my feet. I missed my cool home and rivers so much that day. I regretted why I had come to the coast.

Every day we collected the dry nuts, broke open the husks and loaded them onto tractors. We also cut the tall grasses under the coconut trees.

The usage of the day was so different from the way we had been used to back in the village. We started the day strictly at 7:00 a.m. and worked till midday. We then had a short break for lunch and continued till five o'clock.

In the village, there was no partition of time. The day was day and night was night. We were never short of time because we had all the day for ourselves. If we were working and night caught up with us, we wouldn't worry much about the incomplete work because there was always a whole day tomorrow. However, in the coast, we were so short of time that the day was divided into small parts and each part of the day was allocated to a certain task.

At the end of each working day, we would gather at the meeting area and the supervisors would run through the names one by one. When one of the names went unanswered, his workload the next day was doubled, meaning he didn't enjoy a few moments of sunlight that afternoon.

After each check, some men ran off to the beach to refresh themselves while others would sit around in groups to enjoy a few jokes and tobacco. Occasionally, a few of the boys would sneak off to the nearby villages to search for the pretty Tolai girls, those girls who walked the beaches with their long hair blown away by the sea breezes.

While we blended well with the others, we sometimes had arguments with the supervisors especially when we defied their orders. They pronounced orders and we were expected to obey.

Our immediate supervisor saw us as like one of the copra milling machines which worked nonstop. He barked orders and expected us to follow. He didn't know how to appreciate our work.

One payday Friday, the plantation manager visited us at lunchtime when we were clearing a huge area of grass. He was impressed with the work and asked us to take the afternoon off. He usually came once in a while to see how the work progressed and often appreciated our work with comments and praises.

It was a relief for us to call off the day early that day after a long week of heavy work.

Pepena and I decided to go for a swim that afternoon and hunt wild pigs at night.

Now as we were cleaning our knives and were about to leave, our immediate supervisor screeched to a stop on his motorbike.

"Cut those tall grasses over there," said the supervisor, pointing to a thick area of cowgrass near the sea.

"Master, the big boss has just asked us to leave," I said.

The supervisor took a few steps closer to me and had his head levelled with mine.

"You do as I say," said the supervisor, resting his arms on his hips and looking straight into my eyes.

"We are not working," I protested.

"Now, tell me" he said, shaking my shoulders. "Who is the boss here? You or me? You primitive."

"But sir…", said Pepena who came to my aid.

"Shut up. Both of you" shouted the supervisor. "Is my order not sinking into your black heads? Get back to work before I teach both of you a very good lesson."

The supervisor shot out of our sight on his motorbike, leaving behind a trail of smoke and dust.

Pepena and I said nothing. The other young men were silent too. We slashed the grass in silence but a young man from Sepik wasn't as pleased as us.

"Look," said the Sepik, "the white man is barking orders as if we don't know how to

work. Are we people without brains?"

"We are human beings," said Pepena. "They can't treat us like animals. Wait, I'll kill that bastard."

"You better be careful with the white supervisor," said a man from Kerowagi to Pepena. "He will kill you before you slit his throat. These people always have their guns with them."

But it was me who attacked the white supervisor.

The supervisor created a perfect opportunity for me to vent my anger, and I grabbed it with both hands.

Chapter 24

One day when I came back from work, Anis and Laipe informed me that the same supervisor had killed our pig.

I won the pig in a card game a year ago from a Sepik guy. No one knew where he got the piglet but the Sepik lost all his money on cards and sold his piglet for twenty cents. I bought the piglet for less than half of the price and we fed the pig with the leftover food and coconut that over time, it grew into a huge pig.

The pig lived with us and knew us like a child. It followed us everywhere we went and everyone knew our pig. Even the plantation manager came to buy it one day but I said we were raising it for our feast when we returned home.

"Why did he kill the pig?" I asked the two boys.

"The supervisor gunned it down. He said he was getting rid of pests."

"Where is the dead pig then?"

"The boys helped us to carry it back. It's under the coconut trees."

"Then take it to the mumu area."

The thought of its brain being spilt made my blood boil with anger. I went over and over my head about how I would pay back the supervisor. At last, an idea flashed into my mind.

I roughly slashed off the leaves of a fallen coconut frond with the remains sticking out like a fish's backbone. I also chopped off a bending branch, quite a heavy one. Holding both weapons in one hand and the bush knife in the other, I headed towards the supervisor's house.

The supervisor was outside the veranda enjoying some tea but when he saw me, he set his cup aside and called his dogs over. The two dogs (one was black and the other brown) stood before him and waged their tails as if they were ready to carry out their master's orders. The supervisor pointed to me and set his dogs on me.

The dogs barked and jumped off the verandah and sprinted across the loan with their tails folded behind them and eyes fixed on me. They were of a good breed. Their heights would reach a man's waist. If they were to hunt a wild pig, they wouldn't need the help from other dogs.

As they approached me, I stood still and observed. They both stopped right in front of me and stared at me for a while as if to locate which part of me would be the easiest for them to sink their teeth first. They barked for a while and then one got behind me and the other started barking right in front of me.

At my right hand was a tree but I couldn't run to it because I was already within the dogs' reach. They gnashed their sharp teeth and started barking again. Suddenly the one in front flew to me, aiming for my heart with its arms stretched in front of it. I had no choice but to protect myself.

While the dog was in the space, I swung the knife from my right to the left in full strength. The flying knife whistled across the space like a wind, and when it came into contact with the dog, the whistle changed into a whisper as if it was slicing through some watermelon or something soft.

Two pieces of the same species fell to my feet with the insides spilling out onto the loan. Blood shot up into the skies and sprayed everywhere like light rain.

The dog's friend behind me needed not to be told of its own safety. It was not before I wiped the bloody knife on the grass when the dog was out of sight. It had lost all courage to take revenge for its fallen companion.

Wiping away the blood drops on my face, I quickly walked over to the veranda. The supervisor screamed for help on the telephone.

"Hurry up or else he'll kill me too," said the supervisor over the phone.

I slammed my bush knife hard on the telephone and cut the lines off before I grabbed it and sent it flying over the loan.

"Why did you kill my pig?" I shouted, seizing the supervisor by the collar of his shirt and dragging him out to the loan.

"It ate my soap."

"Na soap yu putim insait or arosait?" (The soap, you left it inside or outside?)

"Inside," said the supervisor, struggling to breathe.

"Na you givim key long em?" (Did you give your key to the pig?) I placed my arm on his throat and pulled him closer to me.

His breath increased rapidly. He was shaking.

"Why did you set your dog on me then?"

"I saw you almost killed a co-worker last time."

Before he could say anything further, broken pieces of the coconut frond flew everywhere, splitting and splattering blood. The coconut frond was soon exhausted. I allowed the stick to have its share in the revenge as well.

The supervisor begged for mercy, but my senses were so focused on the revenge that I couldn't hear his pleadings.

The beatings continued until the poor man lay flat on his stomach with blood all around him.

Now the sun poured its last rays of the day weakly over the coconut trees. A noiseless wind caused the leaves to dance a little. I was satisfied that justice was served. A sense of accomplishment rested on me.

I left the badly injured man and as I was about to exit the loan, a thick smoke of dust rose and fell on the horizon. The dust followed the road like a snake. I climbed back onto the verandah. The police vehicle which was known for beating people up, screeched to a stop in front of the supervisor's gate.

Four native policemen jumped out of the vehicle and quickly surrounded the house. Like desperate hunting dogs, they cast their investigative eyes here and there as they hurried towards the house.

I jumped off the verandah and leaned near the fence where there was a thick bed of overgrown flowers. The policemen stopped over the slaughtered dog and expressed their disbelief at seeing the insides spilt out.

"He must have slaughtered its father too," said one of the policemen.

"We have to track him down before he escapes," said another. "Search around the house. We'll teach him a very good lesson."

Two of the policemen entered the house while the other two went to either side of the house. One of them was approaching my hiding place near the fence. They spotted me.

"Hurry up, seize him before he escapes," said the man and ran towards me.

One of them was holding a gun while the other two were sprinting ahead of him. The fourth man stepped back to man the exit.

I was on my own. I had already decided to beat the white man. Now, I was not free of its consequences. Whatever that came out of that decision would fall entirely on me. I had thrown myself into the water. I had to swim my way out.

All around me was the fence and the policemen were closing in on me. I either had to defend myself or give in. If I were to give in, I wasn't a true son of Yano.

"First the white man, next is you," I said, pointing my bush knife at the policeman with the gun.

"Put your knife down or else I'll blow your head away," shouted the gunman, moving closer to me with his gun pointing at me. He was pleased to showcase his fighting skills. I was also happy to show him what a bush knife was truly made for.

Anger shot through my veins and the bush knife shook in my hand as the policemen neared me. I did the right thing by correcting the supervisor but the policemen were taking sides with him. That was also a mistake I determined to correct there. If I consulted my knife, it would agree with me and would be happy to take sides with me.

The policemen continued to approach me despite my threat but they stopped near the verandah and turned their eyes away towards the road.

"Why is it coming here instead of the mills?" said the man with the gun with his eyes fixed on the road.

The sound of an engine caught my ears. A little while later, the plantation tractor sped towards the supervisor's house and stopped near the police truck. Someone must have alerted him of my plight. Laipe neglected his duty to rescue me. He was a true son of Yano who remembered our fathers' words. He didn't forget his brother in trouble. He whistled and waved his hands for me to go over.

I brandished the bush knife and sprinted straight to the policeman in front of me. I knocked him down with all my might. The two other policemen stepped aside and created a little space just enough for me to get past them. The policeman with the gun recollected himself, picked up his gun, fired several unaimed shots and barked orders for me to stop. The one at the exit threw himself in but I swung my knife and missed his fingers by a small space.

He pulled his head back quickly and hit the back of his head against the iron post at the gate.

I jumped onto the waiting tractor and Laipe pulled out of the supervisor's residence and headed towards the company office. The policemen lifted the injured supervisor onto the police truck and pursued us.

They caught up with us midway through the office and ordered us to stop the tractor.

"Should I stop?" said a panicking Laipe.

"Just hit the road straight," I said to him. "They won't do anything."

We continued our cat and rat chase down the narrow road until we reached a section where the road was wide enough for them to overtake us. They drove to our left and then to our right but Laipe swung the tractor in their way as they were about to overtake us. The truck driver stopped the truck hard behind us and two of the angry policemen jumped off the truck and climbed onto the tractor.

Laipe swung the tractor to the right and then to the left to shed them off but they managed to climb the tractor and made their way to the front. When they were about to leave the trailer and jump over to us, I loosened the pin that held the tractor-trailer to the tractor. The trailer got detached from the head and blocked off the road. The two policemen clenched their teeth and kicked the air with their fists as we drove away.

The plantation manager was leaving the office when we arrived. He must have been wondering why the tractor was returning to the office empty instead of the mills. He threw a puzzling look at the tractor and then at our sweating bodies. The policemen arrived soon and quickly brought the wounded supervisor down the truck.

"What happened?" cried the manager, casting a curious look at the blood-covered supervisor.

"That Simbu man killed the boss," said the policemen, pointing to me. The manager looked at the blood-covered supervisor and shook his head.

"All of you come inside the office," said the manager and went back to his office.

Laipe and I entered first and the injured was brought in after us. The manager asked me why I had beaten the supervisor.

"He kill my pig. I kill him," I said.

"Is that the pig I came to buy last moon?" asked the manager.

"Yessir"

"Why did you kill the pig?" the manager asked the supervisor.

"It ate my soap."

"Soap? Where did you put the soap?" asked the manager.

"Oh, my ears," groaned the supervisor, placing his right hand on his ear. He could not pronounce the words clearly because the coconut frond had disfigured his mouth. His eyes swelled to a full moon.

"I left the soap on the loan," said the supervisor after a while.

"Ah, my friend you have made a mistake,' said the manager. "You should've kept it somewhere safe."

"It was just near the door," said the supervisor.

"Pigs don't reason out things like humans," said the manager. "You were a fool to leave your soap outside. Now go back and pack your things and get ready for the next ship to Australia."

"And you," said the manager, turning to me, "lock him up in prison."

The supervisor was sent home and I was jailed for six moons. I did not present my side of the story. Laipe escaped the prison after I lied that I had threatened him with a bush knife to take me to the office.

Chapter 25

Our prison was a narrow brick house with blocks of rooms separated by thick brick walls. Each room accommodated up to four inmates. It was dark inside but a tiny sunlight spilt in through a gap under the roof between two bricks. A little toilet sat near the wall.

Most of the prisoners were those who rebelled against the government and those plantation workers who defied bosses' orders. I joined two prisoners, Yanape, a middle-aged man from Tari and Camillus, a native of Yangoru in Sepik. Both had spent over half of their terms when I arrived.

Yanape was slapped with a six-moon sentence for resisting arrest after he set fire to some young coconut trees. He said he smoked and threw away the butt onto some dry grasses near the road. A fire quickly developed from it and spread to the young trees before the plantation workers intervened and killed it.

"You should not have been jailed if the fire destroyed nothing," observed Camillus.

"I was jailed for evading arrest," said Yanape. "I ran away to the villages when they chased me. The more they chased me, the more I made their arrest difficult. They chased me all day and caught me at the beach at sunset. That angered them so much that they increased the jail term to six moons. If I had surrendered, I would have been reprimanded and released."

"The fire didn't even touch a young coconut tree, did it?" I said.

"No. I told you no," said Yanape.

"Why did you run away then? asked Camillus.

"I dreaded going to prison, even for a few days," said Yanape.

Camillus's eyes widened. He was about to ask when Yanape cleared his confusion.

"If I were to be sent to jail, I would miss my girl so much. But I had made a terrible mistake. Instead of running away, I ran straight into the jaws of prison and lost my freedom, lost my girl."

"Who is she? Are you married to a local girl?" I asked Yanape.

"Yes … but… oh no, sorry," he said, forcing the words out one by one.

"What do you mean by yes but oh no, sorry?" I asked.

"Oh boy," replied Yanape, taking a deep breath. "I mean, I have two wives and seven children back in Tari, but I need someone here to keep me company, to share my loneliness."

"Man, how could you resist a beautiful woman when she says marry me, marry me?" said Camillus.

Yanape smiled and said nothing. He appeared to have forgotten his children and women at home for a moment. His thoughts seemed to revolve around his newfound love. He leaned his back against the wall and took a nap.

When I was unmarried, I would wonder why men ignored their beautiful wives and hung around with younger women, but later I realised that I was not an exception. Only a strong man stands the seduction of a young woman. A man's greatest weakness is women.

Before I was sent to prison, I dated a beautiful Tolai girl. The first thing I missed in the prison was her. I met her a few moons before I was cast into jail. I would sneak off in the evenings to meet her under a forest of tall coconut trees near the beach. It was not long before I uncovered her red blouse and enjoyed the feel of her beautiful shape. I would look forward to the day to end quickly so I could be at her side and allow the world to slip off my shoulders. We would melt in each other's arms. Like Yanape, the prison cut her off from me as well.

Camillus's story was different. He said he was imprisoned for dislocating the jaw of a co-worker over a half-empty bottle of beer. He said one tipped and spilt the other's beer. An argument flared up between them when alcohol took over the senses and reasoning stepped aside. A full-scale fistfight ensued. Camillus was too strong for the other and he came out victorious over the other. He sent his opponent kissing the cement floor and he woke up with a dislocated jaw.

"If I had controlled my temper, I wouldn't be spending these lonely moons here," said Camillus.

"In Madang where I first worked," said Yanape, "we drank beer which had brains. It did not cause a lot of noise and shouting. We enjoyed every pint of it. But looks like the beer we drink here does not have any brain at all."

"People don't drink beer these days. Beer drinks people," said Camillus. "That's why whenever men meet with beer, their voices rise when beer takes over all their senses. Beer does all their talking; beer does all their thinking."

"But what does beer do when you get into a problem?" asked Yanape. Camillus said nothing.

"When you get into trouble," continued Yanape, "your friend beer folds its hands and steps aside. Beer is innocent. You get all the blame."

"That's what happened to me," admitted Camillus. "I drank as if I was swallowing the bottle too. I got so drunk that I didn't know what I was doing. I allowed beer to drink me and drink my senses out. But you know what? Not a single bottle; even an empty one accompanied me to prison. When the police caught me with their guns, it stripped my strength to the ashes and brought me back to my senses."

Later that night when they learned of how I had beaten the white supervisor and how I had avoided the police, they said I was a real hero. They said I was not only courageous enough to avoid the policemen but successfully forced the white man back to his homeland.

The discussions of the different paths we took to end up in the same place took us straight to midnight.

Our time in the prison was monotonous but we made it interesting because we had each other's company. We would tell stories to pass the time. One night Camillus recalled a great battle in his village where two groups of white men attacked and killed each other with guns.

"Our village became the battlefield for the white and yellow men," said Camillus. "I was a little boy when our village was invaded. The white men took away my father and uncles. Me, my mother and my baby sister hid for a few days in the jungle and only returned to the village when the fight moved on to the next village."

"Why didn't they fight in their land?" asked Yanape.

"I don't know. Probably they didn't have battlefields of their own that were big enough for them to fight. They fought everywhere, on the mountains, over the sea, in the forest, whenever they met."

"Who were these fighters, again?" I asked Camillus.

"The yellow men were called Japanese. They were smaller in stature and more aggressive. The white men were called Australians or Americans, I'm not sure which one is correct. They were bigger and appeared stronger than the Japanese. But many of these

Australians were very very young and inexperienced fighters."

"Did your father return after the battles?" I asked.

Camillus turned his head away towards the wall. He remained quiet for some time before he spoke again.

"My uncles and others returned, weary and exhausted with their skins retreating to their bones. I never saw my father again."

"He must have fallen with the Australians," observed Yanape

"That was what the returned men told us" said Camillus. "Unfortunately the white men's guns failed to distinguish our men from theirs. They killed Australians, they killed New Guineans".

"My fathers joined the Australians. They equally shared death, hunger and sickness with the Australians. Food supplies dropped from the planes landed in the wrong places- places where there was no mouth, bombs failed to reach the targets, guns intended for enemies missed their targets."

"My fathers were carriers. They shouldered the food bags for the Australians to stay alive and fight. They dug tunnels for the Australians so that they could hide from the Japanese and fight them back".

"The wounded soldiers had no choice but to submit to my fathers to treat their wounds. And those who were unable to walk, my fathers carried them up the mountains and through the swamps, and across flooded rivers. Unfortunately, many of them died and were buried in my land".

"The strange and the funny thing about the battle was this," continued Camillus. "My fathers and uncles never knew why they were helping but they helped the Australians to fight against an enemy we never knew."

Every day when the birds welcomed a new day, Yanape marked a stick on the wall with charcoal. He said he was moving closer and closer to his Freedom Day with the passage of a each day. Camillus said he had a moon remaining. I had four moons remaining but I doubted whether I would be released at all because the whites enjoyed keeping the natives in the prison.

One morning when I was into my third moon, the prison gate was kicked open and a tall white man appeared with two prison guards. They called Camillus out. We never saw him again. Camillus took all the sunlight and laughter away with him. Several days later, Yanape was also released.

The prison grew cold without my brothers. They took the laughter and warmth away with them, leaving me with nothing but walls above and around me. One won't realise the value of a person until he is gone.

Many days and nights after my fellow prisoners were gone, the guard who brought us food informed me that our contract had ended and the men were leaving.

"I was watching on the hillsides when the ship pulled into the wharf yesterday evening," said the guard. "The workers are busy preparing to leave for Madang in two days."

I was unaware the contract would expire that soon. All we were told was that we would go home after working for some time on the coast.

"What about the prisoners?" I asked.

"I don't know," said the guard and walked away.

I had left behind a little boy, who hardly walked and his young mother, being pregnant with our second child, and my ageing mother. I had no chance of seeing them again.

There was also no way I could learn of home. The prison cut me off from the outside world.

Thoughts which existed in isolation before came looking for me. Until then I realised how dear my wife and son were to me. I took family for granted when in liberty. Within the confines of the prison walls, my dreams were crushed, my hopes were extinguished and life ceased even with a beating heart.

Next morning two guards came to my prison quickly and handcuffed me.

"Since you are the only one here, you'll be with two other prisoners in the next cell," said the guards and led me away.

We walked across a wide lawn and instead of turning left towards the prison blocks, we entered a half-opened door of another building. The guards left me inside the building and disappeared into one of the rooms at the end of the corridor.

There was a counter in front of me and behind it sat a beautiful young woman. She was sorting some papers but when we arrived, she laid the papers aside and threw her bright eyes (the sharpest eyes I had ever seen) at me and smiled.

The young lady resumed her work but she appeared lost.

"Oh, where have I left off?" she said to herself. Her words were as soft as whispers but I caught them before they died on those beautiful lips. She stared at me for some time but when I beheld her, she looked away. Moments later when she realised that I was still leaning against the wall, she advised me to sit on one of the two worn-out chairs placed against the wall.

All this time, she didn't take her eyes away from me. I once caught her smiling at me. Oh, I couldn't get my eyes off her. I should come back for her someday.

Outside the building, the place was quiet and still. It was a cloudless day. A soft breeze gently flipped through the coconut trees and the sun shone brighter than it used to be in many mornings. It was the kind of day that makes one's mind wander off to the forest and rivers. Home was far away and here I was far away from home. The boys would leave the next morning. I was imprisoned in a foreign land.

At the end of the building, noises rose and fell as if people were arguing. The noises grew louder and louder until it was clear. There was a commotion somewhere inside one of the huge rooms.

"It's coming from the boss's office," said the pretty young lady. "Some Simbu men came here this morning to plead for one of their brothers whom they said was a prisoner here. They said they couldn't go back to Hagen without him. Oh, Mt Hagen, I wish I could go there."

"Have they left the building?"

"No. Maybe they are the ones arguing with the boss."

"Oh oh oh," said the young lady turning her face towards the boss's office, "they are coming out."

The boss's door flung open and several young men were pushed out, quite roughly.

"There is your man," said the bearded boss, pointing in my direction and throwing a key to the boys. "Take him and go away. You are causing me a lot of headaches."

All our boys, Pepena, Poi, Anis, Laipe and Genemba threw their eyes everywhere like hunting dogs looking for their prey. Once they spotted me, they raced along the narrow corridor, bumping each other against the walls. Pepena and Poi unlocked the handcuffs and lifted me off the chair and carried me out.

"We have been arguing with the prison boss since this morning for him to release you," said Pepena.

"The ship has arrived days ago. We are going home tomorrow," said Laipe.

I was surprised to see Genemba with them. We had left him because he was away in his mother's land when we left home.

Chapter 26

The day passed slowly like a river in a swamp. We couldn't wait to go home.

Pepena suggested if we could grab some drinks at the club to pass the time. Pepena's idea pleased us. We strolled away to the club.

The club was away from the living quarters. It was frequented by drunkards mostly on Friday nights when workers got their pay. Men would drink in their tribal groups and when alcohol took over, the quiet place would become noisy. Voices would rise and fall in languages unknown to us.

Beer was said to have a crazy spirit hidden in the liquid. It smelled like urine but after a few tastes of it, you won't part with it because it would forever want to be your friend. Some young men said the crazy spirit could chase your loneliness and worries away as it worked through the veins.

We took a little space in the corner where the light failed to reach the floor. Others came in, grabbed their drinks and occupied the empty spaces in the huge building. We were already talking loudly after a few drinks. The crazy spirit in the beer made our heads spin after a few bottles.

We talked about different things, including our encounter with white men and the clash of our cultures. Memories of the battles we fought a long time ago rushed back fresh as if it were yesterday. Genemba stopped his beer and cried for a while.

"I wish I could go to the battlefield again," said Genemba. "The government and the white men have built jails and used their guns to weaken our muscles."

Talks about Tolai women seemed unending and most interesting. We learnt that each young man had known at least one local woman during their stay on the coast.

Throwing an empty bottle away, Poi asked how Genemba had come to Rabaul.

"Oh, my head is crazy," said Genemba. "The beer is making my thoughts wander like the waves in the sea. I don't know where to start. Maybe I'll tell you the whole story when my correct senses find me again."

"You mean you've lost your memory?" asked Poi who was eager to know about home.

"It was my old man," said Genemba, clearing his voice and coughing out some of the beer. "He wanted me to marry a girl and settle down but I ran away to the coast instead."

"Maybe you didn't like the girl eh," said Poi.

"How could I marry her and stay home while you all are travelling and seeing places? I was thinking of following you to the coast so I asked my parents to send the girl away. However, my father went ahead and paid the bride price. He said the girl would look after him and mother well."

"Why did you run away from her?" asked Poi. "You should have stayed home with her."

"He must already have seen her," laughed Laipe.

Genemba ignored the boys and continued his story.

"I did not run away from her. Two moons after you left for the coast, I travelled to
Madang with Kepambo's brother-in-law.

"Oh yes, yes. I remember that tall Jika guy," said Pepena "I met him during
Kepambo's bride price. He is such a nice young man. What's his name? Palme?"

"Yes, that was the guy," said Genemba. He stopped the story and bowed. Tears choked his throat.

"What happened to Palme," asked Pepena.

"I don't like to call his name," said Genemba. It saddens me every time I think of him."

"What happened to Palme?" asked Pepen again.

"We lost this fine gentleman in a car crash. He was working as a truck driver before he died. The truck was overloaded with over fifty men when they were ascending a mountain. The driver was an old man from Tari called Wandane. When Palme and I came down to the coast, it was Wandane who accommodated us when we were looking for work."

"After staying with Wandane for a moon, we were found to be illegal dwellers. The company kicked us out of the quarters. Wandane however took us under his wings. He fought for us. "They are my sons," said Wandane to the plantation bosses. "How could you chase my sons away like this?"

"Wandane threatened to quit the job so we were allowed to stay with him in his cubicle for a while until we found jobs".

"I worked as a construction worker while Wandane took Palme as an apprentice. Wandane said he was 'molding' Palme to take over his job when he retired. Soon Palme picked up all the tricks from Wandane to handle the huge truck. Palme was an assistant driver to Wandane when they both died.

"Wandane died as well?" asked Poi.

"Yes. When the truck veered off the road and was heading for the creek, Wandane urged Palme to jump out for safety. However, Palme replied, "I won't jump without you. How could I let you die alone in the river?"

"When the truck's back tyres left the edges of the road...," Genemba stopped for a while and stood.

"What happened next?" asked Poi, moving closer to Genemba.

"Aghh, I'll complete the story later," said Genemba and left to relieve himself.

Most of the men had left as it was already reaching midnight. Below our table were bottles with their lids open. We were no longer interested in those bottles, as we no longer needed them.

Genemba returned a while later and picked up another bottle from the half-closed carton underneath the table. He roughly took the lid away with his two front teeth and spat it out onto the floor. A whitish bubble escaped and gathered around the tip of the bottle. Genemba cleaned the bubbles with his tongue and after raising the bottle to the sky, he poured the contents down his throat in one gulp. When the last drops drained into his mouth, he threw the empty bottle away and got another as if he had been dying of thirst for days.

"The truck veered off the road and plunged into the river," continued Genemba. "Since the creek was very deep, the truck flew in space for a great distance before it smashed into the boulders. Broken pieces of the truck and its occupants scattered everywhere on the riverbed. The river turned red with blood. Even today, I can't take the two men out of my head. I lost the best of friends."

"The shoulders on which I leaned collapsed. I had to leave Madang."

"I am so sorry. I can feel the loss now," cried Pepena. The emotions created by the beer were to much for Pepena to control. We all said we would leave Madang too if we were in the same situation as Genemba.

The remaining bottles and a few more good stories took us past midnight.

It was early next morning when we boarded the ship for Madang. The ship's engine roared and shot streams of clouds into the sky as it floated its way into the deep waters on the back of the waves. It was impossible to imagine how the white men could make such a massive unsinkable object that could cut through the rough seas without sinking. The ship's construction and its complicated workings were beyond my simple mind to understand.

A wave of pity swept over me as the beach and our little home disappeared on the horizon. I wondered whether I would come back to it again. It was my home away from home for a long time. Leaving it behind broke my heart but it was comforting to know that our controlled life on the coast was ending. We would be free, free as the free birds of the skies. We would be free to roam our forests and rivers. We would no longer observe the 7:00 am to 5:00 pm working schedule. We would spend our days in whatever way that pleased us. We would have the entire day for ourselves.

While I was carried away by those thoughts, Genemba said he was looking for Poi.

"He isn't with us," said Genemba searching around the ship.

We looked everywhere but couldn't find him on the ship. We all ran to the deck and checked the seashore. Dressed in his red lap lap was Poi, waving and running along the beach like an ant with his red cloth tied to his waist.

I found out later from the boys that Poi had married a local girl and deliberately avoided the ship to remain with her. He had a baby boy with her. Because women and children were not allowed onto the ship, he was torn into two, whether to stay back with his young family or to travel with us. Sadly, he chose the former. We never heard of him again.

He must have died in Rabaul.

Chapter 27

The ship floated above the waves like a feather and occasionally the angry waves shot pools of water over the deck. Pepena and Genemba clung to the rails and vomited out everything they had drank the previous night.

We reached Madang three days later. While we were waiting for the plane to take us home to Mt Hagen, the men went into a small shop and bought spades and bush knives, clothes and blankets and cooking pots to take home with them. I did not have any money for these things so I quietly slipped away to the beach. While I was enjoying the sight of the beautiful sea, Pepena came running after me.

"Get yourself some things," he said, handing me some money. "The boys contributed the money for you."

"Contribution? Why?"

"We raised the money to take you out of the prison but the boss refused our money."

"How did I come out then?"

"That's a long story. I'll tell you later. Go buy your things or we'll leave you behind like your foolish brother Poi."

I bought a sack of clothes and a small bush knife for my little boy Joseph. I couldn't pronounce his name well. I insisted on another name but Piambil Ambo Mopune said Joseph was the name of a hero in their new religion. She said hero so I allowed him to go with that name. But I called him Dosip instead.

"The boss said you didn't deserve to have a short prison term and refused to let you go," said Pepena when I returned after buying my things.

"What did you do then?"

"Oh, that was simple. We asked him to lock us up as well. We didn't have a choice."

"That must have been a real headache for the white man."

"That probably must have been the smartest idea we proposed," said Pepena. "The boss ordered us out at once."

Pepena said if they returned without me, our fathers would chase them away because I was the only one in the family to take my father's place and ensure the continuity of our family line. They did everything they could to get me out.

At last, the plane arrived. It was midmorning and the weather was clear. We loaded our cargo and headed for Mt Hagen.

Mt Hagen was not the place it used to be. White roofs had replaced the grass huts and most of the grassland had been converted into huge tea and coffee plantations. Some said the Wahgi Mek coffee plantation outside Mt Hagen was the largest in the whole land.

We were relieved to be back home after being strangers in a foreign land. We were so excited that before the plane opened its doors, we cheered.

As soon as the plane opened its door, we collected our bags quickly and rushed out. We were advised to collect something called finish pay in a building nearby.

As each man's name was called, he disappeared inside the building and came out smiling with a small yellow envelope under his hand.

When I went in, there were two white men. One was handing out the envelopes while the other stood behind him as if he were guarding his friend against evil spirits. The man with the envelope looked at me and then at the envelope.

"Are you Maip, the hero?" said the man with the envelopes. I thought they had planned to imprison me. But here I was in my homeland. I wouldn't allow them to imprison me in my homeland. I nodded and said nothing.

"Wait for me there," said the man with the envelopes. "I want a word with you."

Two men came in after me and went away shortly with their shares. I leaned against the wall. Another jail term for me? How could they imprison me in my land?

After the white men gave out all the envelopes, they waved me to them.

"Here is the hero," said the man with the envelopes, without looking at me. "We've got something special for you."

Saying that the man who issued the envelopes produced an envelope from inside his shirt pocket.

"This is your finish pay. And this one I have on my left is for your pig," said the man.

"For the pig?"

"Do you remember you've beaten a white man in Rabaul?" asked the young man as I stood there confused.

I nodded.

"The supervisor had left the money for you. He said he regretted killing your pig and sending you to prison."

I didn't know white men admitted their wrongs.

Several two-pound notes were packed neatly inside the envelope. I didn't know what to do with it. It was more than I had ever beheld in my lifetime. I couldn't imagine the supervisor would do something kind like that. I was glad the supervisor had learnt from his mistake. My victim was a rare breed of white man.

At home when we arrived, a small crowd gathered at the ceremonial ground to welcome us back. Some mothers dropped tears of joy seeing us back safely. Others weren't there. Poe's mother wept bitterly and crawled in the mud when she learnt a coastal girl had taken her son away.

After hugs, tears and embraces, we shared our goods with our people and they went away happily with spades, knives and soaps among others.

No one was at home when I arrived. The place appeared desolated. My mother's gardens near the ceremonial ground which she used to tend every day, now appeared to have been neglected for some time. Long weeds had claimed most of the gardens.

Piambil Ambo Mopune and the children returned soon after we arrived. Joseph carried a small piece of firewood on his shoulder and led the way. His mother walked behind him. A happy little girl hung loosely on top of the bilum on Piambil Ambo Mopune's back. She appeared to have gone to sleep a while ago. Piambil Ambo Mopune held the little girl's arm in one hand and a piglet in another.

When they were spaces away from the house, Joseph pointed towards the house and said something to his mother. Both Joseph and Piambil Ambo Mopune stopped and stared at the house for a while. Piambil Ambo Mopune adjusted the bilum handles and they walked slowly towards the house.

Upon reaching the door, Piambil Ambo Mopune held the little girl by the arms and lowered her slowly to the ground. The little girl smelled the smoke and chattered a little cry of relief.

When Piambil Ambo Mopune saw me, she burst into tears.

"Oh, we thought you would never return," she said, drying her eyes.

The little girl cried along with her mother, not because I came home. She was scared her mother cried in front of a stranger. She sat beside her mother at the other side of the fireplace holding the ends of Piambil Ambo Mopune's grass skirt. She threw curious glances at me whenever I did not see her. But whenever my eyes turned in her direction, she cried and buried her little face in her mother's backside.

"Hi little girl, come here," I said, trying to get her over to my side. But whenever I said something, it frightened the little girl more and more.

"Esther he is your father," said Piambil Ambo Mopune, "go shake hands with him." "Oh, you have given her another strange name," I said.

"Yes, from the same good book. Doesn't she look exactly like her aunty Konopu?" added Piambil Ambo Mopune.

"Yes, exactly like her."

All this time, Joseph was leaning against the wall near the door where we stored firewood and stared at me. He must have been wondering who I was. When I asked him if he remembered me, he shook his head without saying something. Then as if someone had reminded him of who I was, he left his place at the wall and hesitatingly walked over to me and sat on my legs. He studied my face for some time and then put his arms around my neck.

The poor little boy sobbed.

I didn't see my mother and enquired about her the next morning. Piambil Ambo Mopune ignored me. She acted as if I had asked her the wrong question. She remained quiet for a long time. Tears swam inside her eyes. Then she began to cry.

"Oh, my dearest mother," said Piambil Ambo Mopune in between tears. "It's moons now."

"What happened to her?" "She is gone," she said.

"Gone where? To Kepambo in Mt Hagen?"

"Come," said Joseph, taking my hands. He led me out of the house. "I will show you grandma's place."

Joseph led me to the back of the house where my mother and the girls used to sunbathe and weave bilums in the mornings.

"That's where grandma is," said Joseph, pointing to a small clearing under a group of casuarina trees. A little cross marked her grave.

Her fresh memories flooded my mind. I could picture her smiling face, her caring heart, her soft voice.

A stream of sorrow flooded my consciousness. I couldn't imagine how the human heart could accommodate oceans of deep grief. If my heart was located outside the body, it would burst open and empty its sorrows.

Death stole my loved ones before the time was ripe for them, leaving me with nothing but memories that would haunt me for ages.

Piambil Ambo Mopune said my mother passed away three moons after I had left for the coast.

"There was no way we could inform you of her death," she said.

"Did she leave behind any dying words?" I enquired.

"Amboama asked you to look after the church well like an egg for her."

"What? Which church? Like an egg?"

"We have our Sunday Schools every Sunday Father. It's pure joy. Our teacher tells us stories from the bible," said Joseph.

My mother had given away the best part of my land to the church. The church building stood opposite our house. More land meant more gardens and more gardens meant more pigs and more pigs meant more wives. A part of me had been thrown away. I could have burnt down the church but because I didn't want to offend my mother's spirit, I withheld my anger.

"Amboama told us not to worry about her because she has gone to the good place," said Piambil Ambo Mopune.

"Woman, which good place are you talking about?" I shouted at her. "Does a grave offer you a good place? Can't you see what death is doing to this family? Death is taking away all our loved ones while they are not old."

Piambil Ambo Mopune said my mother had gone to a place called Heaven to be with the God the missionaries had brought with them. Before I asked any further questions about that heaven or about the mysterious religion, Piambil Ambo Mopune handed me my breakfast and left for the gardens. But before she left, she stood at the door and said, "Amboama said if you want to see her again, you must accept God."

"My mother was not old enough to die. Who is that God who claims to keep my mother alive in his strange heaven? Woman, you better be careful of what those missionaries are teaching you. They are planting lies in your heads. You better be careful. Their lies will spread and spoil my children as it is doing to your heads."

Chapter 28

During our absence, the foolish ideas of the white men had crept into our village and spoiled our people's minds.

Besides the church, a school was established in Tambul where our children were taken away from our homes and taught the white men's language. The road to Mendi was paved with gravel and a few trucks were transporting huge logs from Nemarep to Mendi. Some small trucks ran between Mt Hagen and Mendi. These changes happened so fast that we couldn't fully comprehend whether those changes were good or bad for us.

When school started Piambil Ambo Mopune said we should send him to school in Tambul like the other little boys. But Tambul was too far for the child. The track was slippery and the fast-flowing creeks were dangerous. Although a wire bridge was pulled over the Kaugel River, it wasn't safe for the children as the chance of slipping into the river was high. I refused to allow Joseph to school.

"But everyone is sending their children to school," said Piambil Ambo Mopune. "Why should we keep the child at home?"

"Should I send my boy to school because everyone else is sending theirs? I don't see why we should send the child away in the cold mornings."

"School is good for the children," she insisted. "They'll learn new things."

"Now tell me, woman! What do you know about schooling? You know nothing about schooling!

"My father had this big land. Joseph will inherit the land after me. If he goes to school, I'm afraid he might not come home at all. See what happened to Dopo, Pundu's son?

School has taken him away. He rarely comes back to the village to visit his mother".

"I need sons, and more sons to occupy the vast land my father had left behind. If you only talk about school and cannot give me more sons, I will look for another woman, probably two, who will bear me sons."

Piambil Ambo Mopune said nothing more of schooling that day. However, when school commenced a few days later, Joseph slipped away while I was away in the men's house.

When Joseph went to school on the second day, Piambil Ambo Mopune saw him off the track and came back crying as the child disappeared behind the mountains. She sobbed as if she was losing him forever. I stopped him in the next few days but he cried and went after the other kids. I realised he was too young to understand things.

Only a fool could send his child away in the cold mornings. I didn't see anything good in school. Whatever they learnt in school would be irrelevant to our village. We had plenty of trees to build our houses, enough land to make our gardens and enough forests to hunt our meat. Maybe, like the church, the white men must have spoiled the reasonings of those parents including Piambil Ambo Mopune who were sending their children to school.

The school lured the young children out of the villages. It came up with an award system to encourage learning and to identify the best students. This encouraged the children to compete with each other to get the prizes. The top performing children were awarded prizes after their school ended every year.

Unfortunately, Joseph was caught up in that trap too. He learned the white men's things quickly. His teacher once told me that Joseph was quicker than his peers in absorbing the white men's knowledge.

The white men were very poor in their language and choice of words that they taught their children how to use the words to articulate their thoughts clearly. This was something we were naturally good at. Our chiefs were great orators. They gave eloquent speeches without even going to school.

Joseph said the white men's new language was hard to learn but his books were making his learning easier. I often found him burying his face between the pages after school and sometimes in the night. Sometimes his mother talked to her God to help Joseph get over the difficulties quickly. His devotion to his studies and probably his mother's God must have helped the child in his studies. When school ended, Joseph collected all the top prices in all the things they were learning in school, including a prize on the white man's language and one that dealt with counting things.

School stopped all the carefree life the children had been enjoying. Like our days in the coast, they had five days for school and a day off. The seventh day was the day of rest where children and their mothers attended church in the village.

Piambil Ambo Mopune and the two kids had been going to church when I was away in the coast. The white missionaries' church had attracted mostly women and children and some old men.

The kids were sent to what they called 'Sunday School' in a separate little church beside the main church building. Another school!

Every morning, Joseph wore his black shorts and a small shirt his mother had bought from the mission's canteen in Tambul. The size of the shorts was too large for his age but he fastened it against his waist with a small rope.

I was curious about the church and asked Piambil Ambo Mopune and the kids one Sunday morning who their God was.

"Has your God come to replace our god, Ola Yemo?" I asked. She did not respond. She took Esther by the arm and hurried away to church.

When our mothers and sisters were converted to the white man's religion, the children followed them by default. For ages, women and children had been left out in our ancestral worships so they were happy to worship the foreign God the missionaries had brought with them.

The church, however, appeared to have something we men didn't find in our spirit house. Every time people came to church, they had smiles all over their faces. It appeared as if they were gathering for a huge pig killing or a moka. They appeared to have no problems in life. Rays of happiness glittered on their happy faces. They would come to their church every Sunday morning and would sit around in small groups in front of the church and sing the songs the missionaries had taught them while waiting for the others to join them. They had no difficulty singing because the songs had been translated into our language.

The new religion had also driven a new sense into our peoples' hearts. The missionaries' message converted some mothers' aggressive hearts. Kenenga was one of the women the message changed so much and so completely. The message was said to have

'taken her anger away'. Kenenga used to be an aggressive woman. Whenever her husband Genemba brought home a woman, she bashed her up so badly that no woman dared to touch her husband. Shortly after we returned from the coast, Kenenga suspected a Yap girl of having an affair with her husband. She met the woman in a waipa circle, scratched her face, punched her nose and dragged her hair in the mud until two boys intervened and saved the young girl.

A few moons after Kenenga got converted, Genemba brought home a young girl from Mele in Pangia. Everyone was expecting Kenenga to break the woman's nose but what she did stunned everyone. No word came out from Kenenga's mouth. It was as if the message had made her incapable of using her aggressive hands and tongue again. She gave her room to the couple and moved to the pigpen with her little daughter. The message came in quietly and softened the vilest of the hearts.

The influence of the 'Word' was contagious. After it claimed the women and children, it spread its spell over to the men and captured some of their hearts too.

I was informed one day that Pepena had been drawn into the women's religion some time ago and was living a secluded life.

"He is secretly going to the women's church," said Genemba. "We need to find out."

I was more concerned when Pepena avoided coming out to the ceremonial ground for over a moon. I cursed the religion and went over to Pepena's house one morning to find out what was wrong with him.

Pepena was staring at the flames as they rose and fell. Perai Wenepo roasted some sweet potatoes over the fire. Outside their house, their two sons were chasing each other and playing with their dog.

Pepena's behaviour changed when the boys chased a piglet into the house. Instead of shouting to Perai Wenepo to take the piglet away, Pepena gently threw a rope at her and asked her to take the piglet away. Pepena's short temper had disappeared. Pepena used to bark orders to Perai Wenepo. This change in his behaviour greatly puzzled me.

"Ah the missionaries have built their church in the village," I said to strike a conversation with him but he said nothing. He appeared disinterested in any conversation regarding the church. Perai Wenepo divided the hot ashes and buried the sweet potatoes inside the fire. Pepena recollected the embers and started the fire again. Then he cleared his voice.

"It was a complicated decision," said Pepena. "My brother we have been the best pair.

We frequented the spirit house and offered sacrifices for the sick. We fought battles together.

We chased girls together. Together we travelled to places. There are many interesting times ahead of us. But something has happened to me. Something has changed me."

He paused for he could not continue. Tears devoured his words. I couldn't believe a simple foreign faith could humble a tough man like Pepena and bring him to tears. How could the religion render Pepena incapable of marrying many wives or beating Perai Wenepo? That was too much for me to digest. I went away before he continued his nonsense talk about his newfound faith.

Pepena and the women believed in a man who was killed a long time ago in a faraway land. They adopted his lifestyle by being obedient and submissive to His word.

How could my people blindly believe in a dead man who couldn't even protect himself? They were said to be living under the counsel of the word they heard from a Good Book which contained the dead man's words and teachings. They said their God had died and had risen from the death. It was this rise from death that was keeping their faith in

Him alive and functioning. They said although they would die someday, they would continue to live with their 'God' in the clouds forever. That was ridiculous! No one makes his home in the clouds!

Three moons later, Pepena's faith in the message was confirmed. He and a few other first converts, including Piambil Ambo Mopune, were submerged underwater. They said the water was washing their past away and that they were beginning a new way of living with their God. This erased every hope of him joining us again in our singsings and mokas-the message of their God ruled a clear line of separation.

Pepena had interesting pursuits ahead of him but he had forgone them all to join the weak religion. I couldn't understand his motives. Probably the message he had heard was so strong for him to resist that he gave in like a soft-hearted woman.

Before Pepena was baptised (as it was called) he pleaded with me to witness his baptism ceremony. I declined his request but since he was my dearest friend, I reluctantly went to the Ambola River near Tambul to witness this strange event.

The weather was fine that morning. People from different villages including some from our enemy tribes turned up at the river.

Before the believers were submerged underwater, they proclaimed their faith and thanked their God for delivering them from their bad habits.

When Pepena's turn came to speak before he was submerged underwater, he said:

"My brothers and fathers, we had great moments fighting battles, chasing girls, killing pigs and making mokas. I have been enjoying those things until recently when I have found a new joy. The joy I have found in God's word surpasses all those other enjoyments.

"I have many exciting times ahead of me to make moka and acquire wives, but the arrow of God has pierced me. It has caught me off guard and bent my will to the command of His Word. I have no choice, but to leave you."

"From now on, I won't be joining you because the word says, come out, be separate, be different. I'm sorry to say that but that is what the word is telling me. God's Word is so powerful that it has cut me off from the ways of our fathers and has brought me into God's tribe. I simply don't know how it happened but all I know is I am changed."

"Since I accepted God, I received light and freedom. A veil of darkness that has been keeping me in the dark for ages has lifted off. I can see light. I am no longer walking and living in the darkness. I am stunned by the light."

"Now that I see the light, I see a new beginning for me and my family. I see my future and hope in the Word. I see enduring promises all wrapped inside the Word."

"God has promised a beautiful place called Heaven for me. I am told that I will never die in that land in the skies. I will inherit a home in the skies. I have therefore forsaken this world in favour of the greater things above. Come and follow me as I follow God."

The baptism ceremony concluded with the songs: 'Yunge Kondo Awilimuni Na Wendo Lgim', 'Kombu Heaven Ya Pa Peangare' (How Beautiful Heaven Must Be) and 'Marimari Bilong God I Sweet Tumas' (Amazing Grace How Sweet the Sound).

Something strange stirred up my heart that day. The testimonies and the songs strangely warmed my heart. I believe the songs inspired, comforted and gave hope to many people. They shook my heart that day.

Chapter 29

Since the church was next to our house, we heard everything that was said in the church.

The believers said His love had plunged them out of the jaws of death and freed them from their slavery. That was ridiculous. How could one be dead in his land while being alive? Who enslaved them and where?

Out of curiosity, I went to church one Sunday morning to find out. The few steps I took from the house to the church were the longest journey I had ever made. It was not the ordinary ground I knew. My childhood playground appeared so strange and foreign to me that I thought I was stepping on an enemy land.

As soon as I stepped inside the church, my bones slackened. The strength in me was leaving. I sat at the end of the building with my head bowed.

The congregation sang two songs and repeated Amazing Grace. The song was about some lonely old man who was lost and was found again. I had this instinct that I was that lost man. But how could I be lost in my land?

I didn't know that my mother and Piambil Ambo Mopune had been praying to their God to change me. I was unaware God was working secretly to arrest my heart. I had this unusual feeling that someone was speaking to me. Yes, it was a small still voice, like a person whispering to my heart.

"Maip," said the small still voice, "I am that unknown God you have been worshipping as Ola Yemo."

"Look at Mt Giluwe," said the gentle voice again. The great mountain stood still. Its tops were lost in the sky. The cloudless sky stretched to infinity above the mountain.

"Do you remember the salt water?" asked the still voice. I recalled the great body of water in the coast and imagined its vastness.

"Now can you imagine Kaugel River? All the streams flow into it yet it doesn't leave its banks. All great rivers empty everything in the sea, yet the sea overflows not, nor does it expand onto the land."

I couldn't believe the sea would hold such water after the mighty rivers discharge themselves into the sea day and night.

"I am who I am," came back the voice again. "I have created the heavens and the earth and the sea. I have created the sun and the moon. I spoke into existence Mt Giluwe. I have commanded Kaugel River to follow its course day and night. I have given word to the sea to stay where it is. The sea respects the boundaries I placed. The rivers and streams follow their courses day and night. I feed all the wild birds and injects. They honour me because I am the great God who created them all."

Everything it said made much sense. The rivers run to the sea yet the sea is never full nor does it refuse to accept the massive waters. The sun rises in the same place and sets in the same place every day without tiring. It observes its position and knows where it rises and when it should set. If the sea respects this God and if the sun obeys Him faithfully day after day, this God must be the greatest of all.

While I was going through all those wonders of creation and was amazed at the way things worked, the still voice came back to me again and this time, it appealed to me.

"Now, will you make me your God?" asked the still voice.

"Oh no, not me," I said. "You must be making a mistake." But the still voice insisted.

"No, I am not making a mistake here, for I never make mistakes. I am speaking to you. I want to make you my special child. Now. Will you accept me?"

The voice paused. My heart began to beat faster. The still voice came back to me again with a demand.

"Now, will you make me your God?"

However hard I tried to avoid it, the still voice came back again and again. I didn't realise the songs had ended.

I resisted and clashed with the gentle voice. However hard I tried to eschew the voice; the voice came back to me. I was still battling with the still voice when the pastor took the altar.

"You are not far from God's love," began the pastor. He was quoting from memory. "His love is deeper than the ocean and taller than Mt Giluwe. His love is wider than the wide sky."

"We have been slaves of our fathers' gods and spirits. Those gods and spirits are all meaningless. They don't understand you. When you call upon your ancestors' spirits, they won't help you because they are dead. But the God I am talking about is the unknown God we have been worshipping without knowing. This God has revealed Himself to us through the missionaries. He is more powerful than all our fathers' gods. Now He wants you to give your life to Him. Does anyone here want to give your life to this God?

"You don't need to bring pigs to God. Why? Because God doesn't need your pigs. He owns all the pigs and cassowaries in the forest. All the fish in the rivers and the sea God owns. What will you give to God, oh poor child? You own nothing.

The songs, the still voice and the pastor all had the same message for me. God was bigger than anything that I could think of.

The words fell like hot charcoal from the pastor's lips and melted my stony heart.

"The time to decide to accept God is 'NOW'. Now is a special word in God's language," continued the pastor.

"Since the day I accepted God, I never looked back or regretted. God is my closest friend and refuge in times of crisis. He walks beside me every day and protects me from my enemies. Today you must say sorry to God for the bad things you have done. That's all God wants from you."

"I want to pray now," said the pastor. "But I am extending this little time in case someone here needs to accept God. I believe God is speaking to someone this morning."

My heart doubled its beat. All those words began to burn me inside out. I sweated. Before I realised it, something lifted me off the ground and deposited me right at the altar.

That must have been the strength that changed Pepena. That must have been the power that melted the stony hearts. That must have been the word that changed Kenenga and my people. I was one of its victims.

The message slackened my bones and brought me to my knees. God melted my stubborn heart and plunged me out of my little world that beautiful Sunday morning. The rest was history.

As I emerged from the pulpit later, a weight slipped off my shoulders. A new day dawned for me and a journey to walk with God began.

God's Word was like water on a thirsty land. Our ancestors had been searching for a true god who would satisfy the deepest longings of the heart. They venerated our ancestral spirits and skulls and offered sacrifices after sacrifices; those gods were unable to meet our needs. They had eyes that never saw our needs. They had ears that never heard our prayers. When we accepted God, He opened our eyes. We realised we had been exhausting our pigs for nothing. We realised we had been calling upon gods who never understood our needs. God's infallible word brought a message of hope. It brought us healing and relief. It provided an escape from death.

While I found everlasting promises and relief in God's Word, the news of my repentance did not go down well with our men. They complained and cursed the new religion.

"How could you do this to us?" How could you forsake your brothers like this?" they said. "How could you suddenly change your allegiance without informing us?"

They knew both Pepena and I would not take part in their moka exchanges or singsings. They even threatened to burn down the church when Pepena and I distanced our brothers. We couldn't join them because the message drew a clear line of separation.

"How could you blindly follow your brother Pepena to the women and children?" said Genemba one morning when he realised that the new religion was drawing me away and away from him. He bashed up his wife that afternoon and warned Piambil Ambo Mopune.

"You women better be careful," he said. "You are convincing all our strong men into your new faith. One of you will get my axe."

If it wasn't for God's great love, it wouldn't have been easy for me to leave my brothers. I would have gone back to my old ways but God's Word ruled my heart and thoughts. He strengthened me day after day. His word became truer and truer. His hands guided and led me every day.

God's word freed me from the fears of death and the fears of tomorrow. He planted His word inside me. When the Word took root and grew in me, my worldly ambitions and fleshly lusts fell off me like dead skin.

The message of hope not only captured my heart. It spread throughout the Kaugel Valley, Kaupena and Tongo River, changing lives, dismantling fears and giving hope to the hopeless. We found our future and hope in God's everlasting Word.

Chapter 30

Moons after I accepted God, a beautiful little girl was born and we called her Akiri after our late aunty who had married to Mendi. Akiri took the likeness of her mother. People joked that all our three children had gone to Piambil Ambo Mopune's side of the family.

"They are like Piambil Ambo Mopune, like Maip," laughed Perai Wenepo.

"It does not matter whether they are like Maip or Piambil Ambo Mopune," added

Pepena. "They are all beautiful like their parents. The two were a perfect match. That's why I reunited Piambil Ambo Mopune to Maip."

As soon as Akiri was weaned, she was sent off to school with Esther. However, when Piambil Ambo Mopune fell pregnant again with our fourth child, Akiri stayed back with her mother and accompanied her everywhere she went. Moons later a baby boy was born and on Akiri's insistence, we called him Daniel after a strong man of prayer in the bible.

The string of births continued soon after Daniel's birth. Daniel was still suckling when Piambil Ambo Mopune fell pregnant again with our fifth child. I guess this was due to men spending less and less time in the men's house. This short spacing of births attracted criticism from the village mothers.

Poikaamb said it was unaccustomed for mothers to fall pregnant while a child was still breastfeeding.

"The two of you should be ashamed of yourselves," said Poikaamb to us. "Do you

have a heart for the little boy?"

Since Piambil Ambo Mopune couldn't continue breastfeeding Daniel while she was pregnant, Poikaamb pulled the child away to Pepena's mother who gave him a special water which quenched the child's thirst for breast milk.

Now as the girls grew up, Piambil Ambo Mopune's work in the house became lighter as she shared the tasks with the girls. Meanwhile, Joseph continued his schooling at Hagen High School.

The fifth-born child was a beautiful little girl whom we called Julie. Piambil Ambo Mopune diverted all her attention from Daniel to Julie. Daniel, however, remained our favourite child because he wasn't strong enough.

Daniel replaced Joseph's place in his mother's heart when Joseph went away to school in Mt Hagen. Piambil Ambo Mopune called Daniel *nanga mondotelim*, meaning the child who was brought up in hard times. She even cried when Daniel went away to start school when he reached schooling age.

One moon after Joseph completed his school in Hagen, Mr Brown, the missionary, came looking for me in the village. He was leaning against the tall casuarina tree at the ceremonial ground when I returned from the forest.

"I've got good news for Joseph," said the missionary with a smile.

He said Joseph was selected to further his schooling at Sogeri National High School in Port Moresby.

"Not only that," he continued. "I have another great news for the boy. I see the young man is cut out for great things. Therefore, I have arranged with a friend of mine for Joseph to attend school in America."

My two girls were in school. That was fine. School could take them away but not Joseph. School had been keeping him away from home for too long. He had already wasted enough time in Mt Hagen.

"When I die," I told the missionary, "Joseph will bury me and inherit all my land and possessions. I will not send him away to school anymore."

Mr. Brown insisted on taking Joseph to America but when I was firm in my decision, he shook his head and walked away without saying anything more. The missionary however returned the next day and said everything was ready for Joseph to leave for America.

"You have to make a decision now," said Mr. Brown.

"I can't lose him in that faraway land," I said. "The children tell me America is a huge landmass where people can easily get lost. What is so special about American schools? There are schools in New Guinea where he can go. He is not going to America because if he goes, his mother and I might not see him again."

"He will school for a few years and return home when school is over" said Mr Brown.

Mr Brown tried a few more times to convince me but when he realised he wouldn't gain any ground, he left.

Piambil Ambo Mopune also persuaded me to let Joseph go.

"What if school holds something special for Joseph? Can't we just give him this chance?" said Piambil Ambo Mopune and broke down in tears.

"I don't have many sons. I will never let him go."

Joseph was a quiet boy like his mother. He had the build and likeness of Piambil Ambo Mopune, very tall with sharp white eyes and dimples on both sides of his cheeks like his mother. At times of distress, he leaned on his mother. He and his mother cried that night but that didn't change my mind.

Two days later, Mr Brown came back the third time with Dopo, the young man who had disappeared to the coast. That was the first time he came back after teaching in a place called Salamaua. Dopo must have been curious to find out what was wrong with me for not letting Joseph go. But there was nothing wrong with me. Both he and Mr Brown were crazy. They were only trying their best to lure my boy to America.

Joseph was Dopo's best friend. When Joseph was young, Dopo was fond of him. He would take Joseph to the Kaugel River to fish. Joseph would come home with bundles of fish or birds. Joseph cried and ran after Dopo went he went away to Goroka to train as a teacher.

Joseph said he would follow Dopo's footprint and become a teacher himself when he grew up. When Dopo received some academic prizes at Tambul Community School, Joseph was cheering at the sides. He was so happy that he hugged Dopo and cried. Dopo gave all his prizes, a book and biros and some shirts to Joseph. Later when Dopo heard that Joseph had topped the school in Hagen High School, he kicked the air with his fists in excitement and said, 'That's my little brother'.

When he came that morning with Mr Brown, Dopo was very angry with me.

"Maip," said Mr Brown. "You know nothing about schooling and its importance. You and your father's times are over. We are living in a time when your little village has opened itself up to the outside world.

"School will enable Joseph to read and write in the white men's language and communicate with white men. School is a powerful tool one can use to learn the world around him and connect with people outside of his home."

"What's the importance of learning the white man's weird language?" I said. "It's better to work in the garden or hunt in the forest than to dream away in a boring classroom, struggling to learn some foreign language."

"Your country needs young men like Joseph to develop," said Mr Brown.

"I don't care whether my country develops or not. I know nothing about development. My son has nothing to do with development too. I'm concerned about what school is doing to our children. School is cutting all ties with this village. It is snatching our young people away from the village. They aren't coming home to look after their ageing parents or work on the land. I'm afraid, someday children might return to a village full of decomposed bodies of the old.

"My two girls are in school. Do you know what your school is doing to them? Let me tell you straight. Your school has weakened their muscles. The school children don't work hard in the gardens as we used to do. The girls are no longer helping their mother in the gardens full-time. They are away from school every day and when they come home, they help their mother quickly and rush back to do what they call 'study'.

I don't know what study will give to the poor girls. Study is taking most of their afternoons.

"Joseph has been away in Hagen for so long. He missed out on all the skills he should have learnt from me. He has been taught by teachers in the classrooms. I don't know what these coastal teachers are putting into his mind.

"I don't see any benefits for Joseph to continue his school. He will lose nothing if he quits school.

"I am my father's only son and all his land belongs to me. We have everything we need here. Our people are always here to support each other in times of crisis and need.

Joseph has a bright future with all we have here."

Seeing that my heart was hard as a rock, they left. Dopo however returned in the afternoon. Joseph was not at home. He sat on a piece of log and recalled what he said were some interesting things while I was working on a new axe handle.

"A wind of change is blowing through the shores of New Guinea," said Dopo, trying to be figurative.

"The government has been given over to us and Michael Somare has been elected the Prime Minister. What the missionary said is true. Times are changing. Our educated men are doing the jobs the whites have been doing."

I couldn't understand most of what Dopo was saying and the changes he was referring to. I allowed him to continue and listened to him because he was speaking about some other things and not about Joseph. Moments later Dopo directed his talks to Joseph again.

"You don't know what the future holds for young Joseph," continued Dopo. "This young country needs well-educated men.

"Fathers all over the land are sending their sons to school. In Salamaua where I teach, fathers send both their sons and daughters to big schools, even outside of New Guinea.

"They send girls to big schools too?" I asked.

"Of course. What's wrong with educating girls?" he asked staring at me.

"Well, girls' place is home. They should help their mothers and when they are old, they will fetch a good bride price for their fathers, have children of their own and support their husbands."

"That is true too but I see you don't care for Joseph's future."

"Son, what do you mean? I'm so concerned about my son and his safety. That's why I can't let him go. I have all my father's land which he will inherit after me. Land is our lifeblood. Not school."

"I understand land is our life and our strength but opportunities like this never come to everyone. Not many fathers have the chance to send their sons to big schools overseas."

Tears formed in the handsome young man's eyes. He must have seen something I was not seeing in school. He was as equally concerned as Mr Brown and Piambil Ambo Mopune for Joseph's school. It appeared that Joseph would lose much if he missed school. I was at loggerheads. What should I do? Should I release him? What if I die when he is still in America? How long will he be in America? Oh no, he shouldn't go.

"If you love your son, then why are you denying his education?" said Dopo. "Do you have enough money to send him to America on your own?

"You are a foolish old man. Do you want to see this bright young man breaking his back in the gardens with his potential laid buried within him?" Dopo's voice rose and his face turned red.

"What a shame it will be when others who had been to school will do big jobs in government? How will you feel like? Things are changing but your stubborn head is too old to understand things."

The young man's words were more than enough for me to bear. I recalled Joseph's joy when he woke up in the mornings and went away to school joyfully. He was so happy to continue his studies. If I stopped him, I would certainly break his heart. I condescended to the young man's pleadings.

"Ok he can go," I said.

Dopo hugged me and went away smiling but I was mad with school. Dopo beat me that afternoon. Education had taught the young tricks to outsmart the old and wise.

Two days before Joseph left, everyone gathered together and we killed a pig to farewell him to the land of the unknown.

It was a still night of doubts and confusion. Joseph's peers embraced him and cried a lot. Some said they would miss him so much. Others doubted whether Joseph would come back again. All sorts of questions, confusions and worries hit my unsettled mind.

Piambil Ambo Mopune was sobbing all this time. She said she would pray for God to take care of the child.

"My girls tell me America is the land of great men," said Piambil Ambo Mopune. "Mama school is taking you to a land our ancestors have never known. We don't know what school holds for you. We don't know what America holds for you too. If there are some good things school gives to those who pursue it, let it give all to you. Let school be your friend."

"You could be the hope for our future. While you are given the chance, do your best and make your mama happy," she broke down in tears for she could not say any further.

"Your Father and I will not be there for you when you need us the most," she continued after wiping her tears away.

Now Akiri who was dropping tears silently, threw her arms around Joseph and sobbed. There was a limit to which her young heart could contain her emotions. After the cries subsided Piambil Ambo Mopune resumed.

"Child, never forget what you have heard in Sunday school. I don't know whether Americans still serve God these days, but beloved, never forget our God. Never forget our God, the God who gave us a future."

"Our God is the great God who exists everywhere. I will pray to God day and night in the gardens, in the church, in my room for Him to look after you."

"God will not forsake you nor will He fail you. God will go with you. God will live with you and will look after you."

"Child I am not coming with you because my girls tell me America is a faraway land, a land far beyond the mountains and rivers. I would come with you and leave you at your new school if it was somewhere near Hagen. You will make the journey yourself, but God will go before you when you walk through the fire. God will go before you when you go through the floods. God will go before you when your feet enter the enemy lands. He will guide your feet and protect you from all enemies. The word that you have received from your Sunday School will guide your feet and lighten your path. Always keep the Word alive and burning in your heart."

Piambil Ambo Mopune's emotional words turned the house into a funeral venue. Joseph's peers knew that was the last night they were together with him. We had no idea how long he would be in America. The power of education was too strong for me to hold him back.

"I have no other son apart from you," I said. "It will take a long time before Daniel reaches your age. I have brought you up to inherit the land after me but things are not working out the way I had expected. Everything and everyone are against me. I don't know maybe they have conspired against me to take my son away."

"Letting you go is the toughest decision I will ever make in my lifetime. I don't want to hear any other story on my boy."

I said the above and wiped my eyes. Joseph embraced me and we sobbed for a long time. The feeling of father and son was so strong that I almost changed my mind again.

"Everyone please come closer to me now," said Piambil Ambo Mopune. "I am going to give something special to Joseph."

The children gathered around her quickly, curious to see what she had for him.

"Mama give it to me, give it to me," cried Daniel.

"Bring the light over here," said Piambil Ambo Mopune to Akiri. They both turned to the room. Akiri stood at the doorway with the light in her hands while her mother disappeared into her room. She searched among the pile of few clothes she had and returned with something in her hands.

"Come here," she said to Joseph.

"The missionaries gave this to me for my sweet potatoes," said Piambil Ambo Mopune, holding the thing up in the light for everyone to see. It was a book!

"There was no salt or cloth to exchange with my sweet potatoes in Tambul so they gave me this book. I was told that God's Word is hidden inside the book. But how will I know what is inside? I am blind but my child will be able to know what's inside. If this book contains the Word of God, then, my child, I am giving you a treasure. Take it with you. It will be your companion and your best friend. In your hard times, this will be your courage. Run to the Word when you have problems. Run to it when you are hit by life's toughest challenges.

The Word will guide your feet and light up your path. You won't get your feet hurt because God's light will be with you and you'll be able to see the path clearly."

"When you school, put this book on top of other books. Before you begin the day, read a word and swallow the message. God's Word will refresh your mind and enlighten your understanding. Let the words in this book sink into your brain and drive your imagination."

School took Joseph away to America on a chilling Monday morning. We never saw him nor heard of him for a long time.

The missionaries gave us the Word but also brought with them a clever device that took our children away. The government blindly built classrooms and encouraged children to receive the white men's knowledge.

Chapter 31

One afternoon it was raining heavily. The creeks flooded their courses and the children came home from school wet and cold.

Akiri and Esther went straight to the other house where they kept their clothes and changed for dry clothes. Daniel did not come home with them. He was in grade two at the Tambul Community School. We wondered what had happened to him.

"Where is the boy," I asked the girls as they warmed themselves over the fire.

"His class left early because their teacher was sick," replied Esther.

The next day came and went by and the children came home without Daniel.

"We haven't spotted him at school," said the girls.

Piambil Ambo Mopune went to Tambul the next day and checked with his teacher. She confirmed the child had been missing for two days.

On the morning of the third day, as we were preparing to check with our distant relatives, a woman who was married to Tekep showed up at our home with tears. We thought her husband had bashed her up.

"Is everything okay?" asked Piambil Ambo Mopune.

The woman hesitated for a moment and then said. "I'm sorry. It is the little boy."

"What?"

"Is your boy here?" asked the woman.

"No. We've been looking for him for the last two days," I said.

Further inquiry revealed that our little boy was killed and dumped into the Ambola River.

Unaware of the existing enmity between the Tekeps and us, Daniel went to the

Tekep's land after school with his Tekep schoolmate, a little boy. The enemies took the child's visit as a chance to vent their age-old revenge. They slaughtered and dumped him into the river at night.

Trials and temptations flooded my life after I had accepted God but this was the biggest. Daniel was in grade two when he was killed. The murder happened so quickly like that in a dream that we couldn't believe we had lost our boy.

The news shot a sharp pain straight through my heart. It was the most devastating moment of my life. His mother and I wept and poured our complaints to God. The children wept all night. The grief was devastating.

Whenever we encountered problems, Piambil Ambo Mopune and I would bring all our cares to God. We prayed to God to strengthen us to endure the trials. We leaned on God when burdens pressed us down. God was the pillar of our strength and the supplier of our needs. Our complete reliance on God lifted our burdens and consoled our weary hearts.

The still voice inside me would assure me that challenges would come but I should not abandon my faith in God.

God supplied enough strength for me to go through such tough times. God's word was my hope and refuge in my hardest times. Whenever I fell and whenever my strength failed me, God picked me up and carried me on His shoulders. If someone had followed me closely on my journey with God, he would see my footprints lost in places where God intervened. Me and God we travelled together. Thank God for His unending love. God comforts His children in their darkest moments.

I went to the church that day and poured my heart over to God "What have I done to deserve this?" I complained to God. "I have forsaken everything to follow you."

That day, God said nothing. It appeared as if He had forgotten me in my hardest time. However, I believed God was always there for me and was seeing me going through the tragedy. The more the tougher challenges came, the higher my confidence in God rose.

Very early the next morning the villagers gathered at the ceremonial ground with their spears, bush knives and axes.

"We want answers," said Laipe. "Why should they chop my boy? What has he done to deserve the axe? They can't get away with this killing."

Genemba and Laipe brandished their bush knives and gathered the boys together at the ceremonial ground. The feeling of revenge ran mad in their veins.

Although light had shone through the valley, people dearly clung to their past. Tribal enmity ran so deep in the blood that people couldn't forget something their enemies had done ages ago. My little boy was killed for the fights that happened a long time ago.

I realised that Laipe and the men were determined to pay back the Tekeps. Daniel's death inflicted great pain in their hearts. I, however, said we would not seek revenge for my boy because God had assured me I would see my little boy in Heaven someday.

"Did your God change us as well?" shouted Genemba.

"He is a Sunday school boy," I said again. "I will see him one day in Heaven. If you want to fight, you can fight but not on my son's bones."

This infuriated Genemba so much that he grabbed a burning firestick and set alight our pig pen. Laipe got another burnt down the other house where the children kept their clothes.

Within moments, our two houses were up in flames. Piambil Ambo Mopune and the children wept as the flames devoured the schoolbooks and their clothes. The men stood around the burning houses for a while and then left when the houses were reduced to ashes. Some of them said it was good the houses were gone.

"I will burn down that church as well. It's giving me a lot of headaches," said Genemba as he and the men walked away, partly satisfied.

We searched for the little boy's body for three days but found nothing. We buried his clothes near our house on the fourth day.

Some moons later, I had a dream and saw our little boy in his new home in heaven. Piambil Ambo Mopune cried and said she was looking forward to meeting Daniel in heaven one day.

"Perhaps it was God's will that Daniel should leave us early," she said.

Amid all these turmoils of misery and death, God's Word never left me. It ruled my heart and brought peace and hope to a heart devastated by death, grief and sorrow. I wished everyone in the valley accepted God. I wished they had this peace which drowned all sorrows and challenges.

After Daniel's death, I cried every night for my boys, one dead and one alive. Daniel's place near the fireplace constantly reminded us of the emptiness he had left in our hearts. Joseph was alive in America but he was still a dead boy to me. I was unsure whether I would ever see him again. America was a fairyland to me.

Whenever little Julie asked for Daniel, Piambil Ambo Mopune would remind her that Daniel had gone to Heaven before us to be with God. The innocent girl wished she could join her brother in heaven too.

One day when Piambil Ambo Mopune got Julie ready for church, Julie asked her mother if she had ever been to America.

"Why?" asked a surprised Piambil Ambo Mopune. "Why do I need to go to America?"

"Don't you want to see my brother? Seems that you and Papa have forgotten him." "Why are you saying that?" asked her mother.

"You never talk about my brother. You must have forgotten him."

"No, my dear. It's not that we've forgotten Joseph. Your father and I don't talk about him often because it just breaks our hearts to even mention his name."

They were still talking about Joseph when Akiri returned from school. She left her books in her room and went over to them with a piece of paper.

"Mama look here. I'll show you where America is," said Akiri. She stretched the paper and placed it on the floor in front of Piambil Ambo Mopune and Julie.

"Oh oh, where is it? Show me," said Piambil Ambo Mopune.

"Joseph," said Akiri, pointing to the paper. It was as if America was right there inside our house.

"How far is my boy from home?" asked Piambil Ambo Mopune.

"Oh, do you see this small island here? said Akiri, directing Julie and Piambil Ambo

Mopune's eyes to a tiny dot on the paper. The two nodded as if they knew the island.

"This is New Guinea," said Akiri.

"And this blue thing around the island? What is it?" asked Piambil Ambo Mopune.

"That's the salt water, the big body of water."

"Oh the island is too small," said Piambil Ambo Mopune.

"I wish I was a fish," said Julie. "I could swim to my brother. Look both America and

New Guinea are very very small. I can squeeze them inside my palm."

Julie stressed her fingers from New Guinea to America. I thought the paper was a mistake because how could someone know the shape of the great land and the wide sea?

"You cannot carry either America or New Guinea on your palms," said Akiri, "because those places are not as small as you see here on the paper. My teacher says the actual places are much bigger than the ones you see in this paper."

"Big like our Mt Giluwe?" asked Julie.

"No, they are much bigger than Mt Giluwe or even Tambul. That's why the white men have come up with this paper which is called map to show places."

"Malke is not here because our home is too small, right?" asked Piambil Ambo Mopune.

By this time the conversation became so interesting that I went and stood over the three. Akiri ran her point finger over a tiny piece of land in the ocean.

"As I have said, this is the Island of New Guinea. Malke should be somewhere inside New Guinea. Malke is a dot like this," said Akiri drawing a small mark on the paper with the pencil.

"And what did you say those blue colours again?" I asked Akiri.

"Ah, that is the sea."

"Oh the sea could easily swallow our small island," I said. I couldn't believe God's Word could cross that ocean to reach New Guinea.

"How far is America from New Guinea?" I asked Akiri.

"It's a long long way. The missionaries took moons to reach New Guinea from America."

"Oh thank you God for His love," said Piambil Ambo Mopune. "He came so far to reach me."

"Joseph," said Akiri, pointing to the paper. It was as if America was right there inside our house.

"How far is my boy from home?" asked Piambil Ambo Mopune.

"Oh, do you see this small island here? said Akiri, directing Julie and Piambil Ambo

Mopune's eyes to a tiny dot on the paper. The two nodded as if they knew the island.

"This is New Guinea," said Akiri.

"And this blue thing around the island? What is it?" asked Piambil Ambo Mopune.

"That's the salt water, the big body of water."

"Oh the island is too small," said Piambil Ambo Mopune.

"I wish I was a fish," said Julie. "I could swim to my brother. Look both America and

New Guinea are very very small. I can squeeze them inside my palm."

Julie stressed her fingers from New Guinea to America. I thought the paper was a mistake because how could someone know the shape of the great land and the wide sea?

"You cannot carry either America or New Guinea on your palms," said Akiri, "because those places are not as small as you see here on the paper. My teacher says the actual places are much bigger than the ones you see in this paper."

"Big like our Mt Giluwe?" asked Julie.

"No, they are much bigger than Mt Giluwe or even Tambul. That's why the white men have come up with this paper which is called map to show places."

"Malke is not here because our home is too small, right?" asked Piambil Ambo Mopune.

By this time the conversation became so interesting that I went and stood over the three. Akiri ran her point finger over a tiny piece of land in the ocean.

"As I have said, this is the Island of New Guinea. Malke should be somewhere inside New Guinea. Malke is a dot like this," said Akiri drawing a small mark on the paper with the pencil.

"And what did you say those blue colours again?" I asked Akiri.

"Ah, that is the sea."

"Oh the sea could easily swallow our small island," I said. I couldn't believe God's Word could cross that ocean to reach New Guinea.

"How far is America from New Guinea?" I asked Akiri.

"It's a long long way. The missionaries took moons to reach New Guinea from America."

"Oh thank you God for His love," said Piambil Ambo Mopune. "He came so far to reach me."

Chapter 32

Two years after Daniel passed away, we gathered for the annual Christmas church service in Tambul. It was a weeklong event where Christians in the entire Kaugel valley gathered to worship God.

The service was held in the night and would end on a Sunday morning. The church in

Tambul was on the other side of the Kaugel River but we had to go in the nights.

We couldn't miss God's word for a single night. God's Word became sweeter and sweeter every day that slippery mountains were no mountains to us; cold nights were no nights to us. We would hide bundles of dry pandanus leaves on the roadsides so that when lights burnt out on our way back, we would replace them with those we hid. We used patched pandanus leaves to shelter us from the heavy downpours.

We enjoyed every single church service in the night and when Sunday came, we woke up with the birds.

The older children dived into the icy waters while mothers bathed their babies and little children in warm water. Everyone was excited to attend the church service because it was the only time of the year when all members of the Bible Mission had a combined church service in Tambul.

When I saw children running ahead of their parents that Sunday morning, it reminded me of Daniel. He used to be the first one to wake up and wash in the creek. He would jump into the creek, unafraid of the cold water. Two years went by but we never forgot our little boy. A strong feeling for Daniel came alive that morning. Piambil Ambo Mopune said she had been thinking of him lately too.

"Maybe he wasn't meant to be with us long," I said. "That's why he has left us early."

"I believe today he's watching from Heaven," said Piambil Ambo Mopune.

I knew I would meet him in Heaven someday but how could I ever forget the bone of my bone and blood of my blood? His death created a lifelong wound in my heart.

The service had already started when we arrived in Tambul. When the songs ended, devoted believers of the Word testified of how God had changed their lives. One old man named Kopel from Kariwi said;

"I am a poor man old man. I was lost in the jungles of Giluwe but my great God has plucked me out among my Kulumindi tribesmen to make me His own. I will be forever grateful for His endless love."

An old woman from Kikuwe said God's Word had provided her an escape from death.

"There is hope beyond the grave," said the old woman. "Death buried my ancestors but it has no power to bury me. Although I may die someday, I will live with my God in Heaven forever."

After a few more testimonies, the pastor took the pulpit. He preached about God's great love for mankind. He said God could forgive all kinds of wrongs. The message of love came so strong that it spoke to different people according to their spiritual needs. The message came to expose wrong, uproot and dismantle fear and sin, and strengthen our faith.

For some people, it was the day God dismantled the lust of the eyes and want of the flesh. For others, it was the day God strengthened their faith in Him. But for me, it was the day my faith in God came under a massive test.

Since I accepted God, one trial after another targeted me but God's grace helped me to soar above all those challenges. That morning, God confirmed that hatred and revenge had perished in my life. His Word confirmed He had changed me completely. Just imagine how could I forgive the one who killed my son?

The preaching ended and people poured into the pulpit to pray. Some of the people remained at the pulpit after the prayers and thanked and acknowledged God for the great things he had done in their lives. Some said they were delivered out from the jaws of death.

Others said God had destroyed the enemy's work in their lives. There was this young man who cried a lot before he spoke.

"I'm sorry," began the young man. "I am standing here as a thief and a murderer. I have already said sorry to those people whose gardens I have stolen food from or those whom I have wronged against. But there is one sin that troubles me deeply every day. I am very guilty, even to think about it. This is something that no one would say under normal conditions. It is a confession, a guilty and shameful confession. I know the person to whom I am directing my apologies isn't here because I have killed him. I'm sorry about that. I believe his relatives are here.

"After I killed him, I dumped the child's body into the Ambola River. Oh, I do not deserve to stay alive."

The smiling little face of Daniel appeared and reappeared in my mind. What crime did he commit to get the edge of the bush knife? Would he defend himself against such a young man?

While he was yet speaking, I stood, I walked, I approached him. People were whispering among themselves. All eyes turned to me. Some mothers even rose with me when I walked up to meet my son's killer.

The world had been waiting to see whether the change the message had done in me was temporary or was subject to situations. The devil too must have been watching with his heart on his throat to see how God had changed me.

Everybody was on their knees to see how I would avenge my son's killer because Daniel's tragic death was the biggest story in the land. However, no one knew what was happening inside me. Did I forget my little boy? No. I couldn't understand where I got this peace to forgive the killer. No single scent of revenge dropped into my mind. Instead, a feeling of compassion engulfed me as the young man was on his knees and pleaded before me for forgiveness.

What stripped off my anger? Where was payback?

"Young man please give me your hand," I said, raising him by his hands. "If God has forgiven you, who am I to hold the hatred? You are a free man now.

"My little boy is in Heaven. He was a Sunday School boy. I will see him one day in heaven. I am dreaming day and night to meet my son."

Now Piambil Ambo Mopune who had been crying all the time came up to the young man. God changed her completely like me too. She hugged the young man and said,

"Son when you killed my little boy, you broke all our hearts and took our little boy out of our lives. If I were to take revenge for my boy by cursing you, that wouldn't bring my boy back to life.

"You didn't know what you were doing then. I am forgiving you."

This news of forgiveness spread like a bushfire in the valley. Even the missionary used this act as an example in his preachings to illustrate how God's word could change a heart.

Some of our men including Genemba and Laipe laughed and said, "Maip is a woman. He is weak. He is incapable of taking revenge. That's why he is using his church to hide his weaknesses."

Despite all those negative comments, I did not forsake God, nor did I disobey Him. The more I obeyed God and stayed true to His Word, my faith in Him strengthened. The devil's dominion and reign in my life crumpled to the ground. God's Word confused the devil's plans.

Chapter 33

By the time Esther completed her high school and went away to train as a teacher and when Akiri entered high school, Julie started school. Just before school started, Mr Brown paid me a surprise visit one afternoon.

I was not expecting the missionary and wondered what had brought him to the house.

I was quite a popular guy after I forgave Daniel's killer.

Julie met the missionary at the track and they talked as they walked towards the house. It was a long time ago when the same Mr. Brown came like that to take Joseph away to America. Since it was first introduced, school has been the source of misfortune and confusion in my family. It caused more damage to me than all those foolish benefits the school promised to children. School was taking my girls away. It stole my boy away to America. I suspected he came that morning to take away one of the girls to school too. However, Mr Brown had a different target at that time. He said he had come to take me to America.

"Maip I have come to take you to America," he said.

"Me to America? Will I see my son?"

Mr Brown said he would pick me up on the Monday of the next week and went away.

At last, when all hopes of seeing my son faded beyond the confusions of education, God made a way for me to see my lost child again.

We had no idea how he was doing in America. We were only informed once sometime back that he had finished his schooling and was working. We had no idea what kind of work he was doing in America too. He sent us some money once, but that was a long time ago. America was only a fairyland to me. The children told me stories of it. They said America was a great land beyond the seas inhabited by great men with their great chiefs.

Next day Pepena and our men slaughtered three huge pigs for me at the village ceremonial ground. All the villagers gathered together to farewell me to America.

We had farewelled Joseph in that same fashion. I remembered how Piambil Ambo Mopune clung to him before he entered the plane in Mt Hagen. She cried her eyes out on her way back home and continued to cry for him in the next few nights. However, when she knew God would take care of him, she dismissed her sorrows and prayed for God to take care of the child in America.

Mr Brown came back on Monday morning with other passengers in a truck and waited for me on the road. They called for me to hurry while I was waiting for the girls to pack a pig head inside a bilum. I would take it to America. Joseph was away for too long and was probably missing pork so much.

Mr Brown threw a puzzled look when I arrived with the bilum.

"What are you doing with that pork?" he asked.

"I'm taking it to America for my boy."

"Ah," said Mr Brown laughing. "America is not a truck's journey. Leave it behind."

"But it's not good to visit him with nothing."

"Don't worry about pork. There are so many pigs in America. You better hurry. We'll miss the plane."

I reluctantly gave the pork back to Akiri. She received the pork but remained clinging to me.

"You have taken away my brother and now you have come to take away my father," said Akiri to Mr. Brown.

Mr Brown didn't hear her because the truck's noise was deafening. Akiri sobbed again. She didn't want to let me go.

"Daughter, I am not going away forever," I said stroking her long black hair. "Mr Brown said I will come back again."

"Papa I will go to Hagen High School when you leave," she said, sounding as if I wasn't aware she was going to high school.

"You know where your aunty Kepambo's house is?'

"Mother and I visited her one day."

"Good. You can stay with her and go to school."

I pushed a two-kina note into her hands and released her slowly. She took the money, hugged me for the last time and strolled over to her mother with both her hands covering her face. She and Julie cried as we left for Mt Hagen.

The sun hit our faces when we reached Mt Hagen. White roofs had replaced the grass tops. Most of the old buildings had disappeared. The streets of Mt Hagen were paved with smooth stones.

We had a quick breakfast in a little shop in town and hurried to the airport. Memories of Joseph came fresh as we waited for the plane to arrive from Port Moresby. We waited at the same place Joseph had sat. He was leaning against the wall, crying. He waved at us before the doors shut him out of sight and out of us forever. He took nothing with him, except his two shorts and a shirt in a little red Coca-Cola plastic bag.

Mr Brown said we would go to a place called Australia before we go to America. When he mentioned Australia, I recalled the poor white supervisor I nearly killed in Rabaul. I was worried because I wouldn't go to Heaven without saying sorry. How would I meet him and apologise to him? Would Mr. Brown help me locate the supervisor?

Seeing me in deep thought, Mr. Brown asked if I was ok. He was probably thinking I was missing my people at home, but when I said I was thinking of a white man I had beat long time ago, he was surprised.

"Which white man?" he asked.

"I beat an Australian supervisor when we were working in Rabaul. He was removed from his job and was sent back to Australia.

"Why did you beat him?"

"He killed my pig. I killed him."

"You killed him?" Mr Brown's eyes widened. His eyebrows moved and he moved closer to me.

"He would have died if the police hadn't intervened. I must apologise to him and seek his forgiveness because God denies me at the Eastern Gate when I go to heaven. Please let me see him when the plane stops in Australia. I believe he must still be living in Australia."

"Australia is a big land," said Mr. Brown. "I don't think we'll be able to locate him.

Besides, we will only stop there for a little while to change planes."

My hopes for seeking forgiveness from my victim were gone. I prayed secretly to God to forgive me. I didn't want to miss Heaven just because of that silly mistake.

The plane landed just a little after midday. We boarded for Port Moresby a few moments later and arrived on a windy afternoon.

Port Moresby's small cities were scattered below the grass-covered hills. We spent the night with a fellow missionary at a place called Konedobu near the beach. We were dropped off at the airport the next morning.

We left Port Moresby in a huge plane called Qantas and shortly arrived in a busy place. The dual noise of the traffic and commuters deafened my ears. I would easily get lost if I were to travel to America by myself.

We pushed our way through the crowd, collected our bags and reached for the waiting area. We threw our bags aside and rested on one of the neatly arranged pews. Mr Brown bought a newspaper and read while I took a nap.

Mr Brown would pause whenever an interesting story caught his attention and shared it with me. But how could I be interested in his boring and unfamiliar stories, stories unrelated to me?

I asked Mr. Brown again if we could locate the supervisor but he ignored me. He continued to read his paper until he came to a particular story which must have interested him.

"Look at this," he said, pointing to the picture of a very tall young man with a smiling face. He was dressed in all white with a strange black hat on his head. That was my time to ignore him but when he called the second time I replied.

"Who is he?"

I didn't know why I had asked him but I was curious because the picture was of a typical Highlander.

"It reads," said Mr. Brown with a smile,

"First Papua New Guinean to Tame Big American Bird."

It was at sunset when we boarded for America. I sat next to Mr Brown. A lovely young woman helped me to fasten my seat belt and lock away my bags above my head. She was so kind to me that I thought all white girls were polite and kind like her. She reminded me of Piambil Ambo Mopune in her young days when her beauty glowed like a bright star. The white lady was like Piambil Ambo Mopune; sharp nose, huge tall legs, beautiful white teeth and long hair, but she was shorter than Piambil Ambo Mopune. Piambil Ambo Mopune was Mopune!

As the plane sped down the runway and lifted off the ground after some crazy demonstrations by those ladies, Mr Brown pulled the young man's picture out again and whispered into my ears:

"He is piloting this plane. He is one of ours from New Guinea."

"You mean this huge plane? The one we are sitting in?"

Mr Brown folded his paper into two and took a nap. I stayed awake for a while and then fell asleep. Moments later, Mr. Brown shook me up.

"Did you hear that?" he said.

"Hear what?"

"The captain speaking?"

"Ah my friend, how would you expect me to understand his message? Even if he speaks loud enough for everyone here, that doesn't make any difference for a deaf man like me."

"I wish you knew my language. You wouldn't miss any of the captain's words."

"Don't worry about your language. I won't miss out on anything."

Mr Brown probably didn't like the idea of me being the only one missing out on the pilot's message so he interpreted the pilot's message for me.

He said Captain Joseph Maip was delighted to welcome everyone on board on his maiden flight to America.

I was stunned by this familiarity in the name. Could this be my Dosip? But how could he be here? It was obvious he was someone from the Highlands of New Guinea because his second name was a typical Highlands name.

The voice came on again a short while later. Mr Brown again interpreted the message for me.

"Captain Maip is delighted to fly his special passenger, his old man to America."

The messages were like a puzzle to me. I couldn't put the clues together to form an identity of the young man. Captain Joseph Maip, his first flight, his old father in the plane, the similarity in the names, all confused me.

I was so absorbed in all those thoughts that I didn't know the pilot had stopped speaking. As I was contemplating on putting those pieces of information together, a hand fell gently on my shoulders. I turned, I saw, I saw him!

The young pilot was smiling with tears swimming in his eyes. Oh, wait. I could see something on his checks. Piambil Ambo Mopune's dimples.

"Father!" he cried.

"Dosip! Are you real? Mr Brown, am I dreaming?" "This cannot be true. Am I seeing you Dosip?"

We embraced each other with tears rolling down our cheeks.

The picture of the little boy we had sent away years ago remained only a faint memory of yesterday. Education and America had transformed my little boy. If it wasn't for his mother's dimples, I wouldn't have recognised him.

The passengers cheered and clapped. Some shook hands with me. Some flashed some bright lights on us. Others patted my shoulders and said some things in their language. Mr Brown later told me they were congratulating me for raising a pilot son. But I said it was all due to Piambil Ambo Mopune's efforts.

The feeling of meeting Joseph there on the plane was so unreal that I cried all the way to America. I could cry a river for my little boy.

When we arrived in America and when everyone was leaving the plane, the pretty lady said something but I couldn't understand. Mr Brown again interpreted the message for me,

"She is saying Captain Maip will meet you at the terminal shortly."

"I am Maip," I said, correcting the young lady who was misquoting my son. And he is Joseph."

"I'm sorry if I have offended you," said the white woman. "But in America, we address persons by their surnames."

I thanked her after I understood her. Everyone left the plane. Joseph still didn't come out. I asked the white woman if Joseph was coming out soon.

"Oh, yes," said the white woman. "You will soon meet your handsome son. I hope you will have a great time here."

When Joseph came out and as we were leaving the plane, several people greeted us and flashed their camera lights on us. Some of the men holding the cameras said a lot of silly things in their language but I couldn't understand anything they said.

"They are asking questions to you regarding Joseph. Would you like to talk to them?" laughed Mr. Brown. He was pulling our baggage on a small truck. "Oh, they are crazy. Do I know their language?"

People threw sharp glances and smiled at us as we walked out of the terminal and over to a sea of cars.

We passed three cars and when we came to the fourth, a beautiful young woman with a baby greeted us. The baby was of mixed parentage.

The young woman kissed Joseph and embraced him for a long time. It appeared that she had been missing him so much. It was an embarrassing thing to kiss someone in public.

The baby appeared to have known Joseph. It smiled wildly and jumped off to Joseph when

Joseph extended his hands. The white woman hugged me and said with tears in her eyes, "Papa, welcome to America." She patted my shoulders and smiled and said again and again how pleased she was by me visiting America. Whenever I spoke, the white girl cried and cried. She had a very soft heart like that of Piambil Ambo Mopune.

I got the baby boy in my arms, stroked the child's tiny hands and handed him back to his mother when we went home.

The road was as smooth as the skins of the white people and the ride was as smooth as the road - one could drink tea while driving. There was not even dirt by the wayside. Enormous buildings with cave-like windows stood still like mountains and obscured the sky in some places.

When we arrived at the house, Mr Brown gave me a picture of Joseph and me inside the plane.

"It appeared in the morning papers," he said.

I brought the picture close to my heart and kissed it.

"What can you say of the picture," asked Mr Brown, smiling.

"Oh, I want to cut this out. I want to take it home to his mother."

Chapter 34

Their home was a two-storey building with a little pool at the back. A short fence ran around the building and a red flowered plant crawled up the fence and bent over the edges. At the back of the house stood a large tree. It threw its shadow over the building. Behind the house was a huge flatland. Many sheep and goats were grazing in the fields under that bright afternoon sun.

We chatted outside on the veranda for the remainder of the afternoon until nightfall. The white woman served dinner, which consisted of some unknown white men's food and rice. I didn't like the food because it tasted sour and strange. I asked if they had any sweet potatoes. Joseph said we would have sweet potato the next day.

After dinner, Joseph was curious to know how his mother was doing at home and how fast his siblings had grown up.

"They are all big children now," I said. "Akiri is in high school. Esther has just gone to train as a teacher in Goroka."

"And Daniel? He must be a big boy now," he said.

"Sorry, your brother passed away after you left."

"How? When?" he pushed the words out quickly.

I did not respond. A feeling of sadness swept over me. My mind went back to the little boy. After drying my eyes, I continued.

"He was killed by the Tekeps."

"Why, why did they kill him?" sobbed Joseph. His wife came over and stood near him. She stared at him with confused eyes. He told the story to her. She broke down in tears. "I was thinking of bringing him here," said Joseph, drying his eyes.

"God gave us another little girl and we called her Julie."

"Oh, that is so relieving. But I am very sad for my little brother."

Next day after Mr Brown had left, I called Joseph over and said I needed to talk to him about his *ambo kondoli*.

"Son, I see you've stolen the white girl."

"Why," said Joseph, laughing. "We loved each other so we got married."

"That's okay. But we should have married her properly in the village."

"That doesn't matter."

"No, we should have paid the bride price."

Joseph laughed again and called his wife over. They talked for a while. Then the white girl patted my shoulders and said something with a smile. Joseph interpreted the message for me.

"Father, Jenny says you don't need to worry about bride price. She says her people don't pay bride price in America."

"Are you telling me you get young girls for free here?"

"Yes."

"I will not take the *ambo kondoli* for free," I said. "We had paid bride price for all your mothers. We never stole girls."

Joseph spoke to her again and turned to me.

"Father Jenny says her people will never mind if we take her to New Guinea for free."

"Does that happen to all other girls here? I mean, are American girls taken away without any single bride price?" I asked.

"Absolutely yes."

"Oh, if I were young and not a Christian, I would take home ten white girls to New Guinea right now," I said laughing.

Jenny listened to Joseph for a while and said,

"Papa not ten. Say one hundred."

"No, no. I have an idea. This is what I would do. I would take ten girls away first, all on the same trip. I would build them a house each and then I would come here again and take the next ten away. I would take ten girls home every time I visit America."

"Papa that would be a problem," said Jenny, "because every time you come here, America loses ten young women. If you take all the young girls away, American men would come looking for wives in New Guinea."

"That's okay. They can take our girls away in exchange," I said. "But I am sorry for the poor white men. When they come to New Guinea looking for their white girls, the white women would refuse to come back even if the white men convince them to return."

"Why is that?" asked a curious Jenny.

"After the white girls set foot in Tambul, I would confuse their minds with Malke Lopalopa. They would instantly forget their mothers and all their people in America when the Malke Lopalopa works in them."

After Joseph explained to Jenny our ancestral love magic and its ability to confuse white girls, Jenny couldn't control herself. She went away laughing and crying at the same time. Joseph also laughed until tears rolled down his eyes.

"Oh, Joseph must have used Malke Lopalopa to marry you," I said.

"Oh, New Guinea, the land of unexpected," said Jenny.

"Please take the Ambo Kondoli home as soon as possible," I reminded Joseph again. "Tell her we will pay her bride price at our ceremonial ground at home. Your mother is also looking after some pigs for the bride price. The tribe will be excited to pay the bride price for an ambo kondoli."

Joseph was out most of the time. He said he was working in some 'faraway places' and came home every two or three days. Jenny also disappeared in the mornings and returned in the afternoons, exhausted. She said she was working but her hands were not soiled or dirty as I expected. I guessed white women worked in clean gardens and never touched the soil.

There was an old woman who looked after the baby boy when the parents were away. She came in the mornings and took care of the baby until Jenny returned in the afternoon.

One morning I was alone in the house. The old woman was yet to arrive. My thoughts flew home and brought back the memories I had left behind. I pictured Akiri grabbing her schoolbag and hurrying away to school and Julie at the pigpen letting out the pigs for the swamps. I was meditating on these when the sound of footsteps brought me back to America.

I thought it was the old woman but what I heard next brought me back to New Guinea. Someone was speaking my language but the voice wasn't Joseph's.

"Are these Kaugel people at home?" said the voice. "I'm looking for lodging for I'm a newcomer here."

I had no idea one of my tribesmen was living in America. I shot out to the door but the person was not there. I flew down the stairs as fast as my legs could carry me. To my great surprise, an exhausted old white man was leaning against the rails.

"My friend come, come here. Let me hug you," said the old man, with his arms wide open. "I have heard you have come to America."

He said all this in my language and I wondered how the old man could speak that fluently.

When I came closer, I realised he was Reverend Gibbs. Reverend Gibbs was one of the two earliest missionaries who came to our land. He was a handsome young man visiting all the churches in the villages in Tambul and Tongo River. Now he was very old. He spent his best young days in New Guinea and only went back to America to die. The other missionary and his daughter who came with him were both dead and were buried in Pabrabuk. I embraced the old missionary and sobbed.

"Was America like this when you came to New Guinea?" I asked him.

"Exactly like this," said the old man. "Can you see those two buildings over there?" he said pointing to two tall buildings near the mountain. "Those were the only new buildings erected when I was in New Guinea. Otherwise, everything else was here; cars, roads, electricity and books."

"Oh, you had everything here. You were in Heaven. Why did you come to New

Guinea?" I cried. "There was nothing good in my land. What attracted you to New Guinea?"

"Oh, my brother," he said, "the love we had for God was so great that it made us go to places we never knew. We were persuaded that there were some lost people on the island who needed the message of hope."

"Were you aware that in New Guinea we never had cars to take you around, no telephones to call your people, no power lights to light your home? Did you know the climate was hot and wet all year round? Did you know diseases killed strangers like you and tribal warfare and payback killings were part of life in New Guinea?"

"This is the crazy thing about loving God," said the old missionary. "When you love God more than your life, you can do crazy things for God. When God called us to New Guinea, nothing could stop us, not even our parents."

"Oh, my dearest brother," I said, kissing his hands. "Thank you so much for giving your young life to my people. God will reward you for all that you've done for my people."

"Just a glimpse of my God will take away all the toils of life," said the old missionary.

Oh, what a man, what a sacrifice! Thank you to the missionaries who left their comfort homes and tribesmen. Thank you to those American parents who 'sent their sons and daughters to die in the unknown New Guinea'.

The old missionary spent the night with us and went back the next day.

Some days later Joseph took me to his old school. I was excited to see the place which lured my son away to America.

"This is where I spent the last two years of my learning," said Joseph when we arrived at the school.

The place was well kept like our revered spirit house. The Americans seemed to have high regard for their school. I asked Joseph why the Americans had built such big schools.

"Oh, these schools are built to teach knowledge," he said.

"What do people do with knowledge?"

"They use knowledge to work."

"How long does it take for one to get the knowledge?"

"It takes three years, five years or sometimes longer."

Oh, crazy Americans! I thought. Why do they build big houses just to learn? We pick up all the life skills of hunting, warfare and gardening through observation or by doing. It never took that long for us to acquire those essential skills. We learn those skills at a very young age so that when we grow up, we will not run here and there like the Americans looking for knowledge.

Americans were not only poor in knowledge. They were poor in everything. They lacked almost everything we had in abundance in New Guinea. They lacked knowledge so they spent many years teaching knowledge to their children. They didn't have enough rivers so they piped a tiny stream into their house. They only had a tiny garden at the back of their houses which never supplied much food and a small pool near the fence. They did not even have a ceremonial ground to host big events. In New Guinea, everything was free and in great abundance. We had big rivers to get water and huge gardens to grow crops. The whole forest was ours to hunt for meat.

One night, a thought flashed into my mind. While it was true the Americans were poor in everything, their lives appeared much easier than ours.

We had many rivers and creeks, yet we walked every day for distances to collect water. We had huge forests, but it took half our mornings to bring in firewood. In contrast, once the Americans brought water into their homes through small pipes, they need not visit the creeks again. They even heated the water inside their house to get hot water. They also cooked with a fire lit by some weird vines connected to the wall without it burning their homes.

The Americans stocked firewood, light, food and even fresh water inside their homes in unimaginable ways. Even the house I was staying in had no signs of ageing. I asked Joseph one night when the house had been built. He said the same roof had seen five generations living and passing under it. I couldn't believe him because how could a house stand that long and withstand the violence of the rains and the fury of the winds? How could they build a house whose roofs and posts knew no scent of decay?

In New Guinea, everything worked against us. The same man built a new house three to four times in his lifetime. Within a short time, one side of the roof would collapse to the earth, leaving the owner with no choice but to run to the forest again to cut posts for his next house.

I was amazed at how the Americans managed to achieve such great wonders. I asked

Joseph how the Americans had managed to make life easier for themselves.

"Oh, it is school," said Joseph. "People go to school to learn how to pipe water into their homes. They go to school to learn how to fly aeroplanes and build houses that can last two hundred years. People go to school to make the pain in the knees go away quickly."

Until then I realised why America treated school as its Koka Maldi (our valuable kina shell). They knew what they were doing and why they valued education above all things. Education enabled Americans to achieve things beyond my imagination.

I realised how we wasted valuable time in New Guinea. We spent half a day solving a marriage dispute while the Americans used half an hour to learn knowledge that made life easier for themselves and for everyone around them.

"What do you do to those who first invent those things, say light?" I asked Joseph.

"Americans celebrate such achievements because such things of extraordinary value would benefit everyone," replied Joseph. "Great honour and respect are bestowed upon those who make significant contributions in educating others."

<h1 style="text-align:center">Chapter 35</h1>

I did not know how long I had been in America. The sun rose in the same place above some low-lying hills and sank behind a lonely mountain. Every day was monotonous and lonely for me without anyone. The little boy was there but how could I talk with him? On these moments of melancholy, I consoled myself thinking about home and my little Julie. I missed my forests and my people so much that one day when Joseph came home, I said I was going home.

"You've been with us for only seven moons. You can stay here as long as you wish,"

he said.

"No, I must go home now. I've been away for too long. My girls might think I am dead in America."

Joseph persuaded me to stay back but I couldn't stay that long.

Three days later Joseph put me on the same plane with a young man from Kotna who was returning home from studies in America. I reminded Jenny that we were a family by marriage and by the Word of God.

"Please come home to New Guinea because you are now from New Guinea. We serve the same God your fathers have given to us. Your God is our God."

After a tearful farewell, I left America. I cried all the way back to New Guinea. The young Kotna man comforted me with his assuring words.

By the time we arrived at another busy airport, it was early morning. We disembarked and waited at the terminal.

Many huge planes landed and took off in what appeared to be the busiest airport in the world. I asked the young man where we were.

"Oh, sorry I forgot to tell you," he said. "We are in Australia. We are waiting for the plane that will take us straight home to Port Moresby."

The glass wall provided a good view. I counted the planes as they landed and took off. After reaching twenty, I ran out of numbers so I only observed the planes. One had a huge jumping wallaby on its tail and another had a fern on its tail. I was still searching for the bird of paradise on our plane when the young man pointed to the runway.

"That's our plane. It has just arrived," he said.

"Which one, I can't see our plane."

The young man directed my eyes to his right. There between two huge planes, was my Air Niugini. It had landed moments ago and was completing its journey when my eyes caught her.

Seeing my plane for the first time in a foreign land, and the fact that it was so small, I cried my eyes out.

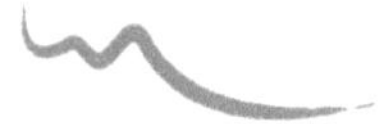

At home, nothing had changed much, However, Piambil Ambo Mopune's pain in the knees had worsened. Akiri had returned for the school holiday and Julie had grown taller.

Our friends came to hear stories of the great land I had visited. I told them everything about America, its high-rise buildings, great schools and its excellent roads and bridges. They couldn't believe any of what I told them.

"How could one build one house on top of another? One roof could collapse onto another," they said.

When everyone was absorbed in the story, I pulled out from my shirt pocket the newspaper cutting and gave it to them.

Piambil Ambo Mopune ran her eyes through the picture but couldn't identify the tall young man with his strange clothes and weird hat on his head. She brought the picture closer to the light and blinked her eyes several times to get a clear look.

"I'm sorry. I can't tell who he is," she said.

I produced another photo, a bright and clear one of Joseph and me standing in front of Joseph's huge plane.

Piambil Ambo Mopune again brought the photo closer to her eyes. The children crowded around her and some stood over her head and blocked the light of the hurricane lamp.

"That is Papa, that is Papa," cried Julie, pointing to me in the picture. And this one?

Who is he?" she said pointing to Joseph.

"Oh, I can see my dimples there. Oh, my child," cried Piambil Ambo Mopune, kissing the photo and placing it on her bosom. She allowed her tears to drop onto the photo. She kissed the picture and placed it on her heart.

"And these ones," I said, handing her two more photos.

"Who is this white woman," asked Akiri, pointing to a photo of Joseph and Jenny with their little boy.

"She is Joseph's wife, an ambo kondoli."

"Joseph married an ambo kondoli?" cried Piambil Ambo Mopune.

"Her name is Jenny." Everyone cheered.

"Please tell Joseph to bring the white girl home," said Pepena. "We will pay the biggest bride price the land has ever seen.

"And is that their little boy?" cried Akiri.

"Oh, look he is smiling. I can't wait to hold this beautiful boy in my hands," cried Julie.

Finally, I showed them Joseph inside his huge plane.

"Where is this?" asked Engaamb.

"That's his plane. He drives the huge plane to so many places of the white men."

"Oh, my little boy," cried Piambil Ambo Mopune. "I never imagined he would go this far."

They cried tears of joy and talked all night about how excited they were about their boy.

Three years after I visited America, Joseph and his young family came home. We paid twenty- seven pigs and 15, 000 kina for Jenny's bride price. We also paid the tribe's prized kina shell, the Koka Maldi to buy the Ambo Kondoli's hand. The villagers said it was an honour for them to give away the tribe's treasure to a white woman. But we were moved to tears when Joseph dismissed it as useless.

Joseph did not understand the value of Koka Maldi. It was the pride of the clan that we had been keeping it safe from great battles over the ages. Our things of value and significance were beginning to lose their significance and value slowly. Money came to dominate bride price payments and settle conflicts. It became the medium of exchange and store of value.

Jenny didn't want any bride price but after we convinced her that it was our way of appreciating a bride's family for raising their daughter, she agreed. She however gave the things back to us, probably because it was too hard for her American people to pull the pigs across the oceans to their land. We killed the pigs and distributed them among the villagers two days after the bride price.

Joseph and his family returned to America three days later.

I encouraged our village kids to embrace school because I had seen school was doing wonders in America. Like Joseph, school would grow wings for one to fly, fly high, higher than Mt Giluwe.

Chapter 36

Piambil Ambo Mopune and I grew old together but she passed away before me, much earlier than we expected. Julie was in her grade six when she died.

She had complications with her breast. After Julie was born, her breasts developed soreness and became painful. Years later when the complications worsened, she frequented her gardens less. We took her to the Tambul Health Centre but it wasn't enough. She passed away at home peacefully. But before she died, she sensed her death and called me over to her one morning.

"Beloved," she said taking my hands into hers, "we have been travelling life's journey together, sharing our pains and happiness. Problems and challenges were part of our lives but God was a big part of our lives. He was so good to us. He gave us His Son and gave us our lovely children. He gives us strength every day to fight the devil and survive."

"My strength has been failing me lately but God has been keeping me alive all those times. This body of mine is so painful but God is supplying me enough strength to bear this pain day and night."

"I am thankful that God is calling me home. I will go home to rest from all the sicknesses of this world and the toils of life. This body of soil and dust will no longer inflict pain and sorrow upon me. It will return to the earth where it was first made from. A new day for me is dawning."

"I never forget what my pastor tells me. I can't wait to go home to that beautiful land where we'll never grow old. Amboama has gone home before me and I am ready to go home now. Amboama and I will be waiting in that beautiful place; I think it must be like America. I don't know."

She stopped for a moment to wipe her tears. She then called for the children. They all came and crowded around her.

"Amboama and I will be waiting for you all at the gate of Heaven. When you come to heaven, we will hold hands and walk into the beautiful home, the home of the pure in heart, the home of those who are washed by the blood of the Lamb. Imagine the joy when we walk into our land of dreams, the land we sing of in our favourite song 'How Beautiful Heaven Must Be'."

Turning to Julie, she said, "My daughter, my body cannot support me anymore on this side of the world. I have been having a lot of pain lately, but that pain must come to an end. My mind is set on the things above, those things I have been working on and waiting for all those times. I am going home to receive my rewards."

Julie held Piambil Ambo Mopune's hands and sobbed.

"Mama no, don't go home now," pleaded Julie. Piambil Ambo Mopune comforted her with her soft assuring words. Akiri and Esther dropped tears silently and sat beside their mother.

"My dear daughters," said Piambil Ambo Mopune, taking the girls' hands. "When I was young, men competed to marry me. I thought beauty and youth would bloom forever in me. I thought I would be young forever. But see how mistaken I was. I see youth has its time; beauty has its time too. They both shine for a while and fade away when age catches up with them. Youth and beauty are gone but God hasn't gone away from me. He has been with me since I accepted Him into my life. He never grows old nor does His strength falter."

"God's great love has been keeping me alive all that time. Thank you to God and thank you also to Pepena who stole me from the Mondikes' hands and brought me to Malke. I am grateful that I am married here. If I had married elsewhere, I don't know whether I would have had the opportunity to hear God's Word."

"Now I am glad that I have lived the life God wanted me to live. I am glad that I have obeyed God all the time. I can't wait to go to drink the water of life and rest under the shade of the Tree of Life."

"I will soon be leaving this painful and old body behind for the earth to feast. It can feast on it however long it wants to feast. I am not worried about it because God is giving me a new body the pains and sickness of this world will never destroy.

"Joseph and his *ambo kondoli* are away. I don't know when Jesus is coming back. But you must be ready all the time because God will come like a thief to take those who are blameless and pure in heart. We all will meet up in the clouds on that glorious morning.

"Akiri, Esther and…., where is my little girl? Julie?"

"I'm here Mama," said Julie, crying. Julie was a big girl but Piambil Ambo Mopune

still called her her little girl.

"Come close, come near to me. Let me feel you with my hand."

Julie stood beside her mother's pillow but soon was down on her knees sobbing.

Piambil Ambo Mopune took Julie's arms and kissed and said to her:

"My little one, I have a message for you. And the message I have for you is this: Look after the flowers around the house for me."

"Yes, Mama."

"Good but not only that," said Piambil Ambo Mopune. "I am passing you something more than the flowers. I want you to take the flowers to the church and decorate the church for me. You must replace the flowers when they die. Water them to keep the flowers fresh.

This is something I want you to do even after you get married and when you are old like me." "Mama I will make sure the church will never be empty of flowers every Sunday," said Julie.

"Good girl. This is so comforting. My heart is at peace that one of my seeds will carry on from where I am leaving."

Now Piambil Ambo Mopune stopped for a while and sobbed.

"Do you have anything to say?" Asked Piambil Ambo Mopune to Julie.

Julie nodded and remained quiet. We waited a while for her to speak.

"Mama," said Julie, "I have one request for you. When you go to heaven and meet

Jesus, tell Him Julie is coming after you. Tell him, I will meet Him in heaven someday soon."

Now Piambil Ambo Mopune released Julie's hands and addressed the girls again.

"I am leaving behind God's Word. It is your resting place. It's your shield of protection."

"God's Word is a two-edged sword. It separates wrong from right and good from evil.

God's Word is light, it is life. It can cut you if you mishandle it. Guard it well with your life.

It is your strength, your hiding place."

"You will marry away to another village. You must obey your man. He should be the head of the family. You must listen to him and take care of him well. By doing that, you will not only gain his respect but God's favour as well. You must not argue with your husband.

God has created you from the man's ribs to help your man."

Piambil Ambo Mopune passed away at home a few days later. Her death was a great loss for us and the church. We grieved her death but celebrated her life as well because God's Word assured us we would see our beloved mother again.

Piambil Ambo Mopune was among the first few early converts to pass away. Her funeral was different. Instead of weeping and worrying too much for her, we celebrated her death with songs and thanksgiving. Our pastor put two neckties, one in front and one at the back during the funeral. He marched around the ceremonial ground before he preached.

"Piambil Ambo Mopune's death is a gain for heaven but a temporary loss for us," said the pastor. "That's why you see me here with two neckties. I am glad that she is one of the first souls to make it to Heaven. I am not serving a dead god. I am preaching the message of a

God whose Word gives hope and life after death."

"Piambil Ambo Mopune followed in her mother-in-law Amboama's footsteps. Like Amboama, Piambil Ambo Mopune plays two important roles in the church. She decorates the church and she is a praying mother. She had been committed to these tasks since the day God called her to be His child.

"Our mother was a pillar of strength for the church. She possessed the weapon of prayer which she executed successfully against the enemy.

Her fervent and ceaseless prayers have been keeping the church warm and alive all those years. Maip and her children are the fruits of her prayers."

"Piambil Ambo Mopune's infectious smiles and kind heart made us all love her so much. Our hearts are broken because we have lost a beautiful mother. Her smiles and her words will never be felt again. However, I want to tell you that she is in heaven today."

"I want to challenge us all, if you want to see our beloved mother again, get what she has left behind. Seize God's Word and treasure it. Follow carefully the teachings of the

Word. Do what the Word tells you to do and do not do what the Word tells you not to do.

Why would you do what God forbids? God's Word draws a clear distinction between wrong and right. Wrong is always wrong, and right is always right. You won't be confused between wrong and right because God has put his law in your hearts. If your heart says something is wrong, then that's wrong. Don't do it, don't touch it, run away from it."

"Look after the message with your life and serve God to the best of your ability today while you are young and strong. Tomorrow when your eyes are dim and when your knees fail to support you, you will sit back and say, 'I have done it in my prime days'."

"Piambil Ambo Mopune kept the faith. She has fought a good fight. She was wounded many times but today she is no longer here fighting. Her days are over. She has gone home a wounded warrior and a heroine of faith. Now she is resting away in the loving arms of her

Father in Heaven."

When the pastor concluded his speech, everyone was silent. Then Genemba stood and said,

"Pastor, I think it's too late for me to give my life to God. I've spent my fruitful years on the things of this world. I am dying someday and I think there is no hope for me after death."

"Who told you you are too late to come to God? Who told you there is no hope for you?" said the pastor. "Come to Him as you are. Today is your day."

Piambil Ambo Mopune's life was a light and true reflection of how God could change a life. Her life touched other people's lives. Genemba and many of our men and young boys repented of their sins and gave their lives to God at Piambil Ambo Mopune's funeral.

One moon later, Genemba's second wife from Mele, Pangia, came to our house with her little daughter. She brought all her things and stayed with the girls when I arrived from the forest.

"Genemba is sending them away," said Julie.

"Why?" I asked.

"Genemba said he has made a mistake by marrying me," said his wife. "After he gave his life to God at Piambil Ambo Mopune's funeral, Genemba said he would go back to his first wife Kengena. I am going away with my little girl. I am leaving his three boys. I haven't brought them with me from Mele."

Genemba's second wife never came back to Malke again. Her daughter must have married elsewhere.

My brother and best friend Pepena and I grew old together but he also died before me.

Pepena was sick and was taken to the Tambul Health Centre. His condition worsened every day and when the nurses there referred him to the Mt Hagen Hospital, he refused. "Why?" asked the nurse. "You need to go to Hagen because you will get better treatment there. We can't keep you longer here because we can't do much here."

"No, I will not go to Hagen," said Pepena from his sickbed. "Do you have anyone else from Malke apart from me here?"

"No, you are the only one here," said the nurse. "Those two mothers over there are from Lower Kaugel."

"So no one in my tribe is here."

"That is true," said the nurse, "but not everyone in Malke is sick. I want you to go to Mt Hagen. The doctors will diagnose your sickness and will treat you better there."

"Don't worry about me, daughter. I know what you must be thinking. You are concerned that I might die. Right?"

"Papa I am worried because your sickness is quite serious."

Pepena took the young nurse's hand, looked straight into her eyes and said, "My daughter, I have been living in this world for too long. My strength has left me. My knees now refuse to support me when I climb a hill or walk down a mountain. My eyes are also telling me that they can only show me half of what they see. All these different parts of my body are telling me that my existence here on earth is coming to an end. My time is drawing nearer and nearer with every passage of the day. I am going home to a better place. I can't wait any longer to go to my new home and get my new body in heaven. I can't even keep my God waiting for me too long too."

The nurse wondered whether she should push her advice further or whether she would allow Pepena to continue his talks.

"Anyway," said Pepena. "Do you have any more medicine left?" The nurse nodded.

"Then give me all the medicines. I will drink my share and my people's shares- all at once, and kill this crazy sickness quickly."

"That will overdose and kill you," said the nurse.

"Ah don't worry about me. If I die, I will still go to Heaven." The nurse shook her head and walked away.

Sadly, Pepena died two days later, leaving behind his old wife Perai Wenepo.

Pepena's death broke my heart one more time. God's Word, however, comforted me once again. It reassured me that Pepena's passing was but just a temporary separation. I would meet my beloved brother on that beautiful morning.

Joseph and his family came home a few years after Piambil Ambo Mopune passed away.

Joseph went straight to his mother's graveyard and broke down in tears. When he returned to the house, he called everyone to him.

"Let me show all of you something," said Joseph. "My mother has given me a priceless gift many years ago. She hid the treasure in her room for a long time and gave it to me when I was ready to receive it."

Joseph felt his inside coat pocket and took out the treasure, wrapped neatly in the same bilum his mother had given to him the night before he left for America.

"She couldn't see what was inside the Good Book but she knew its value," continued Joseph.

"We left the jungles of New Guinea together and together we crossed the great oceans. Together we landed in America."

"From the classrooms to the night skies, we travel. Together we cut through borders and sail through life's challenges. This was not only a gift but a lifelong friend."

Wiping the tears away, Joseph placed the Good Book inside the same bilum and said: "I will live it; I will preach it and I will pass it on to my son when I die. This message of heart purity has been preserved with a lot of prayers, sacrifice and tears."

Mr. Brown died in old age and we buried him in New Guinea. It was sad to see such a handsome young man be buried in a foreign land. But that was his wish. Some time back when he was asked where he would like to be buried, Mr Brown said without hesitation,

"Bury me in New Guinea. This is where my people are. My loved ones are in New Guinea. I will rise with my people in New Guinea when God resurrects the believers on the last day."

I wondered what kind of heart those American parents had for their children. They cut their hearts out and donated to New Guinea. Hearts had to be broken for someone to be saved.

My mother, Piambil Ambo Mopune, Daniel and many loved ones had gone home before me. Their departure broke my heart into pieces, but the grief of loss wouldn't continue to afflict me, because God's amazing grace has made it possible for me to meet my loved ones again.

I am waiting for the day when God will call me home. I will reunite with my God and loved ones. I don't know when my day will come. Moons may come and go, years may slip by but I will forever wait on God's promises because He is a God who not only keeps his promises but fulfils them. My God says a mother can forget her suckling baby but He engraves me on the palm of His hands for I am his child.

I'm dreaming and dreaming of that day when God will call me home. I can't wait to go home and inherit the eternal home God has built with His own hands. I can't wait for that great day of reunion.

My story ends here.

THE END

ACKNOWLEDGEMENTS

Writing is a difficult and lonely pastime. Many people have played a role in my journey as a writer. Without them, this book would not have been written and published.

My beloved mother was the greatest influence in my life. She inspired me to write the book. The character 'Piambil Ambo Mopune' in the book was derived from my mother, and is a mirror reflection of her. Thank you, Mum, for keeping me in your prayers. She and my old man have never been inside a classroom even once. I only wish they could read this book.

I extend my gratitude to my uncles and aunties (many passed on) back at home in Mt Hagen for the beautiful bedtime stories and legends they told me. All those great stories still stay with me up to this day. Here I only tried my best to tell their story.

One's love for literature is often ignited by reading. Many people influenced me to read in my formative years. I pay tribute to some of PNG's finest writers; Sir Paulias Matane, Sir Ignatius Kilage, Daniel Kumbon and Arnold Mundua. Your books not only taught me about our million stories and cultures but challenged me to write my own story, my people's story.

To my boys Gibson John, Raymond Kapoldo, Wakson Wak, Henrick Kaku, Philip Kunz, Jackson Simbura, Jason Pundu, Jessy Tonge, Kingston Mek and Pero Siminji, thank you very much for your valuable feedback and comments to improve the manuscript.

Thank you also to Aiya Dii (Diana John) for providing your constructive feedback after you read the entire manuscript during your busy university days. Your feedback was invaluable.

I also extend my deepest appreciation to my PNG Bible Church family here in Port Moresby and back home in Mt Hagen. Thank you all for keeping me in your prayers.

I would further like to thank my publisher, First Nations Writers Festival International Ltd for publishing my book. Writing and publishing is hard but you have made it possible for my story to reach readers. Thank you and thank you.

Finally, I would like to give special thanks to God. Without God, this book would not have been possible. Thank you for your loving grace, inspiration and protection.

Other books by FNWF